"It wouldn't do for us to catch you lying to us, Miss Underwood."

"She said she knew the last name Cline, but not the man Tynan," Kari's lawyer spoke up. "If you are going to badger her, it will end our cooperation in this little sit-down."

"Maybe you know one of Tynan's relatives?" Detective Grady continued, "His stepdaughter is Sally Cline."

Kari felt suddenly trapped. "I...I...dated one of her sons for a short while. We had a falling-out after our last date."

"Now, that's interesting." Detective Hampton hit her between the eyes with each word. "You just happen to date someone linked to these murders and suddenly you break the story for your newspaper."

"Linked to the murders!" Kari was stunned. "What are you talking about?"

Detective Hampton put a hard stare on Kari. "I think you're holding something back from us. What is it?"

"I'm not holding anything back!" she cried, growing irate. "I've told you everything I know!"

"That's it!" Kari's lawyer said sharply, rising to his feet. "We did not agree to this meeting so you could harass my client."

"Here's a number where you can reach us, Miss Underwood," Grady said, tossing a business card on the table. "Don't let us read about any more surprises in the paper...."

TERRELL L. BOWERS

Raised on farms in the United States, Terrell L. Bowers has been playing cowboys since he learned to walk. After taking up writing as a career he has published more than sixty books. Terrell has been married for over forty years and has two grown-up daughters.

TERRELL L. BOWERS

HEADS I WIN... TAILS YOU *DIE*

W**O**RLDWIDE.

TORONTO • NEW YORK • LONDON
AMSTERDAM • PARIS • SYDNEY • HAMBURG
STOCKHOLM • ATHENS • TOKYO • MILAN
MADRID • WARSAW • BUDAPEST • AUCKLAND

Recycling programs
for this product may
not exist in your area.

ISBN-13: 978-0-373-06273-7

HEADS I WIN...TAILS YOU DIE

Copyright © 2011 by Terrell L. Bowers

A Worldwide Library Suspense/January 2013

First published by Robert Hale Ltd.

www.Harlequin.com

Printed in U.S.A.

HEADS I WIN... TAILS YOU DIE

A very special thanks to Gill Jackson
and the Hale team, without whom this book
would not have been possible.

ONE

JAMISON CLARK GRUMBLED an obscene oath under his breath and followed the two potential car-buyer customers out of the sales office. He watched dejectedly as they walked over to their own car. He had been so close to a sale. Tonya Fenuku was an idiot. Any sales manager worth their weight in breadcrumbs would have signed off on the deal. So what if the company didn't make a fortune on every sale? For hell's sake, a few hundred dollars profit was better than a walk-off customer!

Nicole exited the showroom with her college books tucked under her arm. 'See ya, tomorrow, Jimmy boy,' she chirped.

Forty-five years old and the part-time receptionist calls him *Jimmy boy!*

I should have been a sales manager by now, he reflected bitterly. More than that, he ought to be the owner of his own lot! Instead, he was treated like a loser and even talked down to by the part-time help!

Jamison swore a second time and glared over at Tonya's office window. That simple-minded twit couldn't sell a bucket of water to a man whose pants were on fire! He had put the contract in her hands—the buyers were panting for the car. It was a done deal!

He balled his fists from his ire. How was he supposed to make child support payments when his pea-brained boss sat on her butt like Scrooge and wouldn't allow him to negotiate a deal? The economy was down the pan, so for the past few months he had barely scratched by from one payday to the next. He needed those commissions to survive!

Jamison wistfully considered how good it would feel to walk into Tonya's office and tell her where she could stick this job. Every woman he'd ever known had been a curse to him, one more obstacle in his path to success and happiness! He couldn't recall ever knowing a decent female in his life...not one! From the time his mother had dumped his dad, back when he was six years old, his association with women had gone steadily downhill.

Even the thought of his mother caused him to grimace. She had called his father a bum and a no-good louse, but Jamison learned some time later that *she* was the one who had been cheating on him! And divorce had been an excuse to bring home a host of drunks who ate all the food in the house and then proceeded to knock her around...him too on occasion! The truth was clear—women might have been nurturing and compassionate in days gone by, maybe back in the 50s or early 60s, but they had since mutated into self-satisfying, egocentric whores!

Jamison stomped back inside to his office, tossed his clipboard on the desk and picked up his suit jacket. It was ten minutes until closing, but he was done for the day. He would go home, break out a six-pack of Coors and brood about how a seductive vixen had trapped him into marriage, then given birth to two mongrel brats before he could escape. He would curse the fact he had to fork over a third of his pay for another ten years of child support— more money every time the greedy leech called her lawyer! Three pay raises in four years and he had never seen a dime of the extra money!

She's probably slept with her sleazy lawyer more than she ever did me! he thought sourly.

He started to grind his teeth, only to flinch from a tender tooth. He swore and gently massaged the tooth with his tongue. He couldn't even afford to go to the dentist, because he didn't have the price of the co-payment!

Crossing the lot to his company car—one perk he actually got to enjoy—he mused how a weaker man would have cut his own throat to end his misery.

NEMESIS, AS HE CHOSE to think of himself, got off the bus three stops short of his destination and walked the remaining distance. Attired in nondescript clothing—plain black T-shirt, faded jeans and worn sneakers—he hid most of his face behind sunglasses and a pulled-down Arizona Diamondbacks baseball cap. Unnoticeable to those passing by were the snug-fitting, disposable, medical-grade latex gloves he wore on each hand.

He had previously scoped out the apartment complex and decided it was not a neighborhood he wanted to visit after dark. Better to blend in with the occasional tourist and remain inconspicuous. During rush-hour traffic, with people filing home by the thousands, no one took notice of a man hanging around at a bus stop. He discreetly bided his time until he spied his target.

Jamison's new car, complete with dealer plates, appeared down the street, in the left-turn lane, awaiting the traffic-light arrow. It was all the time needed to walk leisurely from the bus stop, through the apartment complex and climb the stairs. By the time Jamison had parked in his assigned spot and made the ascent to his second-story apartment, Nemesis was in position and ready to act.

As Jamison put his key in the door lock, Nemesis moved out on to the terrace and acted as though he would walk past. Then, just as Jamison pushed open the door, Nemesis thrust a gun against his ribs.

'No noise!' He issued the stern warning. 'Do what I say or I'll blow a hole in your gut.'

'What the hell?' Jamison half-turned so he could look down at the gun. His eyes widened in shock and his complexion blanched. 'Hey, man, I ain't—'

'Move!' Nemesis silenced him with a push and followed him into the dark apartment. He shut and locked the door, while Jamison rotated slowly about and stared fearfully at him.

'What do you want?' The man's voice squeaked with trepidation. 'If this is a robbery, you've got the wrong guy. I don't make enough after paying my ex to even get my teeth worked on.'

'Sit down, Mr Clark,' Nemesis ordered calmly. 'We are going to have us a nice little chat.'

'How do you know—?'

'I said to sit down!' Nemesis commanded more sharply, pointing the gun right at Jamison's nose. The man started toward the couch, but Nemesis stopped him. 'Use a kitchen chair. Put it here.' He indicated the center of the room.

Jamison did as he was told and sat down. Nemesis removed a small roll of duct tape from his back pocket. Wordlessly, he taped Jamison's arms to the back supports on the chair and also ran a couple strips around his chest. Lastly, he used a small piece to tape Jamison's mouth shut.

Standing back to admire his handiwork, Nemesis tucked the pistol inside his waistband and smiled. 'There now... are we quite comfy?' He chortled, a menacing mirth, and glared at his prisoner.

'It took some doing to locate you, Clark,' he told the terrified man. 'Whole bunch of Clarks in the country, you know? It's a good thing your first name isn't Mike or John; I might never have found you.'

Jamison made a face, rolled his eyes and uttered a muffled grunt.

'Yes, yes, I'm getting to it, Mr Clark,' Nemesis said impatiently. 'How can I explain myself if you keep interrupting all the time?'

He snickered at his own humor, but his eyes remained fixed on the man. Leaning over, he asked, 'How's your memory, sport?'

Jamison grunted again.

Nemesis pulled a photo from his shirt pocket and held it out for Jamison to see. He allowed his captive to examine it a few moments before continuing:

'Do you remember the night this was taken?'

Jamison pinched his brows and his head turned back and forth—half negative reaction, half disbelief and confusion.

'Ah, yes,' Nemesis said meaningfully. 'That was a night to remember. Just you and your buddies, having a great old time. Life was one big party back in those days.'

Jamison scowled, unable to comprehend what this was all about.

'Tell me,' Nemesis continued, 'how did you feel the next day? Did the excess of booze, drugs and willing babes leave you hung-over...or did it leave you wanting more?'

Jamison continued to stare dumbly, as if he thought his captor was two cans short of a six-pack. Nemesis sighed resignedly, tucked the photograph away and removed a short length of electric wire from his pocket. The action caused Jamison to strain mightily at the tape constraints. He rocked the chair and would have tipped it over, but Nemesis was too quick. He put a knee across his lap and grabbed him by the hair.

'A good time was had by all—that's right, isn't it!' His voice was harsh and accusatory. 'No consequences for an important guy like Jamison Clark. You and your friends did anything you pleased and no one dared say squat! You were the elite of the class, hot-shot jocks, the coolest dudes around. You were all so special, your group could get away with anything...even murder.'

Jamison emitted agitated muffled sounds, desperately trying to reason or explain, to tell his side of the story. Nemesis had no interest in his babbling or excuses. The man was guilty. He let go of Jamison's hair and produced a quarter with his free hand. He positioned it a few inches from Jamison's nose.

'Of course, you know the significance of this.' He sneered. 'It's what a person's life was worth to you back then.' The fury swelled in his chest. He wanted to pulverize the man's face until it was a bloody mass. But he suppressed the desire and maintained control. He had to be careful. One mistake and all of his planning would be for naught.

'Shall I flip the coin to determine your fate?' he asked, his rage quelled by his sheer strength of will. 'Let's see, heads I win...tails you lose...' Then, with a cruel snicker, 'Your life, that is!'

Jamison wrenched violently against the tape. His rasping moans were more animal than human, his basest instinct for survival reduced to its primeval state. He rocked the chair and exerted all of his strength against the bonds, jerking, twisting, and straining his muscles. But it was wasted energy; he was securely bound.

Nemesis smirked at his efforts—futile and pathetic, evidence of his weakness and cowardly character. He returned the quarter to his pocket and quickly encircled Jamison's neck with the length of electric wire. Moving around behind him, he used his own body for leverage to control the chair, the victim, and the tightening of the wire. He twisted the two ends together and began to snug the noose closed about Jamison's throat.

The man's breathing became labored almost at once. Air whistled through his nose, while his chest heaved from the effort of trying to suck air into his lungs. He gagged forth guttural noises through the tape.

Nemesis gave another few turns of the wire until a mere whisper of air passed through Jamison's windpipe. His face turned from red to nearly blue. The man's eyes bulged, as if they might pop from his head, while veins, thick as strands of yarn, stood out on his forehead. He squeaked out a sorrowful lament, his terrified eyes shining with a glassy sheen. The lack of oxygen rendered him next to unconscious.

'Can you still hear me, Jamison Clark?' He hissed the question, his lips close to the man's ear. 'I am Nemesis and it's time to pay for your sins. Remember what you did and take the memory to your grave!'

TWO

DAGWOOD JASON KEANE—who rigidly avoided any use of his first name—walked through Bally's Hotel and Casino, making his way toward the elevators. He had spent two nights and three days in Las Vegas. Walking around the Strip he had seen the lights and glitz of a major show, watched the sparkling fountains at Bellagio and eaten till he was stuffed at a number of buffets. He hadn't come for the gambling. Nor was he tempted by the occasional warm look from a passing lady while having a drink at one of the fancy clubs. Try as he might, he couldn't put the loss of his wife behind him.

Not that her passing was unexpected. They had entered their relationship knowing their union would be of short duration. With the pressures of his job with the Sutton CID, he had still managed to give as much as possible to their marriage. Doris had understood that he enjoyed his work and she had been loving and supportive. They had laughed and had fun, traveled some, but mostly enjoyed the simple pleasure of being together. She had been courageous and stout of heart, seldom allowing her fear or anxiety to infiltrate their daily lives. To the end she had tried to prop up his spirits with a bravery that would have made a superhero proud.

Jason quickly blinked to prevent tears from forming. It had been over a year since Doris's death, and during her final months she had begged him to find someone else. She didn't wish for him to spend the remainder of his life alone. She wanted him to find a second love…it's the kind of person she was.

He recovered his composure in time to take notice of a violent tussle a short distance from one of the cash centers. A man had grabbed a woman's purse and wrenched it from her grasp. The force of his effort knocked the woman off her feet. He made a break toward the exit as she cried out in alarm. A second lady had witnessed the theft and screamed for security.

The guy had a clear shot through the aisle and moved with the quickness of a startled cat. He dashed madly with his loot, making for the nearest doors. Jason realized that the man had waited until the woman cashed in her winnings, then seized her purse, and was intent on bolting out through the door before security could react. Once outside he would be lost among the hundreds of people on the streets. The daring plan worked perfectly…until a stool suddenly appeared in his path!

He was an agile young man and made a mighty jump over the chair. Ordinarily, that would have been adequate, except Jason sent a second stool spinning in front of him. Leaping the first obstacle only made it worse for the thief when he came down atop the second one. He landed with one leg between the iron bars of the stool and his other knee banging off the seat padding. He sprawled forward and landed with an undignified face-plant against the carpeted floor. Before he could kick free of the chair, Jason sprang upon him and planted a knee in the middle of his back. He grabbed his wrist, then pinned and twisted the arm, so that the would-be purse snatcher was unable even to put up a struggle.

'Hey!' A security guard—whose belly gave proof of too many visits to the buffets—praised Jason's handiwork, panting from his short run. 'Good job, man!'

A second guard arrived on the scene within seconds and they took charge of the lady's purse and the swearing and limping culprit.

'We'd have caught him before he got very far,' the first man boasted to Jason. 'The moment he did the snatch and run we alerted two of our men outside. They were already converging on the exit.'

'Yeah, but this is better,' the second said, showing a proper gratitude. 'Thanks a lot for your help.'

'No bother,' Jason replied. 'I happened to be front and center and witnessed the fellow nick the purse. I'm a police officer myself.'

'Australian cop?' the casino security man asked, hearing Jason's accent.

'Sutton CID; I'm British.'

'Oh, right,' the man said off-handedly, as if anyone with Jason's accent came from the same little corner of the world. 'Is there anything we can help you with to show our thanks?'

'I don't suppose you could tell me where I might get a good cup of tea.'

The man laughed. 'I'm afraid that's one thing that got misplaced during the crossing from England to America.'

The other joined in, 'And what did make it over here got dumped during the Boston Tea Party, back before the Revolutionary War.'

Jason displayed a good-natured grin. 'Yes, I remember...back when we granted you colonials your independence.' The two security guards laughed, he lifted a hand in farewell and proceeded to the elevators.

Arriving at the sixteenth floor, Jason went down the corridor and used the electronic card to enter his room. It was only nine o'clock, but he was still battling the seven-hour time change since leaving London. He decided to take a shower and get his feet up. Perhaps if he watched television for a bit? He hit the remote and discovered the local news was on, so he turned up the sound and began to remove his shoes and socks.

'And local police are investigating the death of a Henderson man who was killed late this afternoon,' the newsman stated. 'The victim, identified as Jamison Clark, had been bound with duct tape and was apparently strangled while at home in his apartment. He was found by one of his neighbors. Police have made no arrests and are asking anyone who might have seen anything unusual in the area to call the LVPD tip line. Jamison Clark was forty-five years old and has been a car salesman in the Las Vegas area for the past five years.'

Jason frowned at hearing the name. He knew two different men by the name of James Clark. However, he'd never met anyone with the first name of Jamison. He dismissed it at once. It was an occupational habit to file away names and faces. It sometimes seemed there was little room in his head for anything else. Some of the guys at the station liked to tease that he had a photographic memory—except the film didn't always develop!

He shrugged out of his sports shirt and pants, headed for the shower and muttered to himself. 'Been on the job so long, every time you hear about a crime you think you have to try and solve it.'

Once under the spray of water Jason considered the journey he would take tomorrow. His grandparents had divorced and each taken a child. His father, Elwood, had been sixteen at the time and remained with his father in London, while his sister, Sally Keane, had been eleven and went to America with her mother. The woman's migration had not been a whim, as she had fallen in love before the separation. Upon arriving in the States she immediately married Tynan Cline. Sally was formally adopted, changed her last name and became an American citizen. A few short years later her mother died of breast cancer. Sally, however, had remained with her new father and stayed in America.

Jason had never met Sally Cline, but she and Elwood never lost touch. He and Sally exchanged letters and phone calls for thirty-five years. Elwood told stories of Sally and Jason thought they might one day meet. It was a sad introduction now, as Elwood had died last month. Sally had little money and was unable to attend the funeral, so it fell to Jason, being the only child, to visit the States and offer the keepsakes and a final letter his father had designated for Sally.

He toweled off and had just slipped on a robe when the phone rang.

'Inspec...' he caught himself before he said *Inspector* and corrected it quickly, 'uh, Jason Keane here.'

'What say, Cousin?' an unfamiliar voice greeted him. 'This is Roger Cline, Sally's number one son.'

'Of course, Sally mentioned you and Reggie to my father in many of her letters. The woman seems to dote on you boys.'

The declaration brought forth a chuckle. 'I just spoke to Mom and she said you would be in town tomorrow. We're planning a family dinner at her place.'

'Sounds good to me. What time am I expected?'

'Supper will be about six o'clock. Can you make it by then?'

'It's what, about seven or eight hours to West Jordan from Las Vegas?'

'About that. But remember the time change. Once you cross into Utah, you lose an hour.'

'So it will be an hour later there than it is here.'

'That's right. I'm in Portland, Oregon, at the moment,

but I've got an early flight in the morning. I'll be there. Oh, and I'm bringing a girl along too.' He made an inaudible grunt, the kind men use when they are explaining everything in detail without the use of verbal communication. 'I'd already asked her before I knew you were coming.'

'That's fine.'

'Reggie will be there too. He's a trucker—don't know if you knew that or not. If I'd have had the number of your cell phone, you could have caught a ride with him and saved renting a car. He passed through Vegas earlier today on his way home.'

'That's all right. I've paid for the room and already have a car rented for the duration of my stay.'

'How's the weather compare to what you're used to?'

'A hot day around London is when it passes the eighty-degree mark. Bit of a shock to the system to be here and feel this hundred-degree dry heat. After a few minutes on the walk outside, I have a strong empathy with a pot roast.'

Roger laughed. 'Why'd you fly into Vegas instead of Salt Lake?'

'It was much less expensive for a round-trip ticket. I suspect the casinos offer the best deals, hoping a person will spend a portion of their time and money at the gambling tables. Also, I wanted to visit America's "Sin City" while I'm here.'

'I hear you,' Roger said. 'Anyway, I'll look forward to meeting you tomorrow. Mom said you were going to stay around for a couple weeks?'

'Yes. I don't know when or if I'll ever get over here again. I'd like to take in some of the sights.'

'We've got plenty of those. We're only a day's drive from Yellowstone or the Grand Canyon, and there's tons to see around Salt Lake too.' Roger snickered. 'Naturally, we also have some of the prettiest women anywhere in the world.'

'We've our share of those back home too.'

'So many women, so little time...right?'

Jason offered a mild laugh. 'Yes.'

'OK, then, I'll look forward to seeing you.'

'Thanks for calling, Roger. Until tomorrow.'

IT WAS SUNDAY AFTERNOON. Kari Underwood was understandably nervous. She was going to meet Roger Cline's mother. She had donned a black silk-chiffon dress, had meticulously applied her make-up, and not a hair was out of place.

She hurried across the room at the ring of the doorbell and pulled the door open.

Roger Cline stood in the apartment hallway. He wore a gray knit sweater over a white, open-at-the-throat shirt, with black slacks. His shoes were smartly polished and his thick hair was impeccably groomed. His natural smile displayed perfect teeth, while his hazel eyes roamed over her, glowing with satisfaction.

'You're a vision to behold,' he said silkily. 'God must have employed a host of angels to help him the day he created you.'

An apprehensive tingle raced along Kari's spine. She concealed the shiver by smiling at his flattery. 'A comment like that borders on blasphemy, Roger. Aren't you afraid of being hit by a lightning bolt?'

'God would not have made you so striking, if He did not wish for we mere mortals to enjoy your beauty.'

'Yes, I'm sure.'

'No, I mean it,' he argued. 'A pretty woman serves a significant purpose.' With a wry simper, 'It's indisputable proof that God is a male presence.'

She laughed. 'And all this time I thought the proof was labor in childbirth, menopause and hormonal mood swings.'

'That too,' he agreed.

'I'm probably overdressed for tonight,' she worried. 'I wasn't sure what to wear.'

'I forewarned my mother you weren't exactly the home-liest girl in the world,' he teased. 'But I didn't mention the fact you also had exquisite taste in your choice of clothes.'

'And your brother? He's going to be there too?'

'Yes, my little brother, Reggie,' he said. 'He will be completely cowed by your presence.'

Roger had not talked much about his twin brother. Although they had spent many hours together, Roger's family life was a subject about which he seldom elaborated. She knew he adored his mother and had never known his father, but had learned little else.

'You call him your little brother,' she pursued the train of conversation, 'but you're twins.'

Roger smiled. 'We're fraternal, not identical. He's my little brother because I was delivered first and I happen to be a little taller than him.' The smile broadened. 'And it goes without saying, I'm the better-looking one.'

Kari laughed and quipped: 'He is obviously the one with the humility in the family.'

'A rare quality indeed.' Roger joined the fun. 'In truth, we're like two peas in a pod.' He stepped back, feigning surprise. 'Oh, wait! We are two peas from the same pod.'

'How charming,' she retorted, 'referring to your mother's womb as a pod.'

'I'll trust you to not mention my indelicate metaphor to either Mom or Reggie tonight.' Then he added, 'Oh, and a cousin will be there too, all the way from England. He has come to visit with my mother. She and his father were separated when Mom was ten or eleven years old.'

'Now I'm really starting to feel antsy about this dinner.'

'Not to worry.' Roger showed a smirk. 'He will also be dazzled by your presence.'

Rather than reply to the flattery, Kari grabbed her handbag, stepped out into the hall and closed the door to her apartment. As they began to walk together, she gave Roger a hesitant look. 'It's been some time since I met a date's family.'

'I don't imagine you get out much...considering the people you deal with at the newspaper are mostly *dying* to get their names in print.'

'Funny,' she said drily, 'but writing obituaries for the newspaper is a stepping-stone. I intend to do some actual stories one of these days.'

'Could I be dating the next Barbara Walters?'

'I don't expect that kind of notoriety, but I would like to be a serious journalist or reporter. Perhaps I will even have a syndicated column one day.'

'I've no doubt you will achieve your goals, Kari. I think you are capable of doing whatever you set your mind to.'

His confident remark lifted her spirits. She thanked her lucky stars again for having met Roger Cline. He was upbeat, charismatic, handsome...much more than any man she had ever dared hope to meet. And best of all, he seemed to be falling in love with her!

THREE

JASON PULLED UP at the house. An older model Toyota and a Ford Ranger pick-up were parked in the driveway. There was room for a third vehicle, but he parked at the curb. Climbing out of the rental car, he decided to visit first and deal with the box of keepsakes later. A young man met him in the doorway: five-ten, finely textured brown hair and of average build. A smile of greeting immediately appeared on his face.

'Cousin Dagwood?'

Jason winced at the name, but walked forward to shake his hand. 'I prefer Jason,' he said, immediately liking the gentle, earnest look of the man.

'Reggie,' he answered back. 'My brother and his date haven't arrived yet. You're a little early.'

'Habit of mine; I tend to be punctual.'

'You're bigger than I imagined,' Reggie said, surveying Jason's six-foot athletic frame. 'And you're what…a couple years older than me and Roger too.'

'I'll be thirty in a couple of months.'

'Three years. Your father must have married young too.'

Jason nodded. 'Yes, poor Father. He often said he couldn't wait to make the biggest mistake of his life. Mum left when I was at primary school.'

'Seems both our families had trouble that way,' Reggie commented, leading the way into the house. 'Those who didn't run off died while much too young.' He realized the personal effect of his statement and quickly apologized.

'I'm sorry, Jason. I didn't mean…I know your wife passed away a year or two back.'

'It's all right. I know you were speaking more about your father and grandmother.'

'Did I hear a car door?' clamored a woman's abrasive voice. 'Is your brother here?'

Reggie escorted Jason to the kitchen. 'It wasn't Roger, Mom,' he informed her. 'It's Cousin Jason.'

Aunt Sally turned from the stove and looked at him. The woman was wearing an orange blouse and black slacks, the outfit protected by a colorful brown, yellow and red apron. She had once been strikingly attractive, but the years had not been kind to her. Rather buxom, she was a little overweight, with age lines creasing the corners of her eyes and mouth. A deep furrow appeared as she studied him intensely.

She abruptly put down a spatula she had been holding, wiped her hands on her apron, then stepped over and gave him a hug. It was a short embrace, more of a greeting than a handshake, less than a kiss on the cheek.

'Jason…I remember Elly' (Sally's nickname for his father) 'saying you hated the name Dagwood,' she began, gazing into his face. 'You look a little bit like my brother did when he was young.'

'I've heard it said,' he admitted.

'It's sad that we couldn't have gotten together before his death. I always thought there would be more time.'

'Yes, Father stayed quite active until his accident. He had often dreamed of making the trip to see you.'

'I'm going to miss his letters and talking to him on the phone.' Sally returned to watching over the stove and said, 'Roger called last night and said he was going to telephone you.'

'Yes, he rang me up at the hotel.'

'He should be here any time.' She flicked a glance at Reggie. 'I hope this new girl Roger is bringing to dinner isn't as dopey as the last one.' She sighed. 'The whole time she was here she giggled and fawned over every word he said. I swear she acted as if she didn't have half a brain.'

'I never met her,' Reggie interjected softly. 'I was out of town the last time he brought a girl to meet you.'

'He broke up with her a couple weeks after the visit anyway,' his mother admitted. Then, with a scowl at Reggie, 'Why is it Roger brings home a different girl every few months and you have never brought a single one to dinner?'

Jason felt uncomfortable being in the middle of a private conversation. However, he could do little more than remain silent.

Reggie flushed with embarrassment, being confronted in such a way, but laughed it off. 'Driving truck, I don't meet a lot of girls.'

'You ought to ask Roger to line you up. You know he—'

'I've got the game on in the other room,' Reggie interrupted, stopping that line of conversation. 'Let's leave Mom to the cooking and see how the Broncos are doing.'

'Football?'

'You ever watch it over in England?'

'I watched a little of the Super Bowl one time. It's a bit like rugby.' He grinned. 'Except you Americans seem to need helmets and a lot more padding.'

Reggie laughed. 'Yes, bunch of sissies, us Yanks.' He led him to the sitting room. He sat down on the couch and Jason settled into a worn easy chair.

'Oh, that's good,' Reggie said, his eyes focused on the television, taking note of the score. 'The Broncos got a field goal while we were in the other room. They're up by ten points now.'

'What innings is it?'

Reggie turned to explain that innings were in base-ball, but caught the smirk on Jason's face. 'Yeah, right.' He showed a good-natured smile. 'Game's about over. It's almost the two-minute warning.'

The sound of a car entering the driveway caused them both to turn their attention to the window.

'They're here!' Reggie called to his mother.

Jason saw the silver Infinity come to a stop. A girl quickly climbed out of the passenger side. When she closed the door her shoulder-length sandy-blond hair was tickled by the wind, as was the skirt portion of her flowing black dress. The hem fluttered with the breeze an inch or two above her knees to reveal sleek, shapely legs. When the young lady smiled at the handsome man—Roger Cline, undoubtedly—Jason discovered he was holding his breath. The girl wasn't glamorous, it was more an innocent beauty.

'There she is.' Reggie spoke under his breath to Jason. 'Roger's next conquest! He brings them home to Mom, so she can inspect and approve his choice. Then, if his record holds true, he will sample the girl's charms for a time, and drop her flat.'

The notion struck an exposed nerve. 'You're saying your brother is a cad?'

'That's too nice a word,' Reggie told him, still keep-ing his voice from reaching his mother. 'Along the high-way of romance, Roger leaves broken hearts like so many mile-markers. He doesn't want a commitment, only another prize for his trophy case!'

'Is his new girlfriend with him?' Sally called from the next room.

'Yes,' Reggie answered her gravely. 'Another lamb for slaughter.'

'Don't you go belittling your brother, Reggie. At least, he's out there trying to find a girl to settle down with.'

Reggie remained skeptical. 'Yeah, I can hardly wait to hear his wedding plans.'

'Get washed for dinner,' Sally called. 'It'll be on the table in five minutes.'

Reggie rose from the couch and switched off the TV. Jason inhaled deeply and let out the air quietly. This could turn out to be one long, awkward night.

KARI WAS A LITTLE overwhelmed to be sharing the table with two strange men and Roger's mother. Jason Keane was introduced as the cousin from England. He was easily as tall as Roger, had pleasing features and cloudy gray eyes. Slightly older than the Cline twins, he wore his maturity like a comfortable jacket and seemed at ease with everyone. He didn't try to assume command of the conversation, but made an effort to be part of the table chatter. She enjoyed his speech, not so much to hear his English accent, but because he had a nice voice and was very articulate.

As for the others, she suffered misgivings concerning Roger's mother. She was an odd sort of bird, negative, bitter, with few good things to say on any subject. When she turned her verbal guns on her taciturn son, Reggie, fussing about him not having a girlfriend, Kari attempted to laugh off her remarks.

'I'm sure Reggie has plenty of choices for a girlfriend,' she said. 'Good men are in short supply these days.'

Roger also took up for him. 'Reggie would be a good catch for a woman,' he agreed. 'The problem with Reggie is, he's one of those rare men who doesn't intend to get serious about a girl until he meets the right one.' With a chuckle, 'And it'll be up to the girl to convince him she is the right one.'

Reggie smiled, but a subtle irritation glowed from within his dark eyes.

'And what about you, Jason?' Kari rescued Reggie from further chagrin. 'Do you have a chorus line of girls in your little black book?'

'His wife died a coupla years back,' Sally informed her bluntly, before he could reply.

Kari felt the fires of embarrassment rush to her face, but Jason smiled politely. 'It was not an unexpected loss, but I haven't actually begun going out with women again.'

'Leukemia,' Sally again spoke for him. 'My brother wrote me all about it. Said they knew she had it from before the two of them started dating.'

'How sad,' Kari murmured.

'We had a happy, albeit short life together,' Jason said.

Kari returned to finishing the meal. The food was passable, but certainly nothing to rave about. Dessert was a piece of Marie Calendar's apple pie, fresh out of the box. As it was served, Kari made an effort to engage the silent brother again.

'Roger tells me you're a truck driver, Reggie,' she said. 'You must see a lot of the country.'

'Some,' was his laconic reply.

'I was expecting you two to look more alike. It's something of a surprise to find a pair of twins who are so different.'

'In all sorts of ways,' Roger interjected. 'Reggie has always been the serious one in the family. If he was to start telling jokes and take center stage at a party, everyone would think he'd been possessed by an alien.'

Kari smiled. 'I'm sure you are exaggerating, Roger.'

'It's for the best,' he assured her. 'Back when we were in school, good old Reggie was always looking out for me. If I had a problem with my homework, he would help me with the answers. If I got into trouble with the neighbors, he would make it right with them. I once mouthed off to a bully and he came after me with blood in his eyes. Reggie showed up and it was the bully who ended up crawling away with his tail between his legs.'

'So Reggie is the fighter in the family?'

'Only because he grew up with me around.' Roger uttered a jovial laugh. 'Otherwise, he would never have had to learn.'

'Reggie looked after you and fought your battles,' Kari deduced. 'So what did you do for him?'

Roger grinned. 'I kept him from getting bored.'

Mrs Cline took the opportunity to enter the conversation. 'They kept me worrying all the time, hon. I can tell you, those boys made an old woman out of me—turned my hair gray and gave me a ton of wrinkles before my time. They were more work than a dozen ordinary kids.'

'I've always thought twins would be a handful to raise,' Kari politely agreed.

'Believe it, hon,' Mrs Cline replied. 'Those two took over my life. I never had a minute's rest from the time they were born, not to this day.'

Kari didn't know how to reply to that, so she left the subject alone.

After a short span of time had passed Mrs Cline rose from her chair, removed her apron and put a hand to the small of her back. 'I'm feeling a bit poorly tonight, Reggie. Would you be a good boy and clean up?'

'I'll take care of it,' he said. 'You go ahead and take it easy.'

'If you're not feeling well, I can come back for a visit at some other time,' Jason offered.

'No, no, it's nothing. Really.'

'Are you sure, Mom?' Roger was quick to ask. 'You haven't been overdoing it at work again, have you?'

She paused to reward his concern with a warm and caring smile. 'No, Roger, I think I might have twisted wrong or something. I'm a little stiff and I've got a slight head-ache. It's nothing to worry about.'

'If you need something...?'

She waved her hand to dismiss the notion. 'It's only a touch of stress, Roger, honey. You go ahead and have a good time. I'll take some medicine and sit down for a while. I'm sure it will pass.'

'If you say so.' Roger continued to show a genuine worry. 'But if you need anything at all, don't hesitate to give a holler.'

Kari watched Mrs Cline go to the living room. The woman plopped down on the sofa, and the next instant the television blared to life. It occurred to her that Roger was a dutiful son, while Reggie appeared more casual, as if this was the norm.

'Well, that takes care of Mom for the evening.' Roger returned his attention to Kari. 'Once she sits down in front of the tube she doesn't move till bedtime. What say you and I go out back? There's a porch swing I've been want-ing to test drive.'

Kari nixed the idea at once. 'I can't let your brother do the dishes by himself. It wouldn't be right.'

'I'll lend a hand,' Jason told her. 'I've been living a bachelor's life recently. I'm not completely inept at wash-ing or drying dishes.'

Roger laughed. 'See?' He spoke to Kari. 'These two gentlemen have the matter well in hand.'

Reggie said, 'You two go ahead. Jason and I will take care of the cleaning up.'

Kari thanked the two of them and followed Roger out the back door to a large porch swing. They watched the last of the sun disappear over the Oquirrh Mountain range which rose along the western sky over the Salt Lake City valley. After the final streaks were nothing more than a faint glow Reggie leaned over and kissed her, a lingering contact, warm, moist and delightful. When he broke it off, Kari gasped for air.

'Gracious!' she panted. 'I need to catch my breath.'

Roger laughed softly. 'This is hardly the place for privacy. Why don't we go back to your place?'

Kari hesitated. There could be no misinterpreting his suggestion of privacy. Roger was satisfied that they had graduated from the primary stage of their relationship. He had been patient with her and brought her home to meet his family.

He expects more than a mere kiss tonight!

ROGER AND KARI entered long enough to say goodbye. No sooner had the door closed than Reggie groaned an empathetic misery. 'That poor kid. She has no idea.'

'Maybe she's the one Roger will choose to have a serious relationship with.'

'There's always the chance…' Reggie's cell phone rang. It was located in a pouch on his leather belt. He plucked it out and propped it to his ear before the thing had a chance to ring a second time.

'Reggie here.'

He listened for a moment. 'You're kidding,' he said unhappily. His face twisted into a grimace. 'And he's going to be off all week?' After a few more seconds he sighed dejectedly. 'Yeah, OK, I'll pick up my rig and hit the highway. I should be able to make it before loading time.'

Jason waited as Reggie put the phone away. Before he could explain, his mother called from the sitting room. 'Reggie? You still here?'

'Yeah, Mom.'

'This bottle didn't have but a drop left in it. How about bringing me one from the cupboard?'

He shook his head at Jason and spoke softly, so his words would not carry into the living room. 'Sounded like a request, as if I could refuse or talk her out of it, but don't you believe it. Withholding liquor from Mom has the same effect as taking a baby-bottle away from a hungry infant... except that my mother screams a whole lot louder!'

Jason smiled at his example.

Reggie retrieved a quart of Scotch from the cabinet above the sink and carried it in to his mother. Sally looked away from the television long enough to pour a little in a glass. She looked past both him and Jason.

'Where's Roger and his friend?'

'They just left. He called to you from the door. I guess you didn't hear him.'

She set down the bottle, not bothering to put the cap back on.

'I've got to make a run to Reno tonight,' Reggie told her, after she had taken a sizeable swig from her glass. 'One of the drivers is down with the flu or something. He didn't tell dispatch until a couple hours ago. The load has to be picked up first thing in the morning.'

'Then you're leaving me too?'

'Yeah, it's just you and Jason this evening.'

She didn't reply and Jason followed Reggie to the door. The young man turned and stuck out his hand before making his exit.

'Sorry to run off and leave you like this.'

'I've got a box of items that my father wanted me to give your mother. I'll get them from the car and spend some time here.'

'Mom will appreciate that.' He shrugged. 'Might even

slow down her drinking for this evening. She sometimes overdoes it.'

'I'll do my best to entertain her.'

Reggie headed for his pick-up truck and Jason retrieved the box from the back seat of the rental car. He carried it inside and joined Sally. She shut off the television as he sat down next to her on the couch.

Sally went through the items in the box. Besides the letter there were some pictures, a little hand-carved statue of a horse, and a piece of jewelry. She read the letter and explained the significance of each of the items. When finished, she went into an adjacent room and returned with a photo album and a second book.

After going through the family album, Sally opened the other book, a high-school yearbook. The next thirty minutes were spent with her turning the pages and pointing out her special memories from her senior year. There were many.

Sally had been a cheerleader and involved in dance. She appeared in no fewer than two dozen pictures and many of the teachers had signed their names under their own photographs.

Jason put on his professional face and feigned interest in every detail or picture she pointed out. When her finger rested on a rather handsome boy named Warren Lloyd he felt genuine sympathy for her.

'The father of my two boys,' she said gravely. 'We had already planned to get married after graduation. Warren's father ran a business over in Murray and he would have gone to work for him. I still wanted to dance, but then we crossed the line one night and I ended up in a family way. Everything was changed by that one mistake.'

'It appears you were very popular.'

She smiled. 'I was head cheerleader. I and the others

represented our school at every sporting event. We were the heart and spirit of the school. When we went to the state finals in football, our quarterback and running back wouldn't have gotten half as much notice without us. We made the names *Kenny* and *Clark* the most well-known high-school stars in the state.'

'Whatever happened to them?'

'They both went off to college. However, Kenny ended up getting busted for drugs and lost his scholarship. It wasn't but a few months later that Clark hurt his arm while pitching for the BYU baseball team. He was never able to throw another pass. Neither of them finished college.'

'Dashed hopes for fame and fortune,' Jason remarked. 'That's a shame.'

Surprisingly, Sally didn't dwell on the two boys; she returned to the present. 'That was a pretty girl Roger brought home,' she commented, closing the yearbook. 'What was her name?'

'Kari Underwood,' Jason replied. 'Her ambition is to be a reporter. At present she writes death notices—obituaries—for the local newspaper.'

'I wonder if Roger is serious this time,' Sally said, a hopeful note apparent in her voice. 'This could be the girl he'll want for a lasting relationship.'

'Reggie didn't seem to think so.'

The remark caused Sally to frown. 'Reggie is always negative about Roger's relationships.' She lifted her glass and drained the last swallow. She took a moment to refill it from the bottle and returned to speaking of her sons and the miseries of a single mother. The death of Warren Lloyd and having twins had cheated her of her youth and destroyed a promising dancing career.

Exhaustion weighed Jason down like a heavy suit of armor. About the third time Sally began to ramble on about her lost love, Jason shut out her voice. He almost nodded off, caught himself, and grew alert once more.

Steady on, Jason, you came all this way to visit your aunt. Be patient a little while longer.

FOUR

NEMESIS WAS ON the prowl again. How quickly the satisfaction of dealing with Jamison Clark had faded. The first step had been one fearfully taken, an uncertainty, a virgin experience. Yet the invigoration and adrenaline rush of success far exceeded any thrill ride or the dangerous high a person got from some brain-numbing drug. Nemesis's visit to a second target would be free from the jitters of his first kill. He dismissed the car salesman mentally from both his list and memory. Jamison's death would not pose a problem. It was destined to be one of the many unsolved murders—no clues, no witnesses, no motive—eventually ending up as an unhappy statistic for the Las Vegas Police Department.

The moon peeked through a few powdery clouds. It was late…or early, depending upon how one chose to think of the time between midnight and one in the morning. Midvale, a municipality a few miles south of Salt Lake City, was mostly quiet at this hour. There was the occasional car on the main roads, but nothing stirring down the side streets or alleyways.

Nemesis moved soundlessly, a shadow within the darkness. He reached the faded sign over the rear entrance to the bar and took up a position to keep watch.

Immobile as a portrait, Nemesis was calm and poised, awaiting his prey with the patience of a spider. Scattered pieces of litter had been strewn about in the passageway, although a trash Dumpster was located next to Pacheco's Club door.

People are such slobs, Nemesis thought. Why couldn't they take a second or two and clean up after themselves? Would that have been so hard?

The rear door of the bar suddenly popped open and a man appeared. He was in his mid-forties, shorter than Nemesis by six inches, and carried a roll of fat around his middle, which jiggled with each step. In his hands was a cardboard box which appeared to be filled with paper and trash. He started toward the Dumpster, shook his head and pulled a face.

'Cabron!' he muttered. 'Smells worse'n a backed-up crapper out here.'

Nemesis watched and awaited his chance. When the man turned his back to toss the box in the trash bin, Nemesis moved quickly. With the waste discarded, the man rotated around.

'Whoa!' He grunted, startled to discover Nemesis standing behind him. 'Where the hell did you come from, buddy?'

'Paul Pacheco, I've been wanting to talk to you.'

'Come back when the bar's open. I ain't got—'

Nemesis removed the .38 Smith & Wesson from his waistband and pointed it at him. 'Now, Paul,' he said, a cool warning in his voice, 'you can make time for me, can't you?'

Paul clumsily backed up against the Dumpster and threw up both hands. His face skewed up in a look of complete shock. He shook his head violently back and forth and sputtered: 'What do you want?'

'Let's step inside.'

'If this is a robbery, you won't have much luck. I sent the deposit with my night girl. It's already in the bank by this time.'

'I only came to talk to you,' Nemesis told him. 'Do as you're told and I promise I won't shoot you.'

Paul's wide, anxious eyes fixed on the gun in Nemesis's hand. 'Who are you? Why do you want to go inside?'

Studying the man's terrified reaction caused Nemesis to smile. 'And here I thought I was the one with the questions.'

'I'll give you the money from the cash register!' Paul desperately negotiated. 'I've got a few dollars on me too. You can take whatever you want. Just don't hurt me!'

Nemesis sighed his impatience. 'Inside, Paul,' he warned, 'or I might become unpleasant. You wouldn't like that.'

'All right, I'm going. I'm going!'

Nemesis stayed alert and close enough to prevent Paul from reaching for a weapon or trying to jump him. Once inside the building, the odor of the bar filled his nostrils. The air was heavy from stale liquor, the sweat of drunks and unwashed bodies. This was not a high-class establishment.

'You've done pretty well for yourself, Paul,' Nemesis told him. 'You own a bar, have a wife and four kids—only one teenager left at home—but you gave them a roof over their heads and always put food on the table.'

'I've been a good provider, yeah.'

'Sit down on one of the chairs.'

'You going to tie me up?'

'Only so our chat doesn't get out of hand. I deplore violence.'

Paul tipped his head at the weapon in his hand. 'That why you brung along a gun?'

'Exactly,' Nemesis replied. 'Now sit down and let your arms hang at your sides. I'm going to tape your wrists to the chair. I wouldn't want you trying something silly before we have a chance to have our conversation.'

Paul didn't argue. A few seconds later he was securely bound. Nemesis put away the gun and tore a short strip of duct tape for his mouth. Paul's eyes widened fearfully.

'Wait!' the man wailed. He shook his head back and forth. 'Tell me, mister! What's this all about?'

Nemesis silenced his protests, roughly covering his mouth with the tape. Once secured, he picked up one of the centerpiece candles from a nearby table and, using its dim glow of light, held out the same picture he had shown Jamison Clark.

'You remember the night this was taken?'

Paul stared hard at the photo. From the immediate furrow along his brow, he was trying to understand what the picture meant. Recognition entered his mien and he squinted up at Nemesis. He blinked back tears of fright and possibly remorse—which rushed to fill his eyes—and turned his head from side to side.

'I can see you remember, Paul,' Nemesis said, putting away the photo. 'That's good.' Deliberately, he removed the wire from his back pocket. 'As I was saying before, you've had a good life…wife, kids, a business of your own…much more than someone like you deserved.'

Paul began to struggle, grunting from the effort of trying to pull his arms free. He blubbered muted words, unable to speak through the tape.

But Nemesis had no interest in listening to his lies or pitiful pleas for mercy. He and his friends more than deserved their punishment. Leaning over, he glared at the man and hissed his words.

'I am Nemesis and it's time for you to pay for your sins. Remember what you did and take the memory to your grave!'

He moved behind Paul, cinched the wire snug about his neck and began to twist the ends together. When the body no longer trembled, Nemesis relaxed from his vengeful posture and stepped around to stare at the lifeless form.

'Not as much fun being the victim is it, Paul?' he mocked him.

Taking a moment to cut a slit in the tape across Paul's mouth, he shoved a coin between the man's teeth. Satisfied with his handiwork, Nemesis took a final look around to ensure he had left nothing to incriminate himself.

'That's two crossed from the list,' he said aloud. 'It's almost too easy.'

KARI STOOD UNDER the shower stream and lathered herself with body wash. She had taken a shower before going to bed but still felt dirty. Dirty, used, disgusted, revolted... every unclean term she could think of.

Gads, I couldn't have been a bigger fool! She fought to keep the tears from starting to flow again. She had been blinded by the desire to have what every person on the planet wanted—to be loved, to have a special someone in their life.

And I chose Roger Cline—king of the vilest Lotharios on earth!

The sob rose in her throat but she swallowed angrily! No! She was done crying. This was not her fault. Roger had played upon her naïveté and used her trusting nature against her. Their relationship had been a chess match, with calculated and deliberate moves, except she had not known it was a game. Thinking back, his every word and action had been a ploy, a deception to win her trust and placate her ego. She had thought him considerate, not to rush into demanding sex, but he had savored each stage of seduction for his ultimate victory.

Kari rinsed and quickly dried herself off, rubbing much

harder than necessary with the towel. She wished to remove every memory of his touch.

Glancing at the clock, she discarded all thoughts but
those of getting dressed and rushing off to work. She had
to hurry. It wouldn't do to arrive tardy, not after all the
months of being punctual and having never missed a single
day at work. She would throw herself into the job, work
harder than ever before, do whatever it took never again
to think of Roger Cline!

A UNIFORMED POLICEMAN was there to meet the two detectives. Deroy Hampton had been on the force for sixteen
years and had earned the reputation of being a hardcase,
because he took both the job and regulations seriously.
His junior partner, Louis Grady, was a well-liked family
man with an easy-going disposition. They had worked as
a team for three years, solving a number of cases without
incurring any serious reprimands.

The police officer pointed toward the rear of the bar.
'The killer entered from the back door. It was still ajar
when Juanita—she's the bar owner's niece—arrived to do
the cleaning. I kept everyone out except for her and she
claimed she never touched the body or back door.'

'Good job…' Grady glanced at his nametag, '…Officer
Pike. Do we have an ETA on the coroner?'

'He and the crime scene team are en route,' Pike answered. 'You're the first to arrive.'

'Let's have a look, Ham.' Grady spoke to his partner.

'There are a few muddy prints by the rear door,' Pike
informed them. 'I was careful not to go further than the
body. Soon as I verified the man was dead, I came out here
and made the call.'

Grady gave him a nod of approval. 'We'll watch our
step.' Turning to his partner, 'Ready for a peek?'

'Everything by the book,' Hampton replied. 'We don't move or touch anything till the crime techs finish their jobs.'

Grady looked down the block. 'Long way around to the rear alley from this side, but we need to have a look back there. The killer might have waited for a time and left something behind...cigarette stub, chewing gum, a bit of hair or something from his clothes. We'll also need to check the Dumpsters.'

'You're younger and in better shape than me,' Hampton replied. 'You want to walk two blocks to get to the alley, be my guest.'

Grady opened his mouth to reply, hesitated, and then tipped his head at an approaching van. 'Here's the crime scene boys now. I guess the back alley can wait a few minutes for them to do their thing.'

Hampton put his attention on Officer Pike. 'This place on your usual beat?'

'When I'm on the night shift I do a drive-by of the Midvale businesses.'

'Any place open after midnight, other than this joint?'

'There's another bar, a café that often stays open till about midnight, but nothing else closer than the twenty-four-hour gas station on the main drag.'

'So much for witnesses,' Hampton said. 'No surveillance cameras either.'

'Unless he lives close by, our perp had to get here some way,' Grady suggested. 'A bus driver or taxi might remember dropping a man off close by. If the killer drove here, he might have parked outside someone's house.'

'We'll check that and get people busy canvassing the area. There are some apartments close by and, even though the nearby stores were closed, someone might have been working late.'

'OK, Ham, you radio for more uniforms while I call in to the office. Soon as the crime scene team finishes up, we'll get a look inside and out in the back alley.'

FIVE

JASON DECIDED TO check out some sights. He started by driving out to see the Bonneville Salt Flats, where land speeds were set beginning in the year 1949, and included records of 300 to 600 miles per hour.

Becoming accustomed to thinking of miles, instead of kilometers, and growing more comfortable with people driving on the wrong side of the road, he returned to Salt Lake and headed north to a place called Antelope Island. A brochure advertised it to be the largest island in the largest salt lake in the western hemisphere. Populating the island were bison, pronghorn, coyote and bighorn sheep, along with numerous other smaller animals.

Driving the narrow winding road on the island, he spied all of the aforementioned, although the coyote was a long way off, as were the sheep. After touring and sightseeing for a couple hours, he stopped at a small beach that offered showers and went for a swim.

Well, it had been intended as a swim, but the salt content in the lake was much greater than that in the ocean. He waded out into deep water—which was no less than a hundred meters from shore—until he was about to his armpits. Within another step or two his feet simply stopped touching the bottom. There was no need to flail about or paddle to stay afloat. The human body simply did not sink in such heavy salt water! It was like wearing a flotation device, bobbing about with no effort whatsoever.

After imitating a cork for fifteen minutes, he returned

to shore. The convenience of a shower for rinsing was a great help. The dip in the cool water had left a coating of fine granules over his body and it took some time to remove the salt film.

He called it a day and picked up some Asian take-away before reaching his motel. At least, they offered tea along with the meal. When he got to his room he took another shower and then sat down to eat while watching the nightly news. He paused from dipping an egg roll in a small container of sweet-and-sour sauce when he heard news of a murder.

'...said today there are no leads in the homicide of a Midvale business owner, Paul Pacheco. The police have no suspects at this time and have not yet determined a motive for the killing.' The newscaster continued, 'Mr Pacheco was found taped to a chair this morning and had been strangled to death in his own small nightclub.'

Jason stared at the tube, totally engrossed, but the news coverage changed to a traffic accident.

Paul Pacheco...Paul Pacheco. Why does that name sound familiar?

He considered the information surrounding his death. Bound in a chair with tape and strangled—the same MO as he had heard about on his last night in Las Vegas. That victim had also been bound and strangled. He had been a car dealer or salesman. Yes, he remembered, him now— Clark, Jamison Clark.

Jason muted the sound on the TV and tried to place the two names together. Paul Pacheco and Jamison Clark. There was nothing—no light bulb switched on in his memory, no hint that he had ever personally met or read about either of the men. Perhaps he should contact the local authorities and inform them of the similarities.

He frowned at the idea. He had been in law enforcement long enough to know that the local police department wouldn't want a visiting CID man sticking his nose into their investigation.

Then he had another thought: a wild, ridiculous notion came into his head. Kari Underwood worked for the newspaper and she wrote obituaries! She could very likely research the two men and tell him if there was any obvious connection between them in a matter of minutes.

There was a telephone directory in the room so he was able to find the correct name without much difficulty. It helped to know that she had mentioned living in West Jordan and there was only one Underwood listed with the initial K.

The phone rang twice before a feminine voice came on the line and said, 'Hello. This is Kari.'

'Miss Underwood? Jason Keane here. We met at Sally Cline's home.'

'What do you want?' Her voice lacked any trace of warmth.

'Did I catch you at a bad time?'

'If you're calling to ask if I'm all right, the answer is yes. I'm a big girl. I can take care of myself.'

'I'm sorry,' he said quickly. 'I don't know—'

'What do you want?' she asked for the second time.

'It's something Roger said about your job...how you worked for the newspaper, editing and compiling obituaries.'

'I'll gladly put Roger's name in the paper!' she snapped in an icy tone of voice. 'But I'll want proof he is dead and that a stake has been driven through his heart, so he won't rise to walk again! Anything else?'

Her utter fury and the volume of her delivery caused Jason to move the receiver from up next to his ear. 'Uh, no,' he said quietly. 'I didn't mean to trouble you.'

Instead of a reply the line went suddenly dead. She had hung up on him.

Jason sat in confusion for a moment and then pulled out a small notepad he always carried. He had the personal information of the Cline family, so he found Reggie's number and punched it in.

Reggie answered. When he heard Jason on the line, he was instantly friendly.

'So how did it go after I left you with Mom?' he asked. 'I figured she would drink you under the table by midnight.'

'I never was much of a drinker,' Jason admitted. 'I was not in the running after the second round.'

'I'm sorry I had to desert you.'

'You didn't have a choice, and it gave us the time together that I had intended. My father asked me to deliver some keepsakes and your mother and I had a nice long chat.'

'That's good.'

'The reason I'm calling, I rang up Roger's girlfriend— Miss Kari Underwood? I thought she might provide an answer to a question. But when I spoke to her, she was both abrupt and abrasive concerning Roger. I wondered if you know what that is all about?'

Reggie sighed loudly. 'Roger dumped her. I spoke to him a little while ago, when I noticed he had stolen another of my shirts.'

'He takes your shirts?'

'Yeah, well, only when he has a plane to catch or an early meeting.' Reggie allowed a hint of understanding to his tone. 'He lives up East and my apartment is a lot closer to his company and the airport. Anyway, I asked him about Kari, and he said he had broken up with her.'

'That's why Miss Underwood was curt with me,' Jason said. 'Roger called off their relationship.'

'After bringing her to dinner with Mom.' His voice was laced with ire. 'And trust me, Roger does much worse than call off a relationship. When he breaks up with a girl, he makes sure they know it's over. I've seen some of the hate mail he's gotten from ex-girlfriends, and he's had to change his phone number more than once. One was vindictive enough that she scratched a few choice names on his car with a screwdriver.'

'Yet you two seem to get along.'

'I know, I know. But we've been best friends all our lives, and we still have great fun when we're together. The only thing we fight about is how he treats women…and his borrowing my shirts.'

'I understand.'

'Why did you want to speak to Kari?'

'A bit of research. I'm rather good at remembering names, and I heard a couple that seem familiar. I thought she might give me a background check on them so I could put the idea out of my head.'

'You're a long way from home to be investigating.'

'It's nothing formal, Reggie. I was trying to place the names Jamison Clark and Paul Pacheco.'

Reggie was in silent thought for a moment. 'I'm not sure about Pacheco, but Mom used to hang with a guy named Jamison Clark. He was one of the kids who was on the high-school football team.'

Jason immediately remembered hearing the name on Sunday night. 'Yes, of course—Kenny and Clark! He was one of the players.'

'He's the only Jamison Clark I know.'

'Thank you, Reggie. You've been a great help.'

'Sure thing,' he said. Then he asked, 'What do you say we get together one of these next days, the three of us, while you're still in town?'

'That would be great.'

'I'll talk to Roger and get back to you about a time and place.'

Jason said his farewell to Reggie, placed the telephone receiver back on to its cradle and made a decision. OK, so Jamison Clark might be the same guy who had gone to school with Sally. The name Paul Pacheco, however, was still drawing a blank. He decided to mention it to his aunt, he would see if she recognized the name.

'ANY LEADS ON the Pacheco murder?' the captain asked, pausing at Hampton's desk.

'Forensics has been working day and night, but we've got nothing to this point,' Hampton replied.

'No one remembers him having any arguments or fights with anyone lately,' Grady put in from his desk, a short distance away. 'We've talked to everyone in the neighborhood—friends, neighbors, acquaintances, his wife and family. His sister, Maria, said she hadn't seen or talked to her brother since Christmas. We basically have zilch.'

The captain frowned. 'You get anything from the tape or wire used?'

'Ordinary duct tape and the electrical wire was light enough gauge to have strength yet is easy to roll into a wad. The perp could have picked them up at any store with a hardware section.'

'How about the coin?'

'A 2005 quarter with no prints or smudges,' Hampton said.

'So our killer is careful.'

'We found some footprints in the alley behind the bar. Standard sneaker, pretty well worn from the markings—a size eleven,' Grady reported.

'That give us anything?'

Grady grunted. 'Nothing concrete, Capt'n. The guy could be six-four or better, if he was wearing shoes that fit.'

'Yeah,' Hampton agreed, 'our man could have picked up the shoes from a thrift store for this job. If he did, they might not be his size and they're probably on their way to the landfill by this time.'

'Nothing else?'

Hampton replied. 'There are a thousand prints, hairs and DNA from every customer who passed through Pacheco's joint, but nothing at all on the duct tape. That means the guy wore gloves and was very careful.'

Grady bobbed his head in agreement. 'The only real clue—if you can call it that—there was still a little money in the till and the vic had close to a hundred dollars in his wallet. Plus he was wearing a ring worth maybe a grand on his finger. We can rule out robbery.'

'In point of fact,' Hampton mused, 'Pacheco actually ended up a quarter richer...if you count the coin in his mouth.'

The captain scowled at his humor. 'Keep at it. I have to report something to the chief that he can pass along to the reporters. I'll say we're following up on a number of tips and leads.'

'You'd have made a good farmer, Capt'n,' Grady teased. 'You shovel manure with the best of them.'

'Find me something better for the next report or we all might end up working on a farm.'

As he walked over to his office, Grady and Hampton exchanged looks.

'I would guess he's catching some heat on this, Ham.'

'Good thing it was a bar owner and not some high-end businessman,' Hampton agreed. 'If we don't catch a break, this murder is going to end up stuck on a shelf with a good many other cold cases.'

'Yeah, and the chief is likely to tell the captain to put us on traffic duty or crowd control for the next rock festival that comes around.'

KARI'S DARK MOOD had not gone unnoticed by her best friend at work. Dee was a little on the overweight side, matronly, and worked in want-ads. Although in her fifties, she and Kari had bonded like sisters. Dee naturally assumed the role as the eldest. Notwithstanding their difference in age, Dee was young at heart, fun to be around and possessed an infectious laugh. The two of them could talk for hours and seldom disagreed on anything of importance.

'You going to 'fess up about why you're so down in the dumps lately?' Dee asked at their morning coffee break. 'Or do I have to order us the Fiesta Plate Special at Freddie's Taco Shack for lunch?'

Forcing the semblance of a smile, Kari arduously suppressed her despondency. 'Eating isn't the answer to everything.'

'Wait a few years, kiddo!'

Kari sighed. 'I'm sorry for being such a Gloomy Gus lately.'

'So give, what's the problem?'

Kari had bottled up her feelings and the hurt was so intense…she needed a relief valve or she might burst. Dee had often been her sounding-board when she felt the need to confide in someone. With little care or control, Kari blurted out the details of her relationship with Roger.

'Gadfry, Dee!' she exclaimed, finishing the story. 'How could I have been so wrong about him? He led me to the gallows and I cheerfully put the noose around my own neck!'

Dee was vehement. 'He sounds like one smooth talkin', heartless scumbag, Kari. It's a crying shame a sweetheart like you got mixed up with such a cold-blooded hunk of slime.'

Kari suffered a renewed chagrin at the ugly memory. 'I was a tramp for giving him what he wanted, and he would have called me a deceitful tease if I hadn't given in!'

'You were screwed either way, kiddo—and that's no pun,' Dee lamented.

'I feel so used,' Kari said, battling a sob which threatened to surface. 'I don't sleep around and I've never had a one-night stand. I...' but she couldn't continue.

'I hope the rotten vermin fries in hell!' Dee declared harshly. 'There are a thousand hussies out there on the prowl every night and he picks a trusting, innocent thing like you to degrade and humiliate. If I were a man...' her face contorted into a mask of fury. 'To hell with being a man! Tell me where to find Rat-maggot (she christened him with a name) and I'll rip out his heart with my teeth!'

Dee's rage worked as a sedative for Kari. She mustered up a smile. 'I always knew you were a real lady.'

'*Lady, smady!* I'll kick that sleazy gigolo so hard in his family jewels that every member of his family will double over!'

Kari couldn't help herself, she laughed out loud. Dee frowned at her reaction and then broke into laughter too. It was the first light moment Kari had enjoyed since Sunday night. Maybe there was hope for the future after all.

NEMESIS MOVED SILENTLY to the front of the house. It added risk to kill twice in such a short period of time, but it was necessary. The cops would eventually figure out his list of victims. They might even discover the motive. It was expected, but it wouldn't do for them to catch on too quickly. He dismissed thoughts concerning future plans and checked the ground for dampness. The lawn had not been watered lately so he wouldn't leave any readable prints. Besides which, he had on another pair of two dollar shoes—two sizes too big—purchased from a thrift store on the other side of town.

Easing in behind a shrub, his heart raced at his own pluck. Was it bold and daring to risk entering a man's house while his family slept, or was it the impulsive act of a fool? One missed step, one tinkle of glass and he would be discovered.

Yet he had studied this mark, knew his habits well. In a few minutes he would be up and moving about. He had come to the kitchen on each of the three nights that Nemesis had been outside watching his house. The man was hardly ever alone…except for his nightly trip in the wee hours of the morning.

Nemesis knew the doors and windows were securely locked. Having planned ahead, he moved like a wisp of smoke to the window he had selected, the one furthest from the bedrooms. There he stopped and removed two items from his black bag. He first applied a suction cup to the window pane, then traced a circle with the glass-cutter. Wrapping his rubber-gloved hand with a clean rag, it took only a very soft tap and the cut-out section popped free. He removed the glass and quickly placed the cutter, rag and suction cup back into the knapsack. Then he reached through and released the window latch. There was no alarm—his unwary prey was a law-abiding man with nothing to fear.

He opened the window and climbed through on to the living-room carpet. He quietly made his way to the kitchen and took a moment to place a chair out in the open. Next, he padded softly to a point where he could remain hidden in the shadows until his victim put in an appearance.

The wait was not a long one. Steve Kenny got out of bed

for his nightly fix—yogurt or Maalox and milk—to soothe his ulcer. Nemesis doubted his stomach condition had anything to do with the picture in his shirt pocket. Men like Kenny would not have lingering regrets over something so trivial. After all, he was a member of today's enlightened society, the one which holds no one responsible for their own actions. Every despicable act can be blamed on someone or something else.

Steve Kenny entered the room and flipped on the light. He reached for the refrigerator door before he noticed the kitchen chair out of place.

'What the...?'

Nemesis stepped out with gun in hand. 'One sound,' he rasped in a hushed voice, 'and I'll put a bullet in your head!'

Steve's hands shot upward and he stumbled back against the kitchen counter. 'What's the meaning of this?' He whined like a little girl. 'Who are you?'

'Keep your voice down!' Nemesis warned. 'If you wake up the house, I'll kill you and anyone else who sees me.'

The man's face worked, settling on a mask of confusion and fear. To his credit, he lowered his voice. 'What do you want?'

'I'm only here to talk to you.'

'If this is about a bill or some breakdown with your car, I'm sure we can—'

'Sit in the chair,' Nemesis ordered.

As with the other two subjects, Nemesis quickly secured him with tape and applied a final strip over his mouth. Once the frightened man stopped struggling and had control of his wits, Nemesis showed him the picture.

Steve frowned and grunted, trying to ask what Nemesis wanted.

'You remember this, don't you?' Nemesis asked. 'I want

the events which surrounded this photo and all that happened afterwards clear in your memory.'

The man's eyes grew large with a curious fascination.

'I'm glad you remember,' Nemesis said. 'You've hidden the truth all these years, but I'm here to collect the debt.'

The gagged and bound man slowly turned his head from side to side, as if to deny his culpability. It only made it easier for Nemesis to finish the job.

'ANY CHANCE THIS IS only a bizarre coincidence?' Detective Hampton asked Grady. He reached out and turned the dead man's head a few inches. 'See it? There in his mouth?'

Grady whistled under his breath. 'Duct tape, electrical wire…it's an instant replay of the Pacheco murder.'

'You ever hear of an MO like this?'

'No, but it duplicates our nightclub owner—right down to the coin left between his teeth!' Grady rubbed his hands together. 'What do you think, he leaves a quarter as a sicko calling card, or is our killer sending a message?'

Hampton scrutinized the coin. 'It's showing tails. Wonder if that means anything in itself?'

'If memory serves, the last one was also tails. I can check my notes, but I'm pretty certain it was the side facing up.'

'Maybe he wants us to tag him with the name *Coin Killer* or some such thing?'

'Two murders with no apparent motive. Instead of leaving us enough money for half a pay-phone call, why doesn't this s.o.b. scrawl us a message on the wall?'

'Be especially considerate of him if he would also sign his name at the bottom of the message,' Hampton joked.

'Pacheco could have made any number of enemies.' Grady waved one hand in a furtive gesture. 'You know, it could have been some underage kids who tried to get served in his club. It doesn't take much for a punk or banger to think he has a reason to kill someone.'

'Yeah, and this guy was an auto mechanic. Do you know anyone who doesn't have a beef about some mechanic? He probably ruined a transmission or overcharged someone for a repair.'

'So we're looking for a guy with a grudge against a bartender and an auto mechanic, who also has a pocket full of quarters.'

Hampton sorted cynically, 'Put out an APB, for any of the local arcade gangs whose car broke down at this guy's place, and then was refused a drink at Pacheco's bar. We ought to have our killer in custody by nightfall.'

'We'd better cross our fingers instead,' Grady replied, growing serious. 'We need for the ME or crime scene crew to find us something to work with.' He glanced around the room. 'Looks the same as the bar owner—our victim didn't put up a fight. He's wearing pajamas too, so he was obviously taken by surprise. Probably kept quiet so as not to wake the others in the house.'

'We've got a couple smudges of shoe prints on the floor and by the window the guy used for access, Ham. One of the crime lab boys took a measurement and said it's a size larger than the prints we got at the alley behind the bar.'

'Guy probably buys shoes at some thrift store and then tosses them,' Hampton surmised. 'No prints or fibers, not even a piece of lint on the window sill or piece of glass he removed. Not much chance of DNA either, because the perp doesn't touch the victim. Except for the duct tape, he kills without ever making physical contact.'

Grady gave a head bob in agreement. 'Back-to-back murders, with not a clue left behind. We had better hope this guy doesn't have a long list of people he wants to kill.'

'*If* it is a list and not random.'

'Got to be specific vics, Ham. Why waste a quarter on a perfect stranger?'

Hampton gave a grunt of agreement and slowly perused the room. 'Not a thing out of place that I can see. Our perp probably uses a knife or gun to get his victims to sit quietly while he tapes them to a chair.'

'Might tell them he only wants to talk,' Grady replied.

'That's a possibility.'

'We sure need to find something. Anything!' Grady complained. 'Two murders and we've nothing but a couple smeared footprints—which might not even be the right size. He wiped the last quarter clean and I'll bet you a cup of coffee this place is free of his prints as well.'

'There's a popular expression about the creek we're up right now!' Hampton gave a shake of his head. 'Ask the guy's wife to look around and see if anything is missing. This doesn't appear to have been a robbery, but it's possible our killer took a keepsake or something. Meanwhile, I'll call the office and have them start a background check on this guy. Maybe something will link him and Pacheco.'

'I'm betting we won't get any help with witnesses,' Grady said. 'The coroner puts the time of death between midnight and two in the morning. Most people in this neighborhood were in bed asleep at the time of the murder.'

Hampton felt equally helpless. 'Yeah, all we can do is work our tails off, pray this guy doesn't kill again, and hope we catch a break. Heck of a way to run an investigation.'

SIX

KARI WAS FEELING a little more upbeat at work that morning. She sipped a swallow of her morning fix—Pepsi over ice—while she organized an obituary on her computer. The phone rep who took the information was either a temp or had been hired out of desperation. Cause of Death: *cronic newmonia!* Didn't the rep know how to use spell-check?

A shadow fell over her desk and she glanced up at Dee. 'Hey!' she said, displaying an enthusiasm she didn't feel, 'What's going on, girlfriend?'

Dee didn't respond to the greeting but appeared unusually serious. 'Did you hear about the excitement in my neighborhood last night?'

Kari pushed back from the monitor. 'No, what happened?'

'Right up the street—not three blocks from my house—a guy was strangled to death in his own home.'

'I didn't listen to the news this morning. I'll probably get my first look at the victim when his obit crosses my desk.'

'Left a wife and two kids.' Dee skewed her expression. 'No, check that—two wives and one kid. He had remarried once.' She put her hands on her hips, pausing to stare off into space. 'I had him work on my car a couple times. He didn't seem like a bad sort and did a good job.'

'I've never known a person who got murdered,' Kari admitted. 'It always seems to happen far away—you know, to someone else.'

'I wonder who will get the story,' Dee said, relating the death back to their company's normal business. 'Probably that catty back-stabber, Charise. It seems like she's always getting her face in the paper or on the evening news.'

Kari suffered a pang of envy. She desperately wanted to be a reporter—an ambition made even more important, now that her love life had turned to dust.

'I'd gladly forgo the television interview or my picture at the top of the article,' she told Dee wistfully. 'Just give me a chance to write the story and see my own byline in print.'

'Maybe you should ask old lady Taylor if you can cover the murder. You could go over there, inspect the scene, wade around in the blood and make a nuisance of yourself.'

'Fat chance of that. The management here doesn't even know I exist.'

'You'll get your chance, Kari. You just have to hang on.'

'I feel like I'm hanging all right…out to dry!' She picked up a pencil and stared at it. 'A year and a half in the newspaper business and I've done nothing but edit, proof read and compose a thousand obituaries.' She grasped the pencil with both hands like a strangle-hold and shook it. 'Sometimes, I'd like to wring the neck of the teacher who told me I'd make a good journalist. I'm sick of doing the garbage work and going nowhere!'

'Everyone has to start at the bottom,' a bass, female voice sounded off from behind the two of them. 'Having a piece of paper on your wall saying you graduated college doesn't make you a reporter.'

Kari dropped the pencil as if it had burned her fingers. 'It's been a bad week,' she explained meekly, rotating around in her chair to look at her supervisor. 'I was just venting, Miss Taylor.'

'*Miss?*' She lifted a neatly sculpted eyebrow. 'What year did you graduate?'

'Sorry about the slip, *Ms* Taylor. I wasn't being disrespectful.' She sought vindication. 'I tend to think of *Ms* as a title for a much older woman. I let the *miss* thing slip because you've always seemed so youthful.'

Taylor narrowed her gaze. 'Nice recovery, Ms Underwood. Would you be trying to suck up to me?'

Kari displayed an innocent mien. 'Certainly not. I was shocked the day someone told me you were more than two score in years. I would have guessed you at closer to thirty—no more than twenty-nine.'

A crooked smile crept on to the woman's blood-red, painted lips. 'I see you've learned that sucking up is best served with an adequate helping of sincerity.'

'Yes, ma'am.'

Becoming businesslike again, the faint smile disappeared. 'As for your desire to get into investigative journalism,' she appeared to choose her words carefully, 'there is a rumor you might be given a chance in the near future.'

The cloud of gloom that had been over Kari's desk all morning split open to allow in a ray of sunshine. 'Really?' She remained guarded. 'You're not teasing me?'

A scowl darkened Taylor's expression. 'Is this the face of someone who indulges in childish teasing?'

'No, ma'am.'

'When you've paid all of your dues and are ready, you'll get your chance,' she declared. 'That's as much as I can tell you.'

'Thank you, Ms Taylor. I appreciate the consideration.'

The woman strode out of the room without another word. Kari glanced at Dee and recognized her friend was about to break into a fit of giggles. Sometimes Dee behaved more like a teenager than a wife and mother of two grown children.

'Thanks for not saying anything to warn me!' Kari scolded her. 'I didn't know Taylor was within hearing distance.'

'That woman is always within hearing distance. She's got the ears of a bat!'

'Did you hear what she said?' Kari asked, unable to hide a tremor of excitement. 'Do you think maybe I'll soon get a chance to do a story on something like last night's murder?'

'More likely, they'll send you to a dull PTA meeting.'

Kari gibed: 'I doubt that. There are too many touchy topics when it comes to teachers, parents and children.'

'You're right,' Dee agreed. 'They'll no doubt start you off with something elementary, like the opening of a new restaurant…though nothing too fancy. Maybe a library or new grocery store.'

'Gee, thanks for the support.'

'Think nothing of it, kiddo.'

'Yes, I will…' Kari quipped. 'Think nothing of it, that is!'

JASON HAD VISITED Sally for a couple of hours on the previous day, and then driven the thirty miles up to Park City, where the Sundance Film Festival was held each year. The day was laid back, and he picked up some tea at a herb and organic-food store. His room had a setup for coffee, so he could use the hot water and make himself a passable cup of tea. Reggie telephoned that evening, but it was just a courtesy call and a promise they would get together again.

The following morning Jason again met Sally for breakfast—she was working late shift at the store—and he brought up Jamison Clark's death. It was only in passing conversation and she showed little interest in the details.

Jason also queried her about Paul Pacheco. She remembered a boy of that name from school. He had been an artist and vague acquaintance, but she hadn't seen him or Jamison Clark since graduation. The remainder of his short visit yielded no further information. She bid him farewell and went off to work, so he made a trip up to see the Kennecott copper mine.

Tynan Cline, Sally's stepfather, had worked there for nearly thirty years before retiring. It was vaunted to be the World's Largest Man-Excavated Mine. Visible from anywhere in the Salt Lake Valley, it was an awesome sight from the overlook. Two-and-one-half-miles wide and three-quarters of a mile deep. They had been extracting copper from the Bingham mine for over a hundred years.

Jason had put the two mysterious deaths on the back burner of his mind, until he turned on the television to watch the five o'clock news. It didn't take long before the reporter had his full attention.

'Police are investigating the homicide of a West Valley man. Steven Kenny was found strangled in his own home. A statement by the police department confirmed the murder of this man was very similar to the murder of a bar owner, Paul Pacheco, earlier in the week. They have found no connection between the two victims, but say it is likely the same killer targeted the two men. If you have any information concerning either man's death, please contact the Salt Lake City Police Department.'

Jason's mind was spinning. Another murder victim? Strangled in his own home? He focused on the accompanying picture which flashed on the television screen. He didn't recognize the face, but there could be no doubt about the name! It sent an icy chill skating along Jason's spine.

He flipped to another channel, as the local news was on four different stations. He learned little more, other than that there were no signs of a struggle. Steve Kenny had been killed by an unknown assailant, while the family had not been harmed or even awakened during the slaying.

The man's name bounced about in his head like a loose tennis ball. *Steven Kenny!* It must be the same Kenny who had played ball with Clark. There was no mention of Jamison Clark yet, but he would soon be added to the list. As a responsible citizen…well, tourist, he should call the police and let them know about Jamison.

This is none of your business, his subconscious warned. *You're not on the case. You're only visiting your aunt. Local law enforcement doesn't appreciate it when someone from the outside comes in and…*

Jason suddenly had a thought. It certainly wasn't ethical, but it could serve his purpose. First, he needed to make a stop at his aunt's house.

KARI WISHED SHE HAD taken her father up on his invite for dinner, but doubted she would have been good company. She had begged out of the meal, but promised to visit her parents soon.

'Maybe you were a little too hasty,' she chided to herself while removing the plastic bag from the freezer. Fried chicken and all the fixings, her father had promised. Now, she would settle for a portion of frozen hash browns, a small slice of ham and toast. She had not felt like eating since being jilted, but she was hungry this evening. Perhaps the appetite was a sign of recovery.

She started to pour a small portion of virgin olive oil into her fry pan when the doorbell rang. She set down the bottle, turned off the burner and padded over to the door. Pausing to look out the peephole, she ventured, *Maybe I can pretend to not be home.*

Spying the man in the hall, she gasped in shock. A

constriction tightened within her chest, accompanied by a poignant ache in her heart. She wavered, consumed by uncertainty and mortification.

Jason Keane! What was he doing here?

Kari sought the icy fortitude to walk back to the stove and ignore the man at the door. She wanted nothing more to do with anyone remotely connected to the Cline family. The misery was too great. However, curiosity was a part of her make-up, a trait needed to be a good reporter. Besides which, she had never been the sort to hide from a problem. She took a deep breath, slid back the dead-bolt and opened the door a crack.

'Jason.' She put no warmth or greeting in her voice. 'What do you want?'

A look of urgency was on his face. 'I don't wish to intrude, Miss Underwood, but I need to speak to you. It's important.'

'I'm not in the mood for company, and I've got supper on the stove,' she told him curtly. 'Maybe some other time.'

'This can't wait.' His eyes shone with a peculiar excitement. 'Believe me, it's well worth your time. I came here to offer my help.'

'Help?' She uttered a grunt of disgust. 'I don't need any help to get over breaking up with Roger.' With a sneer, 'You can tell him I said he could go to hell—the sooner the better! It might crush his monumental ego, but I'm not the sort to go suicidal over losing the perfect man!'

Jason bore into her with a gravely serious expression. 'This has nothing whatsoever to do with Roger.'

The statement removed some of the heat from her roiling temper. 'Then what?'

He looked up and down the hall, as if afraid someone might overhear their conversation, then whispered: 'I've discovered something that might allow you a step-up towards becoming a reporter. If you have the cheek, it could be a story for you, perhaps a major one!'

That sparked her interest. She was still wary, but Jason seemed sincere.

'Five minutes,' she told him firmly. 'Then I want you gone.'

'It shall be as you wish.'

Kari stepped back and allowed Jason to enter. He had a book tucked under his arm and stopped to make a quick inspection of her apartment. She closed the door and casually wondered what he thought of her unpretentious decor. Not exactly lavish furnishings, a second-hand pink love-seat, a rectangular coffee table, and a small entertainment center, which sported a 27-inch television and a combination VCR-DVD machine. Next to the kitchen was a plain, round dinner table with three inexpensive chairs. Fortunately, he couldn't see into the untidy bedroom, as the door was closed.

Kari stepped around in front of him and purposely looked at her watch. 'The clock is ticking,' she warned. 'What's so important?'

'Look here,' he said, opening the book he had brought with him. Kari glanced at it. 'A high-school yearbook?'

'Yes,' Jason replied. 'I've discovered something rather important.'

'What are you talking about?'

Jason flipped to a page and pointed to a row of pictures. 'See this man?' At her glance, he read the name: 'Paul Pacheco.'

Kari regarded him with an inquisitive look. 'So it's Paul Pacheco, so what?'

Jason turned back a page, indicated another picture and announced, 'Steven Kenny.'

Kari made a more careful inspection this time, wondering what she was missing. 'OK, so those two guys were in the same graduating class.'

'The two recent unsolved murders here in the valley,' Jason clarified. 'Both of whom have been on the news lately. Paul was found strangled to death in his pub and Steve was murdered last night in the same fashion.'

A shrill alarm sounded within Kari's brain. The names were suddenly familiar, names torn from the headlines of the newspaper where she worked. A tingle of anticipation seeped into her calm demeanor.

'You're saying there's a connection, because both of the murdered men graduated from the same school and in the same year?' She clung to her composure and gave her head a negative toss. 'It's probably only a coincidence.'

'I'm sure that's what the local police think,' Jason said, his expression stoic. 'But there's something else, something I don't believe the police know yet.'

Kari was intent now, moving to stand at Jason's side, as he flipped through another several pages. He found the one he wanted and said: 'See this fellow?'

She leaned close enough to detect a slight fragrance of Jason's aftershave. In some remote region of her mind she knew he had freshly shaved before coming to visit.

Dismissing the notion, she studied the picture indicated and stated the name: 'Jamison Clark. Who's he?'

Jason displayed a grim satisfaction. 'Jamison Clark was bound and strangled to death at his home in Las Vegas last week.' He gave her a meaningful look. 'It was on the local news while I was staying at Bally's Hotel and Casino. They reported that the police had no suspects in his murder.'

Kari was on board now and her heart began to race. 'Three of them! All from the same graduating class!' She was breathless. 'All murdered within a matter of days!'

'Yes,' Jason confirmed. 'And each was strangled to death, after being bound with duct tape!'

'Good lord!' Kari exclaimed. 'Jason, do you know what this means?'

'It means you have an opportunity to write your first story.'

'Yes!' She gulped back her enthusiasm. 'I mean, no! It's the fact that someone is killing off guys who were in the same graduation class. It can't be a coincidence. There has to be a connection—three victims, all murdered in the same way!'

'That's where the police come in. You release the story and they use the information to proceed with their investigation.'

Kari began to pace the room, turning over ideas and options in her head. This was a major break. Bringing the story to light could do wonders for her career, but did she dare write about an ongoing investigation? And what about the newly uncovered facts? Who would believe she had come up with the information on her own?

'I don't know, Jason,' she said, thinking aloud. 'We shouldn't withhold the third man's connection from the police.'

'You won't be withholding anything. I've seen the same thing many times at home. A reporter writes a story and the authorities beat down your door to get to you.'

'What about when they ask me how I put together these facts?'

Jason shrugged. 'Tell them you did some digging and discovered it on your own. I prefer not to be involved.'

'You *are* involved!' she exclaimed. 'You're the one who found a common link between the murders. This is your discovery!'

'The local police would think I was interfering in their

investigation. With you, they will suspect you are using the information as a tool to get ahead in your job.'

Kari began to turn ideas over in her head. 'OK,' she said as if talking to herself, 'I'm sure I can keep you out of it.'

'Good.'

Then she stopped and stared at him. 'While on the subject, how did you happen to piece together this information?'

'Aunt Sally showed me the yearbook after our Sunday dinner. I have an eye for names and faces. The second man, Pacheco, I recalled seeing his name in print, but I did not place him until Kenny was killed.'

Kari pulled a face. 'The three of them graduated twenty-seven years ago—a year before I was born. Why would anyone be killing them now?' She stared at him in puzzlement. 'And how did Sally Cline happen to have the yearbook with all three victims?'

He sighed, flipped the page on the yearbook and pointed. Kari glanced at the picture of a pretty girl: Sally Cline!

'This is my aunt's yearbook,' Jason told her. 'She was in the same graduating class as the three victims.'

Kari gasped. 'That's incredible!'

'She told me about Clark and Kenny, and how they were destined to become football stars.'

'What about the third man, Mr Pacheco?'

'He was something of an artist, although he never used his talent professionally. I looked through the yearbook and he isn't listed on any of the sports rosters.'

'So this doesn't necessarily have anything to do with the football team?'

'No, but it can't be a coincidence, not three victims from the same graduating class, all strangled to death in the same manner.'

'Oh, Jason!' She was unable to suppress her excitement.

'This is such a…it's so considerate of you! You don't know how much this means to me.'

'I hoped it might be something you could use to your advantage.'

Kari moved over, rose up on to her toes and kissed him on the cheek. She smiled at the immediate flush of embarrassment which filtered into his features.

'Thank you. Thank you so much!'

'Yes, well,' Jason cleared his throat, 'I hope it helps. After the contemptible way Roger treated you, I'm glad I could offer a bit of support in your writing career.'

'Have you eaten yet?'

'No, but I can stop for—'

'I was just throwing together some hash browns, toast and fried ham. Not exactly a feast, but we can have something to eat and discuss my story proposal.'

'No,' he backed up a step. 'It would be awkward if I were to stay.' 'You aren't like your cousin, are you?' she asked bluntly. 'I mean, you did this as a kindness, not so you could try and seduce me…right?'

The words were delivered with such force, Jason replied in kind. 'I find you very attractive, but I'm not the sort of man to take advantage of a lady.'

'Then I'm safe with you?'

'Safe, yes, but…'

She smiled. 'So sit down while I fry the meat and hash browns. I want your input on the story I have to write.'

Who wouldn't enjoy spending some time with a beautiful, intelligent, and very charming girl? Jason capitulated and asked, 'You said ham and potatoes?'

'Yes.'

'If you also have eggs on hand I can fix you a Jason Keane Special.'

Kari arched a single eyebrow. 'A Jason Keane Special?'

'I've seen something like it on menus here in the States. They list it as a skillet dinner, but I don't use so many ingredients. I only need a bit of meat—ham will do nicely— plus potatoes and eggs, a little onion, milk and butter.'

'I have a bottle of onion bits.'

'That will suffice. You start work on your story and I'll prepare the meal.'

Kari smiled her agreement and showed him the kitchen. Jason worked efficiently and the meal was ready in twenty minutes. It tasted much more appetizing than it looked— the fried potatoes and ham smothered in eggs, all mingled together and lightly seasoned.

After another two hours of writing and editing, Kari watched Jason go down the hall to the stairs. She stood at the open door for a moment, curious about the pleasant man. He was nothing like Roger...or any other American she had ever met. Roger had been suave, charismatic, then he'd dumped her like old garbage. Jason had not flirted with her, even though he admitted he found her attractive. He had been completely non-aggressive, polite and a perfect gentleman. Roger had thought nothing of breaking her heart, while Jason felt remorse for his cousin's treatment and tried to make amends for something for which he'd had no part.

Her mind returned to the story she had written. It was a good article, a very good article. Jason had a keen eye for detail and his history in criminal law had helped her to use the right phrase or word on several occasions. She would get credit for the story, but it all derived from his efforts.

Thinking about the news account, she needed to formulate a plan. The story would have to be published quickly, before someone else stumbled on to the same information. She would go to work early and put her plan into motion. This was her big chance. She vowed not to blow it.

SEVEN

Marge Taylor accompanied Kari as they marched up to the managing editor's desk. While Scott Quinn took time to scan her article, Kari quivered inside with anticipatory excitement. Once he lifted his gaze to look at her, she could tell he was pleased.

'Marge and I have discussed the possibility of your moving up within the company, Kari. This is an impressive piece. Do you have the facts to back it up?'

'I saw the high-school yearbook and researched the news article about the murder of Mr Clark in Las Vegas. It's obvious the three murders are connected.'

'And you hit on this yourself?'

She didn't wish to lie to the editor. 'Actually, I was clued in about the third victim by a private source.'

'A private source, you say?'

'Yes. He happened to hear about the first murder when he was staying in Vegas. It's fortunate he recognized the name and put it together with the other two.'

He drummed his fingers on the desk. 'If we break this story, the police are going to want to know how you came up with this.'

Kari frowned. 'The information is out there for anyone to find. There's no reason they should think I didn't discover it on my own.'

'Would you want to have to lie to them?'

'No,' Kari admitted, her pulse beginning to pound.

'But I don't intend to give up my source. He prefers to remain anonymous.'

'What if they threaten you with jail?'

'That seems a little dramatic, considering they could connect the same dots as we did. Besides, there is a sacred trust between a reporter and her source,' she posited. 'I realize it isn't protected by law, but I won't reveal his name.'

Kari could almost see the wheels turning in Scott's head. He swiveled in his chair and stared at Taylor. 'What do you think, Marge?'

'Kari's been dependable and has done a good job for us. I feel comfortable recommending her.'

'Then it's settled.'

Kari looked from one to the other. 'What's settled?'

Scott replied, 'The only way we can legitimately support your writing, or for you to protect a source, is if you are part of our reporting team. We'd have a weak stance defending your journalistic rights while your only professional writing is the obituary column. As of your starting shift today, I'm promoting you to a field reporter.'

Kari did handsprings and shouted with glee—inside. Outwardly, however, she managed to maintain her decorum. 'Also,' Scott continued, 'as you were the one who discovered the details of these murders, I'm assigning you to the story.'

The news nearly caused Kari to faint!

'There will be some disgruntled employees when news about this gets out,' Taylor warned.

'Buzzard fodder!' Scott said staunchly. 'If they were any good they would have found this same information themselves. My motto is to let the one who discovered the story be the one to run with it.'

Kari barely contained her exuberance. 'Thank you, Mr Quinn. I'll do my very best. I promise!'

'Marge will show you to your new desk and introduce you to those who work in research. Keep me posted on whatever else you find.' He eyed her meaningfully. 'Get in there and dig. I want you to attend every news conference given by the police concerning this case. Get me a couple of good follow-up pieces.'

'I'll start right away.'

Scott smiled at her enthusiasm. 'Kari, if these three victims were all murdered by the same killer, there has to be an event or common bond that ties them together. You find out what it is and it'll be front page.'

'Yes, sir. I'll get right on it.'

Scott turned his attention to his computer monitor, so Taylor and Kari left. Once into the outer office, Taylor stopped and gave her a stern look.

'Well, squirt, it appears you managed to slip in through the back door.' Her voice was austere, but there was a slight, upward lift at the corner of her mouth.

Kari laughed, her jubilance barely contained. 'I'm not particular about which entrance I use, so long as I get where I want to go.'

Taylor gave an affirmative bob of her head. 'Spoken like a true reporter. I think you'll do just fine.'

Kari experienced a subtle confidence. Even Taylor thought she had what it took to be a reporter. She was going to get a chance to live her dream. Until Jason put the story in her lap, it had seemed an unreachable goal. Or so far away in the future that she dared not dwell on it. She had to dream no more....

I've arrived! I'm a reporter!

Thirty minutes later Dee stopped by to visit at Kari's new desk. She had a twisted smile on her face, revealing her uneven front teeth, a minor distraction from her otherwise comely features.

'Hail the newest scribe for the emperor!' she teased. 'Does the High Priestess of Baloney need some help moving her stuff?'

Kari laughed, still giddy about the promotion. 'I think I can manage. There isn't much down in obit that I want to remember.'

'Well, don't forget about me. I'm still stuck in that black hole, and who knows what kind of ghoul they'll assign to your old desk.'

'I'm sure you'll get along with the new person just fine,' she said. 'But you might want to keep your garlic and cross handy.'

'Gee, thanks for the encouragement.'

Kari sobered. 'You know the one thing that really blows about this whole deal?'

'What's that?'

'The guy who...' but she stopped. She couldn't reveal her source, not even to someone she trusted. She hurried to alter what she was about to say. 'You remember my telling you that Roger's twin brother and cousin were at the Sunday dinner?'

'I thought you and I agreed to never mention Rat-maggot or his family's name again.'

'We did!' she concurred with vigor. 'But this isn't about...uh, Rat-maggot or his brother.'

Dee scowled. 'So who are we talking about?'

'Their cousin from England, Jason Keane. He's as different from you-know-who as night from day.'

'And likely, twice as sneaky!' Dee wailed. 'I know. You find the accent charming, and the guy is so James Bond!' She fixed a hard stare on Kari. 'But we all know how James Bond treats his women!'

'Actually, Jason doesn't come across as some kind of secret agent. He is very sweet...and considerate.'

'I don't believe it!' Dee cried. 'You're not developing the hots for the cousin of the man who treated you like garbage—you couldn't be that thick-headed!'

The situation seemed crazy to Kari too. How could she explain how she felt to anyone else without sounding mad? She gave up trying to rationalize and confessed. 'He happened to stop by last night to talk.'

'Yes, and you gave him a kick to the rump and sent him on his way,' Dee hypothesized. 'I was just saying to myself what a smart girl you are! Best to put everything connected with that family of losers behind you.'

'That isn't exactly what happened,' Kari admitted. 'Jason felt terrible about the way Rog…Rat-maggot treats women.'

'Oh, wracken-frack!' Dee used one of her made-up expressions (first incorporated to keep from swearing in front of her children). 'You're not going where I think you're going with this?'

'I didn't invite him over. In fact, he's only in the States because his father died and had left some keepsakes for his aunt, Sally Cline.' She heaved her shoulders in an innocent shrug. 'Anyway, we just talked for a bit, and he fixed us a meal—a delicious skillet dinner.'

'Kari, Kari, Kari,' Dee was resolute, 'You don't want to get involved with the cousin of the man who just broke your heart. Besides which, he isn't even American. He lives a few thousand miles across the ocean. Think, girl, think!'

'I am thinking,' Kari replied carefully. 'I'm thinking of inviting him out for a pizza or something.'

'Then back to your apartment, just the two of you, with some romantic music and maybe candlelight?' Dee gave her head a negative shake. 'No way, kiddo. That's the dumbest stunt you could pull.'

'But he's the nicest guy I've met in years.'

'Kari, stop punishing yourself. This isn't about the Brit at all. You're still stuck in limbo over Rat-maggot!'

'No, I'm not.'

'Then try using that solid melon on your shoulders for something other than a hair rack. You were supposedly head-over-heels, crazy in love, up until Sunday night. Now you claim Jason is nothing like your old flame. Rationally, if they are so completely different, you shouldn't have the slightest interest in the man!'

'He's sincere, thoughtful, and very much a gentleman, Dee,' she told her. 'He's not as dashing and handsome as... Rat-maggot, but he's caring and thoughtful. I'm sure he also has a good heart.'

'You're on the rebound, lady,' Dee warned. 'Do you know what happens to a girl's judgment when she's on the rebound—she doesn't have any!'

Kari couldn't argue. She knew Dee was making sense. But Jason had given her the story and asked for nothing in return. She felt she owed him something.

'It's only an invite for pizza and a little conversation, Dee. He deserves to know his encouragement helped me to write the story and allowed me to get the promotion. It wouldn't be a date or anything.'

'Oh, my mistake,' the woman snipped cynically. 'Silly me, I thought meeting a guy and having pizza together constituted a date.'

'Not at all.'

'And there's certainly nothing intimate about allowing a guy to prepare you a meal last night!'

'I was busy writing.'

Dee laughed derisively. 'Kari, you are such an Innocent. Jason is going to take your proposal as a date. And when Rat-maggot finds out he'll think you are using his cousin to try and get back at him. This whole idea is going to blow up in your face!'

Kari uttered a groan. 'I know you are only concerned with my welfare, Dee. That's why I mentioned the idea to you.'

Dee's brows drew inward and she narrowed her gaze. 'Come on, hit me with the *but, Dee* line?'

'But, Dee,' Kari obliged, 'don't you see? I do owe Jason something for his efforts.'

'You don't owe him anything, girl! I'm warning you. This is about as smart as playing chicken with a fast-moving train!'

Kari lowered her head. She was torn by a confusion of emotions, unable to decide which was the better solution. If she didn't make the effort to communicate with Jason, he probably wouldn't contact her again. That would be the end of it. He would return to England and she would never hear from or see him again. On the flip side, if she invited him to meet, it might lead to more than a mere 'thank you' dinner.

Am I ready for that? What if I start liking him a little too much?

On that last notion, dare she consider what would happen should their relationship progress into something more than friendship? He was only visiting. He would be going home soon. Any romance was doomed when she might not see Jason for months or even years at a time.

She resolved to let the matter wait. She would consider the pros and cons of any future relationship with Jason. Once she had taken time to think it over, she could make a responsible and appropriate decision.

'I've got to go clean out my old desk.' She spoke up, changing the subject. 'If you're serious about helping, I'll let you carry all of the heavy stuff.'

'Sure, what are friends for?' Dee replied dourly. 'You take advantage of everything I offer…except my good advice.'

'I haven't made up my mind yet.' Kari smiled. 'Being my friend also means, if my best-laid plans go down the toilet, you will be here with a shoulder for me to cry on—right?'

Dee groaned. 'I should have taken the career choice of my great grandfather. When he first came to America he was a sheep herder. He spent his summers alone in the hills, just a horse and a couple dogs for company. I'll bet they didn't give him half as much stress in a whole season as you give me in one lousy sentence.'

JASON SPENT THE next morning at a library, searching for data on the Internet. He found little information connected with the trio of men, because of the number of years that had passed. The research yielded but a few tidbits from news postings. Most of those with Kenny and Clark had to do with their short careers in sports. Sifting through the archives on Clark, he read enough to know his divorce had been ugly. There had been three calls to police for domestic violence—settled without an arrest—and one restraining order issued. As for Kenny, he parted from his first wife without any bad press. Pacheco had only a few incidents which listed his bar, the usual fights or drunk and disobedient customers. His marriage had been solid.

None of the three had ever served any time in jail. Or, if they had, the record had been expunged. As far as he could deduce, there had been a youthful friendship between Kenny and Clark, but not Pacheco. It was the same as he had seen in the yearbook, Pacheco was odd nut of the three.

Finished with his search, he paid four dollars for a cup of tea—it didn't pay to order tea at a bagel-and-coffee hut!

Plus, the girl had remarked how much she loved *Australia*! However, it was a decent-tasting tea and it allowed him to sit and relax for a few minutes. As was his habit, he let the tea act as a tranquilizer, taking a sip now and again, while his mind was cleared of all thought. It was in such a manner that he would contemplate facts and put things into perspective. With no real clues or additional information about these murders, he didn't have any lightning-strike notions, no revelations of any kind. Still, it was nice to have tea and take a short mental vacation.

With nothing else on his agenda he decided to play tourist and visit the LDS Temple Square, which covers about ten acres. After that, he would drive back to the motel and go for a swim in the pool.

KARI SAT NEXT TO the *Sentinel* lawyer. They were alone in a newspaper conference room, except for the two detectives. She had never been interviewed by the police before. It was exciting and intimidating at the same time.

The pair of detectives looked pretty ordinary. The one called Hampton was the larger of the two. He was a stern-looking sort with piercing brown eyes. He stood a couple inches over six feet and was a robust 200-plus pounds. The other man, Grady, looked more the average family man, about five-ten, with a little extra weight around his middle. He was the more amiable of the two, with a softer way of speaking.

'Thank you for meeting us this morning, Miss Underwood,' Detective Grady said. 'Considering your article in the paper, you might have a big future in criminology.'

'Or maybe you'll get to do a little inside work with real prisoners,' Hampton added pointedly. 'You've heard of withholding evidence, impeding a police investigation, terms like that?'

'My client used readily available information to write her story,' the attorney replied for Kari. 'Anyone could have discovered the same data. It was only necessary to research the backgrounds of the victims.'

'How did you come to learn about the one in Las Vegas?' Grady wanted to know. 'What put you on to that murder?'

'The standard of presumption,' Kari answered in a professional tone of voice. 'The *what if* theory. Once I discovered Pacheco and Kenny had graduated from Jordan High in the same year, I searched the Web for any others who had died recently from the same class.'

'Miss Underwood used to work in the obituary department,' her lawyer explained. 'That particular background work allows her a degree of expertise in researching personal histories.'

Hampton eyed her closely. 'We're not so sure you did this on your own, Miss Underwood. We're thinking you got a tip from someone, perhaps someone who knows a lot more about this case.'

The lawyer again replied for her. 'Even if someone had given her that bit of news, a reporter has an ethical responsibility to protect the identity of their source.'

'There's no written law protecting a reporter's source,' Hampton said sourly. 'And the lady has only been a reporter for two crummy days. Any judge in the country would find Miss Underwood in contempt, should she try to hide behind a flimsy excuse like that.'

'Becoming a reporter is a position I've been working toward for a long time,' Kari defended herself. 'I have a degree in journalism from Utah State.'

'And this is your big break,' Grady noted. 'Very convenient.'

'Yeah, and now we have to deal with the fallout from your article,' Hampton growled. 'We've gotten a dozen phone calls from people who graduated from Jordan High, all concerned they might be the next victim!'

'Do you have any pertinent questions for Miss Underwood?' the lawyer asked.

'How about any other information she might have on the murders?' Grady asked, regarding her with an intense scrutiny. 'Is there anything you're holding back for a follow-up story?'

'The article contains everything I've discovered about the murders so far,' Kari answered. 'I am going to continue my research, but I don't have anything else.'

Hampton continued to glare at her as if she was hiding something. Grady seemed more irate and disgusted. The two men obviously didn't like the fact a reporter had been the one to break the story which linked their two murder victims to a third.

'Do you know a Tynan Cline?' Hampton queried.

Kari could not hide her surprise at hearing the name. 'Cline?' she asked, stalling for time to get her thinking process working.

'Yes, Tynan Cline…Cline, spelled with a "C". He's a retired gentleman who lives up in Copperton.'

'What does Mr Cline have to do with anything?' Kari asked.

'We're asking the questions, Miss Underwood. Is your answer a yes or a no?'

'Does this have to do with the case at hand?' the attorney asked.

Grady was the one to reply. 'When we linked these three victims together, Tynan Cline's name came up.'

Kari was stunned by the news. 'Came up how?'

Hampton grunted with contempt. 'You're the smart girl, the one with all the answers. Why don't you tell us?'

'I don't know anything about Tynan Cline.'

'You seemed to recognize the name,' Hampton said, his hawklike eyes flashing. 'I saw it in your face.'

'I am familiar with a family named Cline, but I've never met Tynan.'

'It wouldn't do for us to catch you lying to us, Miss Underwood.'

'She said she knew the last name, but not the man,' the lawyer spoke up. 'If you are going to badger her, it will end our co-operation in this little sit-down.'

'Maybe you know one of Tynan's relatives?' Grady continued, 'His stepdaughter is Sally Cline. She lives on the west side and is the mother of twin boys.'

Kari felt suddenly trapped. What was going on? Jason had said his aunt was in the same graduating class as the three victims, but what did her father have to do with the murdered men?

'Did you say Mrs Cline is Tynan's daughter-in-law?' she asked, trying to absorb what was being said.

'No. It's not *Mrs* Cline,' Grady corrected. 'The woman has never been married. Cline is her adopted name from when she came to this country as a juvenile.'

'I...I...' Kari battled for rationale and went with the truth. 'I dated one of her sons for a short while. We had a falling out after our last date.'

'Now that's interesting,' Hampton hit her between the eyes with each word. 'You just happen to date someone linked to these murders and suddenly you break the story for your newspaper.'

'Linked to the murders!' She was stunned. 'What are you talking about?'

Grady clarified. 'Mr Pacheco owned a bar. A thorough background search was done on him when he applied for his liquor license. If a formal charge had been made against him it might have cost him a chance to secure his license.

What we discovered was a police incident report with Tynan Cline's name on it.'

'What does this have to do with Miss Underwood?' the lawyer wanted to know. 'She has told you she doesn't know this Tynan person.'

'We are looking for a motive here,' Hampton said. 'She's the one who tied a third murder to the other two. The complaint made by Tynan Cline is the only connection we have found between the first two men. Now we discover it encompasses a third victim.'

'Jamison Clark too?' Kari asked, perplexed by the news. 'You mean he was listed in the same complaint?'

Before either detective could respond, her lawyer asked: 'What was the date of these charges? Mr Pacheco has owned that club in Midvale for many years. This alleged complaint can't be very recent.'

Hampton cleared his throat. 'The date isn't important.'

Her lawyer stuck with the question. 'Then we can assume it has been a long time. More than ten years?'

'That isn't the point.'

'And Jamison Clark has not lived in Utah for nearly twenty years,' Kari's lawyer persisted. 'It has to be a very old complaint to have included him.'

'The date makes no difference,' Hampton argued. 'It ties all three men together.'

'The statute of limitations has obviously long since passed concerning any possible charges from that event— unless you are talking about murder,' her lawyer continued to argue. 'You can't seriously think such an outdated complaint has anything to do with the recent murders or my client.'

'Really, I don't know anything about any charges,' Kari put in. 'I told you, I've never met Mr Cline.'

Hampton put a hard stare on Kari. 'I think you're holding something back from us, Miss Underwood. What is it?'

'I'm not holding anything back!' she cried, growing irate. 'I've told you everything I know!'

'And I think you're lying!' Hampton's voice boomed.

'That's it!' the lawyer said sharply, rising to his feet. 'You clearly have no pertinent questions to ask. We did not agree to this meeting so you could harass my client.'

'We'll be in touch.' Hampton mellowed, but his tone was still cool. 'If you discover any more useful information, you should seriously consider calling us first.'

'Here's a number you can reach us at, Miss Underwood,' Grady added, tossing a business card on to the table. 'Don't let us read about any more surprises in the paper.'

The lawyer waited until the two men had left the room, before he rotated around to look at her.

'You needn't worry, Kari.' He offered up a smile. 'It's the job of those detectives to push buttons and hope to get a response. If they had any serious concerns about you or your source, they would have made threats about jail time and criminal charges. They are naturally upset over having a novice reporter find something they should have discovered on their initial investigation.'

'What about my dating the grandson of a man who has a distant link to something that involved the murdered men?'

'You saw how they backed down. The charges they spoke of must have been made a long time back, possibly when those men were still in school. They are grasping at straws to find a viable motive.'

'You were very well prepared.' She praised his support. 'How did you know so much about the victims?'

He grinned. 'I make it a point to never go before the

court or to a police interview without researching the case or client.'

'Can you find out about the complaint made by Mr Cline?'

'I doubt there is a courthouse record available. As Mr Pacheco was allowed to own and operate a bar, it must have only been a preliminary grievance, one never formally filed in court. I suspect the police have the only copy of that report.'

Kari let out a deep breath. 'Thank you for being here today.'

He reached out and patted her on the shoulder. 'The newspaper didn't want to have one of its reporters ending up on the front page, being charged for refusing to disclose a source.'

The man looked down at his watch. 'I've got to get home. My son is having a soccer match in an hour. If the police contact you again, or you have any questions, feel free to call the office. They can always reach me.'

Kari said goodbye, left the break room and headed back to her desk. With what she had learned, she had no choice but to contact Jason. Of all the bizarre twists, his aunt's stepfather had become a person of interest in this murder case!

EIGHT

'WHAT DO YOU think?' Grady asked Hampton, once they were back in their car. 'Does she know anything more than she put in her story?'

'She struck me as being honest and up front, but naming Cline definitely shook her tree. I wonder if Tynan or his stepdaughter can tell us anything useful?'

'Sure isn't much to go on, when you consider we're talking about a single, outdated, preliminary report, one which never made it to a formal complaint.' Grady snorted. 'And is based on an incident that happened over a quarter century ago.'

'If the motive is from way back then, there has to be more information than was included in the report,' Hampton said. 'Tynan was the man who called the cops, but then the matter was dropped. We need to find out what the whole thing was about.'

'Who handled the complaint on our end?'

'An officer named Summers—died in 2003.'

Grady shrugged. 'Then we have to talk to Tynan and Sally Cline.'

'I suppose someone in the family might still harbor a grudge of some kind. Depends on what we find, but we might have to look at the rest of the family. Beside the old man, there's Sally and her two sons.'

'And absolutely no motive.'

Hampton expelled a sigh. 'I agree, it's probably a waste of time, but I don't know what else we can do. The Cline family is the only lead we have, but it's a stretch to link three murders to something dating from way back to their high school years.'

'On the other hand, those three guys could just be a coincidence. Maybe this coin killer is a high school drop-out after an entire graduating class. There might be other murders where the vic was strangled with electrical wire and had a quarter placed between their teeth.'

'The captain said to keep quiet about the quarter thing, but he did put it on the wire with the other details. If there's any more like the three we know of, it won't take long for us to find out about it. If they should find another vic in a different state, the feds will be all over our case.'

'It isn't a serial killer if he has a hit-list, Ham. We should be able to keep the investigation going from our end.'

Hampton returned to the reporter. 'Did you find any-thing when you dumped Underwood's phone records?'

'Not much. She admitted she had been dating one of the Cline boys. We had some traffic between her and Roger Cline. One odd call recently…from a motel. It was a guy named Jason Keane. It lasted less than a minute, but it could have been agreeing to meet or something.'

'You check it out?'

Grady harrumphed, saying more with that single utter-ance than with any of his words. 'The address on his res-ervation says he's from England.'

'Can't see that tying into our case. Not unless someone hired a hit man from out of the country.'

'Doesn't seem likely.'

Hampton toyed with his ear, a habit when he was doing some hard thinking. 'Maybe the Underwood gal got the information from the mother, Sally Cline? The old lady was at school with all three of our dead men.'

'And maybe she told the truth and did discover the third

murder victim on her own,' Grady suggested. 'She had been working the obituaries and looking to move up. She might have come up with the idea to research the graduating class from that year on her own.'

'You're reaching, my friend.' Hampton nixed the idea. 'When I see something with wings and feathers flying overhead, I call it a bird, not a lucky hunch.'

Grady chuckled. 'Damn! You're so deep sometimes, it's downright scary.'

Hampton grinned. 'The file on the Vegas murder ought to be back at the office by now. Maybe we'll find something in it to connect these three murders.'

'Optimism doesn't suit you, Ham. It's out of character.'

'We'll look over that report and check in with the chief, before we drive up and see Mr Cline. Maybe he or his stepdaughter will shed some light on this case for us.'

'Let's get a cup of coffee first. You do remember it's your turn to buy?'

'Grady, if your memory was as bad about facts concerning a case as it is about who bought coffee last, you'd be driving a golf cart and ticketing illegally parked cars.'

'I've a wife and three kids at home, Ham. Could be I've got more on my mind than a bachelor like you.'

'That's a better excuse than admitting you're a tightwad.'

'If you're going to whine and nag about it I'll pay for the lousy coffee.'

Hampton smiled. 'This case is looking up already. Maybe we're in for a break.'

'Yeah, you keep on dreaming, Ham. You're real good at dreaming.'

NEMESIS PUT DOWN the paper and swore under his breath. Having Jamison Clark linked to the other two murders was going to push up the timetable. He stared at the printing again and frowned—reported by Kari Underwood.

'How did you learn about Jamison?' he asked aloud. 'Did you get lucky on your own or did someone contact you?' He wondered if one of the other potential targets had kept in touch with Clark. It didn't seem likely. Jamison had moved out of Utah shortly after his college career ended because of a bum arm. He might have attended a ten- or twenty-year high-school reunion, but what were the chances anyone would have heard of him being killed?

He paused in thought. Obituaries were often carried in a person's home town, even if the person hadn't lived there in years. Maybe his ex-wife had notified the Salt Lake paper.

It didn't matter now. The connection had been made so he would act accordingly. The nosy reporter linking Clark as the third victim was not important, other than because the information would undoubtedly put the police on to the list. They might put the other two names on the alert or even offer them protection. Still, he doubted anyone had discovered the motive behind the killings yet.

He checked the amount of cash he had—there would be no paper trail—and he had plenty. Having the police involved was not a problem. He had expected them to be on his trail before he finished his job. What he didn't like was having a snoopy reporter in the middle of this. And if Underwood hadn't learned about Jamison on her own, what else did she know and was anyone helping her? He racked his brain, trying to consider someone he might have missed.

There was no one.

She must have seen the obituary, which would list Clark graduating from Jordan High. It didn't take a brilliant mind to see the similarity between his murder and the other two.

Standing with his arms folded and his mind working,

Nemesis smiled. There might be a benefit to having an overeager reporter on the job. If something went amiss with his original plan, he might be able to use her to his advantage. Nothing had changed. Everything was still on schedule.

THE TWO DETECTIVES rode in silence until Hampton spoke up.

'I figured we were wasting our time with the old man. He gave us nothing more than we already knew.'

'Unless the murders are only about one of our vics,' Grady said. 'Maybe the perp wants us to think there's some kind of vendetta going on. He could be using a serial killer style to cover up the fact he only wanted to kill one or two of men.'

'Then why go after Jamison Clark first?' Ham grunted. 'If it hadn't been for that reporter gal, we wouldn't even have matched him with the other two.'

'You're right,' Grady agreed. 'Tynan said it was about a high school Christmas party. His girl came home drunk and he called the cops. The charges were dropped because the kids were all under age.'

'Nothing much to kill anyone over.'

'No,' Grady admitted. 'But a few weeks later, Sally's boyfriend dies in an auto accident. Maybe that's the key. No one is going to kill a bunch of people over a little booze at a party—but what if it had something to do with Warren's death?'

'It would explain why our killer went all the way to Vegas to kill Clark. If the perp wanted us to think this was a serial killer, he would have made certain we tied all three deaths together.'

'You're right, Ham. Clark has to be one of his intended victims. Otherwise why use the same MO?'

'And he killed him first. That might mean something too.'

'What do you want to do about Sally Cline?' Grady asked. 'She might be able to tell us something about the car accident.'

Hampton gave a shrug. 'Let's stop by on our way back to the barn and see what she has to say. Maybe we'll get lucky and she will point us at a suspect.'

'There you go, Ham, dreaming again.'

THE FOLLOWING MORNING, Reggie contacted Jason shortly after Jason had eaten the free breakfast at the motel. It was about the same as he would have eaten at home, cold cereal, a glass of orange juice and an apple. Reggie's call was an invite for him to join him and Roger for a game of pool. Jason had played a little snooker and was familiar with pocket billiard games such as 'eight ball' or 'rotation'. He agreed to meet them and jotted down the address. He was about to leave his room when a second call came in. It was Kari Underwood and she wanted to meet for dinner at a pizza place. He accepted the offer at once and changed his plans for the day.

Actually, it was no contest—dinner with the beautiful and charming Kari Underwood, or a boring couple hours with Aunt Sally before she went to work. As his aunt didn't expect him, he wasn't obliged to call her. In reflection, they had run out of things to talk about.

Jason decided to make use of the exercise room and the swimming pool. He would then make a cup of tea and watch some television until it was time to meet Kari.

KARI AVOIDED THE possibility of more than a friendly liaison by meeting Jason at a nearby pizza place right after work. It was several miles away from her apartment, and she arrived a few minutes early, only to discover he was already parked and waiting.

She pulled up next to Jason's rental car. By the time she had her car stopped and the engine shut off, Jason was there to open her door for her. Kari had donned a casual skirt and blouse for their late afternoon tryst. Careful to keep her knees together, she swung her legs around to get out of the car.

Jason smiled once she was on her feet, and broke the ice. 'I saved a copy of the newspaper and saw the article and your byline,' he said. 'How does it feel to be an actual reporter?'

She laughed politely. 'The pressure is unbelievable. The editor wants a follow-up story, but I haven't found anything worth writing about.'

'Don't the police have any leads yet?'

'Only me,' she said, half-seriously.

'I expected to find them camped in front of my motel room.'

Kari gave her head a negative shake. 'You are my source. As such, I have an obligation to protect your identity.'

Jason laughed. 'Spoken like one of our own snoops. They tend to protect their contacts as well.' When she didn't reply to that, he turned serious.

'At the moment, murder and mayhem needs to take a back seat to the really important issues,' he commented, as they walked together toward the entrance. At her curious look, he finished, 'What kind of toppings do you prefer on your pizza!'

Jason held the door and allowed her to select the table. It was a little early for the evening crowd, so there was only a handful of other patrons. Kari chose a secluded booth, where they could talk privately.

A girl took their order, returned shortly with their drinks

and then left them alone. They sat across from one another and Kari risked opening the conversation by touching on a sensitive subject.

'I must say, Jason, I find you're very easy to be around,' Kari began. 'When I was dating Roger, I never felt quite at ease. I became panicked if even a single strand of hair was out of place. I worried about everything I said, fearful it would come out silly or offend him in some way. For all of our time together, I maintained a façade and attempted to be the perfect woman.'

'You might not believe it, but I understand completely,' Jason replied. 'According to Reggie, when it comes to dating, Roger only has to snap his fingers and choose the one he wants. I've known a chap or two like him.' He grinned. 'Being a rather average bloke, I must admit to a touch of envy.'

Kari didn't mask the loathing in her voice. 'He is very good-looking and has a world of charisma, but it's all on the surface. Underneath the charm, he's as cold as ice, and his heart must be a festering sore. How else could he treat women the way he does?'

'A man or woman who behaves so contemptibly towards the opposite sex is something I've never understood.'

Swallowing her bile, she shifted the conversation. 'And you, Jason? How are you getting along with the Cline family?'

'I haven't spent much time with either of the boys, but they did invite me to a game of pool tonight.'

'I remember you saying you didn't have a girlfriend back home.'

Jason was candid. 'I haven't been out with a woman since my wife died.'

Kari did not miss his solemn expression. 'She must have been quite special.'

'Yes,' he said. 'Doris was diagnosed with leukemia in her teens. She was up front about it when we first started going out. We both knew our time together was limited.'

'It's still very sad.'

'I think it helped us to enjoy each day of our life together. Most people put off doing something until they can afford it or have the time. We did everything we could from the day we were married. We probably got more out of life in our time together than many couples do in a lifetime.'

Kari had no idea how to respond. Jason had married a woman knowing she had a death sentence hanging over her head. Yet he didn't strike her as the type to have done it for martyrdom. She attempted a tactful approach to escape what might be a tender subject.

'It's lucky your wife found someone like you to share those few years with. My mistake was in not discovering what kind of man Roger was, before I let him...' she gulped ignominiously. 'Before he made a fool out of me.'

'Reggie said his brother has a habit of seeking out girls with high morals and then seducing them. It sounds as if you and he went together for some time before you succumbed to his charm.'

Kari groaned. 'I begin to worry about the female of the species. Makes me wonder if Roger ever met a girl he couldn't seduce.'

'Happily, I'm not privy to his actual track record.'

'And what about you and me today?' Kari asked frankly. 'Do you think I'm on the rebound? Is that why I'm here with you?'

Jason was equally forthright. 'I wouldn't venture a guess. Are you?'

Kari lowered her eyes, afraid he would see her own self doubts. She wanted to believe she was strong enough to bounce back from a bad relationship. But it had been less than a week. How could she know her own heart?

'I—I'm not sure, Jason,' she gave him an honest response. 'I haven't had many serious relationships in my life. I thought I was in love when I was seventeen, but it was mostly a yearning for romance, the desire to have someone special in my life. When I attended college, I had a couple short-time boyfriends but it ended without anyone getting hurt. I haven't dated very often since I graduated…that is, until I met your cousin.' She swallowed hard against the shame which sought to constrict her words. 'I truly thought Roger was sincere, that we were both falling in love.'

'You don't have to—' Jason started to interrupt.

'No,' she cut him off softly, 'we need to clear the air between us. I don't want an elephant in the room every time I speak to you.'

'All right,' he acquiesced. 'If you want.'

'I think physical love is too special to be casual about,' she began. 'I actually don't have very much…experience.' The words came out shaky and meek. She hurried to clarify what she wanted to say. 'I'm not a party girl, not now, not back in college or high school. Roger was only the second guy I ever…' she fumbled for the right words, 'I was ever intimate with.'

'I'm sorry you were one of his victims,' Jason said gently.

Kari swallowed her disgrace and forced a reticent smile to her lips. 'Of course, if I hadn't been his mindless puppet, I would not have met you and ended up with a story to write. I guess something good did come of our relationship.'

'That's what they call me around the Sutton CID,' he made a jest, 'a marvelous booby prize.'

'Don't say that.' She used a scolding tone of voice. 'You

are very nice and easy to be around. I told you how I always felt the need to keep up a veneer with Roger, constantly afraid I might do or say the wrong thing. I never really relaxed around him, not the way I do with you.'

'I suspect that's because you consider me in a friendly, handshake sort of way, not as a potential suitor.'

Kari wondered if he was right. Was she one of those desperate creatures on the rebound, eager to find anyone who would show her a little attention or affection? Or did she really see him as no threat, because he wasn't special or important to her.

Gadfry! I sound as cold-hearted as Roger!

She was saved from having to continue as the pizza arrived. Having chosen pepperoni topping, she picked up a slice and took a healthy bite.

Kari immediately had to shift the pizza about in her mouth and try to suck in enough air to cool it down. 'H-hot!' she gasped, waving her hand in front of her open mouth.

Jason smiled at her antics. 'My wife—although a pitiful cook—warned me how things straight from the oven tend to be on the warm side.'

The bite cooled enough so Kari was able to chew her food in a normal manner. 'Good point,' she allowed, pausing to savor the taste. Being more cautious with a second bite, she first cooled it down by blowing on it. Careful to chew without smacking her lips, she placed the wedge of pizza on her plate. There were several napkins provided, so she used one to wipe a bit of sauce from her fingers.

After a couple of sips of Pepsi, she automatically picked up the pizza with her fingers and took another bite. It occurred to her that that was something she wouldn't have done with Roger. The server brought forks with the meal, so she would have probably cut each bite and been less messy…less comfortable.

Covertly, she glanced at Jason and tried to discern what kind of man he was. Honorable, without question, as he had married a terminally ill woman, yet spoke only of how full their life had been together. Some men might have exploited the history, used it as a lure to tempt the next girl they met. But he made no mention of his personal sacrifice. He said that he had not dated since her passing. That beckoned a decency and moral character anyone would admire. She searched for truth. How *did* she feel about him?

Jason glanced up—catching her staring at him—and gazed directly back at her. He regarded her with smoke-colored eyes, eyes that were unexpectedly mysterious, earnest, even inviting. She wondered what he was thinking.

'Regarding your article, I presume the police took a proper notice?' Jason said, his words belying the fervent interest she interpreted in his gaze.

'They swooped in and grilled me over the coals like a prime steak. Thankfully, the newspaper provided an attorney for our interview. He didn't let them push too hard. Plus, I couldn't tell them anything. Everything I knew was in the article we wrote together.'

'You did point out how the story was nothing they couldn't have discovered themselves, had they taken the time to look?'

'Yes,' she agreed, 'but they were concerned I had a source who might know a lot more than he had told me.'

'You wrote everything I had uncovered.'

'Are you sure?' she asked. 'Is there anything else at all, perhaps something you merely suspect?'

The question caused his eyebrows to lift in surprise. 'No, nothing.'

She had no doubt he was telling her the truth. 'Then I

have some information to share with you,' she said. 'The detectives caught me totally off guard when they mentioned Sally's stepfather.'

'What? You mean Tynan Cline?'

She gave an affirmative bob of the head. 'They said he had once called the police to make a complaint, one which involved all three of the murdered men. They wouldn't tell me what it was about, only that no formal charges were ever filed.'

The cop in Jason rose to surface. 'Tynan knew those three men? He actually called the police about them?'

'It sounded as if it was from something which happened a long time ago. My attorney tried to pin the police down about the details, but they wouldn't tell us anything.'

Jason mused, 'I wonder what the call was about?'

'The lawyer determined it had to have been from over twenty years ago.'

'How did the police stumble on such an old report?'

She told him about Pacheco's liquor license and the notation on his application, then continued: 'They asked me if I knew Tynan or Mrs Cline.'

'My aunt? What's her part in any of this?'

'I don't know. I suppose it's because she graduated in the same class. Or it might have had something to do with the charges Tynan made against those three men.'

'Sally never mentioned any trouble during our conversations.'

'But she did know all three victims.'

'Yes, Clark and Kenny are two boys she talked about from her school days. When I asked about Paul Pacheco, she showed me the drawing he had done of her from the Christmas pageant. It was a very good likeness; but he drew several other girls too. There didn't seem to be anything special between him and my aunt.'

Kari considered the news and took another bite of pizza—again careful to blow on it first—before resuming the discussion.

'It sounded as if the police intend to talk to Tynan and maybe your aunt too. I attended their news conference this morning and the spokesman said they were following up on some new leads.'

'From what I've heard of Tynan, he can handle just about anything,' Jason said. 'As far as Aunt Sally goes, they had better get to her before she goes to work.'

'You mean because she has a drinking problem?'

He became pensive. 'Reggie told me he couldn't remember back to a time when she didn't drink. He blames it on broken dreams, the burden of responsibility and raising twin boys mostly on her own. I suppose it was all too much for her.'

'It must have been difficult for her and the boys growing up,' Kari said softly.

Jason gave a slight bob of his head. 'Reggie said she's gotten worse since he and Roger moved out.'

'It's sad.' Kari sympathized with him. 'Sally is still young and attractive enough to start her life again.'

'It's not the life she wanted,' Jason replied. 'Once she had consumed a fair portion of spirits on Sunday night she lamented endlessly about what a great life she would have had if Warren Lloyd—her boyfriend and the father of her boys—hadn't died in a car accident. She said he didn't even know she was pregnant with the twins at the time of his death.'

'Still, it's a shame to be alone. Everyone needs someone in their lives.'

'Roger and she are very close,' he said. 'We can judge him harshly for the way he mistreats every woman he meets, but he seems a dutiful son. He calls her faithfully several times a week and visits her a lot more than Reggie does.'

'Roger boasted about buying her presents. There's a portable dishwasher and two extra chairs in the garage, as well as the fancy patio set out back of the house.'

'He is a generous son,' Jason said.

'Yes, and Sally has never hidden the fact that he was her favorite son either, not since the day the boys were born.'

'It's an odd paradox,' Jason mused, 'how a man can be so cruel and heartless towards women, then take care of his mother so faithfully.'

'One might call it a Freudian contradiction.' She grinned. 'I took psychology my last year in college.'

'Pretty *and* clever; a rather wonderful combination.'

Kari felt a warm glow rise to her cheeks and asked, 'What about you, Jason? Widowered so young, are you now looking for the perfect woman to share the rest of your life with?'

He snickered at the idea. 'The perfect woman would undoubtedly be looking for the perfect man. That leaves me standing at the curb.'

'Cute, but it isn't an answer.'

'Maybe, if you and I happen to cross the line between just being friends and move on to something more, then I might tell you.'

Kari offered him a demure smile but did not reply to his statement. *How can I?* she fretted. *Until I know my own heart, I have to maintain a safe distance. I'm not ready to make a complete fool of myself again, not yet anyway!*

NINE

JASON HAD BID goodbye to Kari after their meal. The parting had been uneventful, no hug, no clasping of hands, only a wave and fleeting farewell. He recalled a longing as she had driven away, something he hadn't felt since losing Doris. He set aside the emotion and met up with the Cline twins later that evening.

Roger was in rare form. He was witty, full of energy and couldn't seem to miss a shot at the billiards table.

'Four straight games!' he announced triumphantly, sinking the last ball on the table. 'Too bad we're not playing for money.'

'The loser pays,' Jason replied drily. 'To those of us on a limited budget, that makes it a game for money.'

Reggie glanced at his watch. 'And I'm about played out. It's time for me to head for the barn.'

Roger ignored their remarks, retrieving the balls and setting them in the rack. He paused a moment and looked at Reggie. 'So, tell me, little brother, what have you been up to lately? Mom said she's spent some time with Jason, but you haven't been around since we all got together for Sunday dinner.'

'I took a Reno haul and a couple short runs. Dispatch has another trip lined up for down south in a day or two. I really hate going to Southern California any more. The highways are always snarled up, either by too much traffic or construction or both.'

Roger winked at Jason. 'This guy went through the

trouble to get his teacher's certificate after college. You have to wonder why he doesn't sell his rig and start teaching math and history at one of the schools.'

'I put in two applications this year,' Reggie made his excuse, 'but neither place was hiring people without experience. I do have a standing offer for my truck, if I should land a teaching job.'

Jason asked, 'Are you interested in teaching at a junior or a secondary school?'

'Anything but junior high—twelve- to fifteen-year-old. I remember those were the worst, most rebellious years for Roger and me. Most all kids in that age bracket are trouble.'

'Yeah,' Roger agreed, 'we raised a lot of hell in junior high. Reggie grew out of it when he became a sophomore in high school, but I didn't buckle down and study until my senior year.'

Reggie chimed in cynically. 'If I remember right, you took a study period, gym class, stagecraft and were in the band. How many real classes did you take in your senior year?'

Roger chuckled at the memory. 'OK, so I coasted through it, but I still got the scholarship I needed.'

'Sports got you the scholarship in college.'

'What can I say? Everybody loves a jock.' He grinned. 'Anyway, I only majored in business and marketing so I could start higher up the ladder in the sales industry. And you have to admit, it's paid big dividends. Five years and several promotions later, and now I've got an impressive title and a liberal expense account. I've made friends with a great number of people with money or power or both. I often ride in their corporate jets, get chauffeured about in their limousines and eat in some of the nicest restaurants in the country. It's not a sin to be friends with people who have money.'

Reggie spoke to Jason, 'Top sales rep in his field. I'll bet my brother could sweet-talk the devil into buying heaters for every soul in Hades.'

'Selling insurance is selling the *intangible*,' Roger corrected. 'A true compliment would be to say I could sell the devil fire insurance.'

'Maybe after you get there,' Reggie quipped.

Roger chuckled. 'Anything else going on in you guys' lives?'

'There might be some excitement,' Jason offered. 'Did you see the article in the paper about the local murder victims?'

'I've been working sixteen hours a day lately, often out of state, selling or settling claims, Cuz. That's how I afford to buy my toys and pay for a luxury apartment with weekly maid service.'

Jason asked: 'Do you remember the names Jamison Clark and Steve Kenny?'

Roger lifted his eyes to stare at the roof. 'Clark and Kenny…the names have a familiar ring. What are they, a comedy act?'

'They are murder victims,' Jason told him.

Roger displayed an immediate shock. 'Cripes, Jason! Is that what being a British cop does to you, you memorize the names of murdered people?'

Reggie filled in the explanation. 'You know them, Roger. They both played football back when Mom was in high school.'

A look of comprehension came over his features. 'Oh, sure! Clark and Kenny, the two guys Mom said she and the other cheerleaders made famous in her senior year.' He smiled at the thought. 'I remember her telling us the opposing team players were too busy ogling her to keep their mind on the game!'

Reggie frowned at Jason. 'You told me about Clark; I hadn't heard about Kenny. He's dead too?'

Jason studied the two closely, but detected little other than surprise in their expressions. 'And there's a third guy from your mother's graduating class, Paul Pacheco. He was the bar owner who was killed earlier this week.'

Roger whistled in disbelief. 'You're kidding! Three guys are dead, all from Mom's class? What a surreal coincidence.'

'It's no coincidence,' Jason replied. 'They all appear to have been murdered by the same killer.'

'The same killer?' Reggie was stunned by the news. 'That *is* weird.'

'I haven't listened to the local news all week,' Roger said. 'Do the police have any idea who is doing the killing?'

'Not so far,' Jason said. 'But I believe the police will talk to your grandfather.'

That hit home with both boys. 'Grandpa?' Roger asked. 'What's he got to do with three dead guys from Mom's high school?'

Jason explained about him calling the police. 'He started to file formal charges against those very three boys at one time, but he withdrew the complaint.'

'Tynan?' Reggie mirrored Roger's disbelief. 'What kind of complaint?'

'I don't know.'

Roger was deadly earnest now. 'How'd you find out about all of this stuff, Cuz?'

'I read most of the details in the paper,' Jason replied.

'And Grandpa is somehow involved?' Reggie asked.

'Not involved but, considering he named all three boys in some kind of complaint with the police, it would be standard procedure to talk to him.' He made a slight shrug. 'Might have already talked to him by now—your mother too.'

Roger swore. 'That makes no sense! Why would the cops want to talk to Mom? What could she possibly know about three guys getting murdered?'

'She probably knows why Grandpa filed the charges,' Reggie guessed.

'Cripes!' Roger howled. 'This is ridiculous. I don't think Mom has heard from any of those guys since she graduated. I doubt she even knows about them being killed. She doesn't subscribe to the paper and she seldom watches the news.'

'Roger's right,' Reggie said. 'Mom never pays any attention to the news.'

'I mentioned Clark's and Paul's deaths to her when we were talking,' Jason told the two boys. 'She didn't seem all that concerned.'

Roger threw his hands up in frustration. 'If the cops start hounding her, it will put her over the edge for a month. She's been promising to cut back on the booze lately. I told her if she lost her job because of her drinking, I was going to make her attend AA meetings.'

'Bet she was thrilled about that idea,' Reggie said.

Roger bobbed his head. 'I'll make her do it. She knows I will.'

'With you being closer to your mother than Reggie,' Jason enquired of Roger, 'do you recall her ever mentioning any trouble between her school chums and your grandfather?'

'Never, and I don't remember ever hearing about someone named Panchecko.'

'It's *Pacheco,* Paul Pacheco.'

'Right. Him I don't remember, only Kenny and Clark,

from her stories from when the football team won the state title.' He glanced at Reggie. 'How about you?'

'I didn't even know Clark or Kenny's first names.'

'Have you called and asked Grandpa about it, Jason?'

'I only learned about the complaint a few hours ago,' Jason told them. 'I've never met Tynan. I thought I'd drive up and visit him tomorrow or one of these next days.'

'I'm booked solid or I'd go with you,' Roger said. 'I've got to process a couple claims tomorrow, and then fly back to New York. Let me know if you find out anything.'

Jason said he would. Roger set down the cue ball and cocked his head at Jason. 'If I get tied up in New York, I might not see you again. What do you and Reggie say to one last game?'

Reggie looked at his watch. 'All right, but this is it for me. Who gets the break?'

'Let's give it to our visiting cousin.'

Jason picked up the pool stick. 'Very sporting of you... considering I've not won a single game.'

'That's me, a real sport,' Roger taunted. 'And for a little incentive—if either of you wins the game, I'll pick up the tab for the night, drinks and all.'

Reggie groaned resignedly. 'The way you've been playing, I think it's a safe bet that Jason and I will split the tab.'

'Show some fighting spirit, boys, and give it your best shot. One of you is about due to win a game.'

Jason chalked up the end of his stick and took careful aim. He knew he would have to be very lucky to beat Roger. He played nearly flawless pool. With a smooth, powerful stroke, he sent the cue ball into the set and the balls scattered across the table. Several rolled close to the pocket, but nothing went in. It was Roger's turn. The game was as good as over.

KARI WAITED PATIENTLY until Sally Cline answered the door. Subsequently, she mustered forth a bright smile of greeting. 'Good morning, Ms Cline. Do you remember me?'

It took a moment before recognition entered Sally's expression. She glanced past Kari, as if expecting to see one of her sons. 'What brings you out this way, hon?'

'May I come in for a short visit?'

'Why not?' Sally replied, pulling her robe together to hide most of her flannel nightgown. 'It's my day off.'

Kari passed through the door and closed it behind her. Sally continued to frown, but there was no animosity in her expression. 'I thought maybe we could have a little chat,' Kari said, trying to break the ice. 'I know the police were out here to visit and hoped you could shed some light on a few things.'

'Stupid clowns!' Sally complained. 'They come around as I'm leaving for work, asking me all kinds of fool questions. As if anything I could tell them about some recent murders was going to help. I haven't seen any of the boys they asked about since high school graduation.'

'You never attended any of the class reunions?'

Sally uttered a grunt of disgust. 'Didn't leave anything or anyone behind worth remembering. My best girlfriend moved away the year after we graduated. I wasn't all that fond of or curious about anyone else.'

They entered the living room and the malodor of hard liquor assailed Kari's sense of smell. She spied a bottle of Scotch and a partly filled glass sitting on the coffee table. When Sally sagged down into the recliner chair, Kari took a seat on the couch across the way.

Sally reached over and picked up the glass. 'Need a little fuel to get me started some days.' She excused her drinking. 'Your life gets flushed down a toilet and it takes a little extra to face each day.'

Kari laughed, as if the woman had told her a joke. 'We all need a little stimulant to keep us going. I drink a gallon of Pepsi or coffee each day. Caffeine is the only way I've found to keep up my energy.'

Admitting to a bad habit was good therapy. Sally immediately appeared more comfortable at Kari's confession. She gave her head a nod toward the kitchen. 'I can heat you some water,' she offered. 'I've got instant coffee in the cupboard.'

'Thanks, but I had a cup before I came here,' Kari replied.

'So what do you want from me, hon?' Sally asked. 'I don't have any control over Roger, if you're looking for a way to tie a ring on his finger.'

'Actually, Roger and I decided to discontinue seeing one another.' Kari's admission did not seem to surprise Sally. Considering her son's cruel behavior, she had probably become used to seldom seeing the same girl twice. Kari continued and watched for her reaction. 'However, I have spent some time with Jason lately.'

The news put an incredulous look on the woman's face. 'You and my British nephew?' She snorted. 'There's a new twist I haven't seen before.'

'What do you mean?' Kari clarified. 'We aren't actually dating.'

'Oh, well, if you were it would be a first for Roger. With poor Reggie, it was always the other way around.'

'What do you mean?'

Sally waved her hand. 'It's been tough on him growing up; Reggie has always lived in his brother's shadow. I remember over the years how, every time he got himself a girl, she would always end up chasing after Roger instead.

Some boys would have been fighting like two dogs over the same bone, but not my sons.'

'You don't think Reggie minded losing his girlfriends to Roger?'

'I asked him about it once.' She ran her fingers through her unkempt hair and scratched her head. 'Seems it was the second time he lost a girl to Roger. Anyhow, he said if they were willing to leave him to chase after Roger, they would likely get more than they bargained for.'

'Because Roger would woo them for a short while and then dump them,' Kari deduced.

Sally shrugged off the statement. 'Well, Roger is a picky sort. He never has found a girl he wanted to settle down with. The boy is like a poor kid in a candy store—he wants a taste of everything, but doesn't want to spend his money!'

Kari laughed at her simile, but experienced a sudden pang from deep within the still open wound in her heart. She was all too aware of how Roger used a girl and then left her flat. She smothered the ache inside and stayed on course.

'You must have had your hands full raising the two boys.'

'They took everything I had,' Sally said, lifting her glass to take a sizeable swig. 'When I graduated high school, I had a scholarship for college,' she continued. 'Do you know how few dance scholarships there were back then? It was almost unheard of.'

'You were a dancer then?'

Sally sobered. 'Yes, until I wound up pregnant at eighteen. Next thing, the father of my boys is killed in a car crash. That pretty much ended my world.'

'It was all very tragic,' Kari sympathized. 'Wasn't there anyone to help?'

The woman's eyes misted. 'My mother died of breast

cancer when I was fifteen years old. I remember how I used to worry about the fact I was well developed.' She uttered a mirthless chuckle. 'It was silly, I know, but I was scared that having breasts as large as my mother's would cause me to get cancer too.'

'Breast cancer is a dread of all women.' Kari excused her fears.

'Anyway, Daddy remarried a couple years later. I think the woman loved him but, when it came to kids, she only put up with me. She lived for the day when I was grown and gone. When I ended up pregnant and without a husband, my stepmother wanted me to have an abortion. Daddy refused. He said I could live at home and they would help me raise the twins.'

'What did you want?'

Sally lifted her shoulders and let them fall. 'You've met my boys. Can you imagine just snuffing out their lives? I didn't really think about it. Those were not simply embryos, they were my twin boys! There's no way I could have destroyed them and not lived to regret it.'

'It's a pity their father died before they were even born.'

A misty sort of look entered her expression. 'Warren was the love of my life. We had talked about having kids and both of us wanted three or four. He was going to work at his father's business and we would have had our own house...'

When she didn't continue, Kari spoke up. 'So you raised the boys at home, with the help of your parents?'

'Not my stepmother. She didn't want to help me raise my babies.' Sally scoffed her contempt. 'The old bat packed up and moved out right before the boys were born. I got a little compensation from social services for being an unwed mother, but that's it. I sacrificed everything for my sons, my career in dance, dating, everything.'

'Surely, there must have been a few men around who wanted to date you? It's obvious you've always been very pretty.'

'I didn't go looking for a man,' she replied. 'I was too broke up about losing Warren. And the boys were such a handful, I never had time for any courtship.'

'You have a nice house.'

'The only good thing my stepmother ever did,' she explained. 'She never remarried and died when the boys were in their junior year in high school. Dad was still listed as co-owner of the property, so he gave me the house and we refinanced the balance of the mortgage in my name. I don't make a lot working for Smith's Food Stores, but I've been able to keep the house and feed my boys.'

'You did very well to put them both through college.'

'Social Services helped some, and Roger and Reggie both worked to help pay their own way. I'm proud of my boys. They both left college with degrees.'

'That's pretty amazing.'

'Yes, my boys are my life. We're a close-knit family. Roger is the special one—he has always been the one who looked out for me the most.'

'I notice Reggie seems quite different.'

'Yes, he's standoffish—you know, the quiet sort. Still, he was a good boy, never got into trouble and did his chores without complaint. If he lacks anything, it's ambition.' She laughed. 'Not exactly something Roger ever had to worry about. Once Roger got his degree, he went into insurance and now he's one of the top men working for his company. He makes friends easily and is smart as can be.'

'Yes, he told me how he often dealt with high powered corporate officers and company CEOs all over the country.'

Sally displayed a proud lift to her chin. 'Sometimes in other countries too.'

Kari decided she had been cordial long enough. 'Can I ask you a rather personal question?'

Sally gave her head a toss. 'Sure, why not?'

'Before the police talked to you, did you already know about the three men from your graduating class?'

'I'll tell you what I told them detectives. I hadn't given those boys a second thought in years. I didn't know about anyone being killed until Jason told me about it.'

'The police said your father had once wanted to file charges against those very same three men. Can you tell me what that was about?'

It was the wrong question. Sally frowned at Kari and put down her glass. 'I remember Roger teasing you about wanting to become a reporter. Your question sounds like something one of them snoops would ask.'

'I'm sorry, I didn't...'

But Sally rose to her feet. 'Them two cops, they wanted to know all about that party too. What's going on? What's this all about?'

Party? She wondered what kind of party, but hurried to reply. 'I only ask the question because of the coincidence.'

'What coincidence?'

'The three men all being named in your father's complaint. I wanted to—'

A knowing look came into Sally's eyes. 'You're looking for a story!' she cut off her explanation. 'You and them two cops are trying to hang a murder rap on someone, and you're both looking at my father!'

'No, it isn't like that.'

Sally rose up out of her chair and snarled her words. 'You've outstayed your welcome, young lady. I'm not saying another word to you.'

'Please don't be angry,' Kari said quickly. 'My only

concern is about why the police were interested in Tynan. I want to help.'

'I don't need any of your help!' Sally snapped defensively. 'I raised my kids alone; I put them through college alone; I can darn well take care of those cops alone!'

Rather than make things worse, Kari gathered up her purse and headed for the door. She attempted another apology on her way out, but Sally slammed the door to cut her off.

Once back in her car Kari worried at the mess she'd made. The only thing she had learned about the police report was that it was a very sensitive subject and might concern a party of some kind.

This visit isn't going to sit well with the twins or Jason.

She wanted to explain herself to Jason, before he heard the news from Sally. Perhaps if she invited him over for dinner? The notion caused an immediate tingle, a subtle rippling which cruised through her body like an unexpected chill. Goose-bumps rose all along her arms and she suffered an involuntary shiver.

Why the intense reaction? Was it because she wanted to see Jason again? Or was it the wintry frost of fear, afraid that admitting she had been prying into his aunt's past might give him a bad impression about her?

Kari was in limbo, unable to determine her own heart. Jason seemed a very nice guy, but it would be foolish to fall for a guy who was only visiting and lived a world away. Making the decision, Kari inhaled a breath of confidence, pulled out her cell phone and punched in his number.

TEN

HAMPTON SAT WITH his chair next to Grady's desk. Both of them had been studying the reports and files scattered about. Grady had a sheet of paper and a pencil in his hand.

'Let's review where we are, Ham. We got nothing with Tynan or Sally Cline, none of our three vics have a record, and there's no evidence of anyone making threats against any of them.'

'This can't be about the complaint,' Hampton summarized. 'Old man Cline didn't want some high-school kids to get busted for underage drinking at a Christmas party, he wanted the supplier punished.'

'You're right, and there was never a follow up to get the person responsible for purchasing the liquor for the party. Sally said there were up to sixty kids there on and off during the night. That much alcohol would cost a sizeable chunk of change.'

'It was a major party, probably paid for by the kids themselves,' Hampton said. 'I can understand no one taking the charge too seriously.' He snorted. 'Besides which, one of those interviewed was the son of an LDS bishop.'

'Seems I saw one was a city councilman's kid, too.'

'If the actual party isn't the motive, Grady, something else has to tie those three together.' He tossed a sheet of paper on to the middle of the desk. 'Here's the report from Vegas PD—they got exactly dick for us. Jamison had a bad marriage, but he was keeping up his child support payments. Otherwise, he had no shady dealings with anyone… not that they could find, anyway.'

Grady glanced through his notebook. 'Sally Cline went to the party because she was lonely. Her boyfriend had gone out of town with his family for the holidays. Maybe that's the key.'

Hampton sat back in his chair and studied his partner. 'Grady, you've got that look on your face like your brain is working overtime.'

'Stay with me on this, Ham,' he said thoughtfully. 'No one ever ratted out the guy who bought the booze for the party. However, Sally Cline told us Steve Kenny's cousin was there and she thought he was quite a bit older than the other kids. She didn't know his first name. Everyone called him Special K.'

'I remember, like the breakfast cereal. But even if Special K bought the beer and liquor, where's the motive for our string of killings?'

'What if we've been looking at the wrong point of interest?'

'Grady, I haven't got a slightest clue what you're talking about.'

'Warren Lloyd.'

Hampton frowned. 'You mean the accident?'

'I just looked over the police report.' He indicated an aged yellow folder on the desk top. 'A couple of witnesses claim the boy was racing—his car and a red, full-size pickup. The cop on the scene said it appeared Lloyd had lost control on the curve and was killed when his car rolled over.'

'I still don't see anything that would start a murder spree twenty-seven years later.'

'It might, if Lloyd *wasn't* racing,' Grady said solemnly. 'What if he was being chased?'

'OK, I catch your drift. A guy comes back after the holidays and learns his girl has been grounded for getting stewed at some party. He might have gone looking for those responsible and ended up getting into a fight.'

'It's what I would have done at his age,' Grady said. 'His sweetheart can't date him for a month—could be her reputation gets slandered too—so Lloyd starts making a lot of noise. He maybe threatens to go to the police or tell Tynan Cline who bought the booze. The boys go to talk to him or threaten him.'

'I don't know, Grady. The drinking and being grounded doesn't seem like anything worth killing over.'

'Special K had to be over twenty-one to buy beer or hard liquor. If he provided the alcohol for the party he might have been sent to prison.'

'Maybe...depends on the judge. Buying liquor for minors isn't high on the list of crimes for which perps get prison time.'

'Vehicular homicide would have been much higher on the list.'

'It wasn't ruled as such,' Hampton argued.

'Because no one talked.'

'I don't know. The car accident could have been just that, an accident. Even if Special K or some of his pals were trying to stop Lloyd. They might have only wanted to throw a scare into him and get him to back off.'

Grady drew his brows together in a frown. 'Unless the truck bumped the car and knocked Lloyd off the road. It could have been intentional.'

'But it was ruled an *accident*,' Hampton insisted. 'Where is the motive for three murders that you're talking about?'

'What if our perp had a record or other warrants out against him? If so, a charge of providing alcohol to minors meant jail time. He goes after Lloyd to reason with the kid and Lloyd ends up dead from the car crash. Now the police add vehicular homicide to the underage alcohol charge and he is looking at ten to fifteen years of hard time.'

'Yes, but over a quarter century has past since that night.'

'There's no statute of limitations on homicide. He could be trying to cover the death of the Lloyd kid.'

'That ain't thin, Grady,' Hampton complained, 'it wouldn't make two-pound-test leader for your fishing rod!'

'Yes, but we don't know who this guy is yet. The accident report does say Warren's car had a streak of red paint on the driver's side door. It could be the truck forced him off the road. We need to find out who bought the liquor for the party and who might have been driving that pick-up truck.'

'Your deductive reasoning is truly amazing,' Hampton said. 'But whether the accident was on purpose or unintentional, it doesn't explain why someone would start killing these guys now.'

'Let's say our victims knew who was driving that truck. Perhaps one or more of them were even riding in the truck, when Lloyd was forced off of the road and was killed.'

'The secret has been safe for all these years. Why would anyone break their silence now?'

'Something might have changed recently,' Grady explained. 'Maybe our killer got worried one of them would let the truth leak out. He could be shutting them up before they can talk.'

'And the quarter? What's it mean?'

'Got me there, Ham. It could be a private joke between him and these other guys. Maybe they flipped a coin to see who would deal with Lloyd.'

'Did I say two-pound-test leader?' Hampton growled. 'I was giving you too much credit.'

'I don't know what could have set off our killer, Ham. I'm only trying to find a motive that fits. The perp might need a clean slate for some reason. Maybe he is taking a job with the government or something and is afraid of a background check.'

Hampton sat up straight and grew thoughtful. 'Another possibility, Grady, is if our killer has come into some money recently. Maybe someone died and left him a load of loot. None of our vics had a lot of dough. He could have been worried about blackmail, or one of the vics might have threatened to expose him.'

'We need to find out who attended that Christmas party and drove a red pick-up truck. If it was Special K, we could have a direction to follow. It's the closest thing to a lead we've managed to this point.'

'Let's start with the list of names of those we know attended the party and see who all they can remember. Someone knows Special K's real name…and whether or not he was the one who bought the liquor.'

Grady tapped his notebook. 'Maria Pacheco attended the party. She would be a good person to talk to again. She's had time to think about her brother's death. We didn't know about the party when we interviewed her after Paul's death.'

'Meanwhile, we better stake out both of the remaining names. If our coin killer goes looking for another on the list, maybe we'll get lucky.'

'Sure haven't had any luck since we started this case, Ham.' Grady looked at his watch. 'How about we grab something to eat before we start?'

'You're always hungry.'

'Come on, Ham, I always stop when you start craving caffeine. Anything beats buying the road-kill sandwiches out of the break room vending machine.'

Hampton grunted. 'Sometimes, you nag worse than my ex-wife.'

'I'm a better cook than your ex-wife too.'

Hampton snorted. 'Who isn't?'

'Only woman I ever knew who could burn boiled water.'

'You got that right, Grady. I lost fifteen pounds during the eighteen months we were together. She could write one of those diet books and make a bundle.'

'Bet you miss having her lying next to you at night though.'

'She could be something special when the mood struck her, but once her mother moved in my life became a living hell.'

'Ever wonder if you would have made a go of it, if not for that old gal's interference?'

'I don't know, but being nagged twenty-four seven by two women, Grady…I never had a moment's peace.'

'So, where do we go for lunch?'

Hampton snorted. 'You tell me. You're the one who is starving!'

KARI WAS WATCHING from her apartment window for Jason. When she saw him park his rental car in the Visitor Only parking stall, she hurried into the bathroom for a final look at her reflection in the mirror. She did a quick touch-up to her hair and was ready when his knock came at the door.

Jason appeared freshly shaven and his hair was well groomed, though he obviously was not the kind of man to style his hair or pluck his eyebrows. He was attired in a gray sports shirt, which was open a single button at the neck, and his black, dress slacks were neatly pressed. Even his shoes were polished.

He glanced over her attire—a modest, saffron-colored, sweater-dress outfit. With a belt of delicate braided silver about her waist, it flattered her womanly contours without being immodest. And he paused to take note that she wasn't wearing any shoes.

She uttered forth a nervous laugh. 'You must think I'm part gypsy, running around without shoes.'

'Not at all. I enjoy a girl in her bare feet.'

'Why?' she asked bluntly. 'Don't you think it puts a woman at a disadvantage?'

'Probably the opposite,' Jason replied. 'There's something very natural and feminine about a girl running around without her shoes.'

'As I suspected, you are a throwback to the caveman era.'

'I've been accused of being chauvinistic at times.'

Kari stepped back and held the door so he would enter. 'What have you been up to since we last met for pizza?'

'I've been busy. Reggie had a delivery to make this afternoon, but he and I went to a sporting goods store this morning. He stocked up on fishing supplies, and then he took me on a short sightseeing tour up a canyon...someplace called Alta, where they do a lot of winter skiing. Anyway, Reggie told me you have beautiful autumns here, but it is too early for the change of colors. Even so, it was quite beautiful.'

She laughed, unable to suppress the mirth. At his curious look, she said, 'I can't remember ever hearing a man use the term *quite beautiful,* except when trying to flatter a woman.'

'It was my wife's favorite expression,' he said, a softness entering his features. 'I don't make a habit of saying it in public.'

'She sounds like a wonderful woman. I can't imagine how difficult it must be, finding such a person and then losing them.'

'There's an adage about a bulb that burns too brightly also burns out the quickest.'

Kari displayed a smile of compassion. 'Yes, I believe that's true in some cases.'

The table setting was for two and the centerpiece was a charming candelabrum with three lighted candles.

'I wouldn't want you getting the wrong idea,' Kari informed him, as she closed the door behind him. 'But just as you were saying about light bulbs, the one above the table burned out when I switched it on. So we're having a candlelight dinner because I don't have a spare bulb in the house.'

Jason came back with a ready retort. 'Now that you've adequately ruined both the effect and my hopeful fantasy, what's for dinner?'

Kari laughed politely at his humor. 'Pork roast, stove-top stuffing, candied carrots and a bean salad. If that doesn't fill you up, I made banana pie for dessert.'

'Banana cream pie?'

'I've a can of whipped cream for the topping.'

He chuckled. 'You may have to roll me out through the door when we've finished. I've a weakness for banana pie.'

The conversation during the meal was light-hearted. They sat across from one another, sharing the meal and growing more comfortable with each other. No teasing barbs, no worldly opinions, only a frivolous and easy-going banter between two newfound friends.

After the main course, Kari pushed the dirty plates and leftovers to one side of the table and set two servings of pie together on the bare end of the table. When she sat down to eat dessert, it made the arrangement more cozy, intimate even.

As they both worked on their slice of pie an odd transformation took place. It seemed the mood, the atmosphere, even the smoky color of Jason's eyes became more enhanced. Kari felt the change, as if they had become closer in their short while together. Then, without warning, the serene comradeship gave way to something else.

Kari had eaten most of her dessert and decided to add more whipped cream to the last couple of bites. Holding up a forkful of pie, she shook the can and attempted to spray the cream directly on the morsel. Her aim was somewhat off center and a little sprayed on to the side of her hand.

'Oops!' she exclaimed. 'I must be getting cross-eyed in my old age.'

Jason reached out and took hold of her wrist. 'Tsk, tsk, madam,' he said, mocking the decorum of an English butler. 'Allow me to tidy that bit of bother for you.'

She giggled with amusement and leaned forward so he could lick off the cream.

Instead, he opened his mouth and took the bite of pie right off of her fork.

'Hey! You thief!' she charged. 'You were supposed to lick my hand!'

'Madam,' he conjured the pious air of a butler again, 'I am not a dog. I don't go about licking people's hands!'

To even the score, she dug her fork into his remaining pie and retrieved a suitable bite. 'Fair is fair,' she retorted haughtily.

He laughed at her pluck and snatched up the can of whipped cream. 'Point taken,' he said. 'Let me spruce that up for you. We both know your aim is not all that good.'

She extended the fork in front of her. He tipped the can—too horizontally to work properly. The result was not a little puff of cream, but a spatter of drops, most of which ended up on her face. She sputtered and blinked from the sprinkle.

'Oh, thank you.' Her voice oozed sarcasm. 'That was so much better than my hitting my own hand.'

Jason picked up a napkin, reached over and dabbed it lightly on her cheeks and forehead, removing the damp spatter. When he paused, she looked undeviatingly into his eyes. There was a warmth and depth within his gaze which she could not fathom. For no apparent reason, her heart began to pound with the cadence of a drum roll.

'Did you get it all?' she asked, her voice curiously husky from the swell of emotion.

'Missed a spot,' he admitted. But instead of using the napkin, he rose to his feet, leaned over, and gently kissed her on the tip of her nose.

Kari quivered slightly at the touch of his lips. She waited, eyes half-lidded, expecting him to kiss her on the mouth. To her surprise, he withdrew, allowing her time to recoup her senses. Tittering uncertainly, she continued to display good-nature about the childish game.

'My turn,' she said, taking the can.

Jason was seated again, outwardly wary, but he remained steadfast. For all he knew, she might intend to spray his whole face. Instead, she put a slight puff on to her finger and dotted it to the end of his nose. He remained completely still, while she moved over and used her lips and tongue to remove the sugary dab. When finished, she sat back in her chair, barely concealing the bolt of anticipation which rocketed through her senses, awaiting his next move.

'Jolly good. I have a grasp of the game now!' Jason quipped, responding to the dare. 'A chance to compare techniques.' And he once more took hold of the can.

'Wait!' she screeched, as he put a small portion on to his finger. 'We're even! You can't—'

But he flipped the gob at her. If she hadn't moved it

would probably have landed on her forehead. By jumping back, it spattered on her throat and slid an inch or two down the side of her neck.

'Oops!' he said in mock dismay. 'This could be something of a challenge.'

'Wait a minute, Jason,' she began, holding up her hands to ward him off. 'I think this juvenile game has gone far enough.'

'Fair is fair, you said.'

Kari did not need a psychic to realize where this was headed. She ought to have taken a napkin and wiped off the smidgeon of cream. Instead, she remained steadfast, tilted her head slightly back and waited.

Jason stepped around and lingered above her. 'Hum, I begin to appreciate a vampire's point of view. You have a most inviting neck.'

Kari held her breath. When his lips touched and caressed her throat, she experienced a shudder of excitement. Jason did not linger, however, and immediately returned to his chair.

Kari knew the next step. If she dared to place a dab of cream on his lips...

'Perhaps we should clear the table,' Jason offered, allowing her an escape route.

'No,' she said a bit too quickly. 'It's my turn.' Rising to her feet, she gave the can a vigorous shake. With a single press, she worked the dispenser stem on the can. It sputtered air and squirted a few tiny drips of liquid. She frowned, shook the container up and down several times and made a second attempt. The result was the same.

'It would appear the game is cancelled due to a lack of ammunition.' Jason tossed out the jest.

Kari laughed, unusually spirited. 'Yes, but I still owe

you one.' She met Jason's gaze and felt another tremor. If only she could know her own heart. The desire was—

At that instant there came the musical jingle of a cell phone!

'That would be me.' Jason grudgingly reached down and removed the gadget from his pocket.

'I understand why some people hate these things,' he said. He switched it on, rose from the table and took a couple steps away from Kari.

'This is Jason.' He listened for a moment. 'Yes, Roger, I thought you were busy tonight?' Another moment to listen. 'Well, I told you what I knew about the story. What is…?'

Kari was stung by a twinge of guilt. She had scarcely broken up with Roger, and here she was, playing and teasing, ready—nay, eager—to be kissed by his cousin. How could anyone not think something was wrong with that!

'She did?' Jason asked. 'No, I didn't know about it. I haven't spoken to Aunt Sally today.'

Kari was overwhelmed with a rush of culpability. Sally had told Roger about her visit. Good Lord! She could not have felt any smaller!

'Yes, it was to be expected that they would get to your grandfather,' Jason was speaking again. 'Reggie and I would have talked to him this morning, but Tynan belongs to a bowling league and wasn't going to be at home.'

Kari's brain was working, trying to sort out the right words to keep this whole mess from ruining their evening. She didn't want Jason angry with her.

'No, not tonight,' Jason was saying. 'I'm having dinner with someone.' A pause. 'Yes, of the female persuasion.' Then, another short pause. 'No, it's nothing serious.'

The last sentence stung. Kari had intended to explain about her visit with Sally, but her chance was lost. She should have told him before they sat down to eat.

Jason spoke into the receiver a last time. 'Fine, I'll talk to you then.'

Kari stared down at her bare feet. She suddenly wished she was wearing six-inch heels. The last thing she needed at the moment was to be at a physical disadvantage. She took a deep breath as he put away the phone.

'I was going to tell you about talking to Sally after we had eaten,' she began.

'Did you learn anything?'

She frowned at his professional demeanor. 'She became upset with me. I was curious as to what questions the police might have asked...because of my story—our story.'

'And?' He prodded her on.

'And nothing!' she exclaimed. 'Sally got defensive and ushered me out of the house. I tried to explain and apologize, but she wouldn't listen.'

Jason paced the room for a moment, as if trying to sort out what he had learned. 'I expected the police might want to speak to Tynan, after what you told me about his filing a complaint against those three men. We can only assume the complaint had something to do with Aunt Sally.'

'That's exactly what I was trying to find out,' Kari interjected.

Jason regarded her with a steady gaze. 'You should have told me about your visit to her right away.'

Kari wrung her hands, desperately searching for a suitable answer. 'I didn't wish to start the evening off by boring you with work. Especially with it being a complete washout. I was going to mention it to you after we finished dinner. Then, the dessert thing began and, well...' She struggled for words. A heat wave bathed her face and she knew she was blushing. 'Well,' she finished with the lame excuse, 'Roger called before I had a chance.'

'Roger saw your byline on the story,' Jason informed her. 'He thinks you might be trying to get even.'

'Only a warped mind like his would work that way,' she said.

'I wouldn't blame you,' he countered. 'The man is a complete louse when it comes to his treatment of women.'

The suggestion gave Kari strength. 'I wouldn't do that!' she flared defensively. 'I was following my story. The visit to your aunt was to learn about the complaint Tynan filed against those men.'

'Too bad you learned nothing worth while.'

'Sally did let slip something about a party, but I don't know what it has to do with anything. She ran me off too quickly. As for Roger, I couldn't care less what he thinks!' She softened her stance and finished with, 'But I do care what you think.'

He stood there, indecisive, as if he had a lot on his mind. After a long moment, he said: 'I should be going.'

Kari was immediately contrite. 'Don't be angry with me for not speaking up right away, Jason.'

He gave a bob of his head. 'Not at all. I understand.' The words were spoken, but there was more at work than his words. 'Would you be upset if I were to leave you with the dirty dishes?'

'No, that's fine,' she replied.

He started for the door. 'Roger asked if I would go and see Sally. He said she sounded pretty upset by all of this and he doesn't want her to drink too much. Reggie would be the better choice, but he's on the road.'

Kari held her breath and asked: 'Will I see you again?'

'You have my number,' he said.

Kari wished she could say something to stop him, but she didn't know the words. The evening had been a wild roller coaster ride. It had started out slow, gaining speed during the meal. The incident with the whipped cream had lifted her skyward to the heavens, only to plummet back to earth when Jason's cell phone had rung. With the man out of sight—perhaps out of her life—the ride was over, the thrill was lost.

ELEVEN

JASON PULLED INTO the driveway around midnight. It had been a wasted trip to visit Sally. By the time he arrived she was sloshed and asleep on the couch. After a few incoherent sentences from her, he had helped her get off to bed. Once she had been tucked in for the night, he had taken a few minutes to wash up the pile of dirty dishes in the sink and clean up the kitchen. When he left, he made sure the doors and windows were locked.

He entered the motel room to see the message light was blinking on the phone in his room. He hit the playback and listened. One of the messages was from Roger. It said he would try his cell phone—the earlier call he'd received. The other was from a Detective Hampton. He requested Jason to call to schedule an appointment for a short interview. Jason decided he would drop by first thing the next morning. Considering he knew very little about the murders or the history of the three men, it ought to be a short conversation.

Jason had picked up his laundry from a place called The Red Hanger so he had a choice of clothing. He laid out a casual shirt and slacks, then got ready for bed. It was going to be a short night and he feared sleeping was not going to come easy.

Fifteen minutes later, lying beneath the covers, he tossed and turned, unable to find a comfortable position. Of course, he knew it wasn't the bed, it was Kari. She refused to get out of his head. He envisioned her captivating smile, the mischievous sparkle in her eyes, and he smiled, recalling the musical lilt to her voice when she was teasing. As for the game with the dessert, it would forever be engraved in his memory. He was still amazed at entering into a contest so juvenile and silly. He hadn't engaged in a game of *I dare you* or a food fight since he was a teenager.

His wife had been what some referred to as a 'stiff Brit', ladylike in every way. She would have scolded him for acting foolishly, although in a pleasant way. Her scoldings usually held little anger. It was more her way of retaining her own puritan femininity and holding him to a higher standard.

Jason rolled over on to his stomach, trying to blot out the frivolous memory, but everything about Kari remained stark and vivid in his mind's eye. He was haunted by the subtle fragrance of her perfume, the effect of having her look at and through him, and most of all, the ready-to-be-kissed look on her face an instant before the cell phone rang. Had he kissed her he would not have been able to walk away. One kiss would have devastated his resolve, weakened his knees and melted his heart. How in the world could Roger jilt someone so...so perfect!

JASON SAT ACROSS FROM the two detectives. They were cordial in their introductions, simply using the names Grady and Hampton. As the two men sat down, they grew serious.

'We tried to get hold of your cousins, but it seems one is out of town on a delivery and the other left on a flight for New York,' Grady said, opening the conversation.

'Yes, they both travel a lot,' Jason told them. 'Roger handles corporate insurance claims for some major companies around the country. As for Reggie, he drives a lorry... uh, truck that is, and makes deliveries as far as the coast.'

'You are what, Sally Cline's nephew, from England?'

'Yes, I'm visiting for a few days.'

'She told us you were a cop of some kind.'

'Yes, an inspector with the Sutton CID.'

The two men exchanged looks. 'Inspector, huh? What field of investigation are you in?'

'Homicide and violent crime mostly. I've been with the CID for almost ten years.'

'You're aware of the homicides we're working on—a trio of murders?'

'I've read a little in the paper. I don't know much else, other than the three men all graduated from the same class as my aunt.'

'Those same three men were also listed in a complaint, filed by her stepfather.' Hampton spoke up for the first time. 'What do you know about that?'

'Nothing,' Jason replied. 'I've never met or talked to Tynan, although I intend to visit him while I'm here. Roger called last night and said you had talked to both him and Sally.'

'What about you?' Grady asked. 'When did you see Sally Cline last?'

Jason said, 'I stopped by last night. Roger was concerned about her. I got there too late to do much good. She had an off-day from work and had been nursing a bottle of Scotch...probably since morning. She didn't say much that made any sense.'

'If the woman has a drinking problem, your cousins ought to try and get her into a program. Could be she's an alcoholic.'

'I'm sure she qualifies as one,' Jason allowed. 'But a person has first to admit they have a problem and want to get better, before they can be treated. Aunt Sally doesn't strike me as a person who is very keen on admitting she is in the wrong.'

'What do you know about the three men who died?'

'Pacheco was a pretty good artist in high school. There's a picture he drew of my aunt in their senior yearbook—he drew some of the other cheerleaders too. As for the other two guys, Aunt Sally talked about them a little. Kenny and Clark were football stars in high school. She said they both encountered difficulties in college, so neither made it to the professional level. That's about it.'

'What about Warren Lloyd?'

'Roger and Reggie's biological father,' Jason replied. 'I take it that you know he died before the boys were born.'

'Some information has come to light since we started our investigation.' Grady spoke in a cordial tone of voice. 'There's an outside chance Lloyd might have been run off the road intentionally.'

Jason frowned. 'Your department is only now getting around to investigating his death?'

'Until now it was assumed to have been an accident.' Grady was defensive.

Hampton took over. 'But there might be a connection with the killer we're looking for.'

'In what way?' Jason queried.

Grady explained how a red pick-up truck had been seen racing with Lloyd. He indicated there had been some red paint found on the side of Lloyd's car and it could have come from the two vehicles hitting each other.

'It was probably an accident,' Hampton retook the lead. 'The two vehicles might have sideswiped as they raced, or the pick-up might have inadvertently forced Lloyd's car off of the road.'

'It could have been intentional too,' Jason postulated. 'How does that explain why someone would murder three guys?'

'We've talked to a lot of people who attended the Christmas party that night. Two different witnesses remember that Steve Kenny's cousin drove a cherry-red Chevy pick-up. Coincidentally, the cousin, Tom Kenny—the kids knew him as Special K—was twenty-one at the time.'

Jason said, 'So there was a Christmas party with underage kids and you think this Tom Kenny is the one who bought alcohol for the kids?'

'We believe so.'

'What does all of this have to do with Tynan Cline?'

'Sally—your aunt—got drunk at the party and Tynan called the police. Warren was at a family reunion at the time. He was probably real unhappy to come home and find out his girlfriend was grounded for a month. He might have threatened Special K…if he discovered he was the one who bought the booze.'

'Then this Special K character, Tom Kenny, decides Lloyd may go to the police?'

'It's all guess-work,' Grady admitted. 'Warren might have gone looking for Tom or maybe Tom wanted to stop him from going to the police.'

'Tom Kenny had an arrest record before that party,' Hampton put in. 'He would have served hard time for supplying booze to all of those kids. It gave him a motive to keep Lloyd from involving the police.'

'What's all that got to do with these latest murders?' Jason wanted to know. 'Lloyd's death was proclaimed an accident and the booze thing is well past the time for being punishable. Do you seriously believe someone is killing these men to hide a truth which had little or no possibility of coming to light?'

'Tom Kenny has spent fifteen of the past twenty-five years behind bars for a number of offenses,' Grady explained. 'He had been in counseling with a shrink for the past ten years and was ordered to take medication for his manic depression. He also suffers from paranoia. The day of his release he dropped out of sight.'

'Sounds totally off his nut, but why kill those people now?'

'We spoke to his psychiatrist,' Grady responded. 'Under the circumstances, the doctor waived the patient confidentiality. He told us Tom stopped coming to his appointments as soon as he hit the streets. If he has ceased taking his medication too, he might be paranoid enough to think even his own cousin might talk to the police.'

Jason gave a shake of his head. 'Unless you've been holding something back, the statements I've seen and read in the news say there are no solid leads or clues. It's difficult to imagine someone so sick in his mind being so careful at a crime scene. Have you got his prints or DNA to confirm he's the killer?'

'We are not at liberty to say what clues we are currently processing. Let's stick with your part of all this.'

'My part?'

'It's why we contacted you, Mr Keane,' Hampton said. 'We've been interviewing people who attended the Christmas party that night. There might be more to this than a few kids getting too drunk to stand up.'

'What do you mean?'

'A good many of the witnesses say the party was innocent, but one or two alluded to having left the party when things got out of hand. Another said they heard rumors about something bad happening...a fight or attack of some kind.'

Grady leaned forward, alert, as if reading Jason's body language and searching for any unusual reaction. 'Are you quite sure your aunt never mentioned anything about the party?'

Jason didn't blink. 'Not a word.'

'Have you heard the names Larry Wilkins or John Beckston?' Grady asked. 'Maybe Sally or one of the boys mentioned their names?'

Jason paused to think. 'No, I don't recognize either of them.'

Grady offered the next question. 'You being an inspector, I know you're more observant than a normal person would be. Do you believe either of the boys knew about the complaint filed by Tynan?'

'First impression, they both seemed genuinely shocked about the whole matter.'

'And you did try and ask your aunt about it last night when you saw her?'

'Yes…she belched in my face and passed out.' He put his forearms on the table and leaned forward. 'What else do you know about this case?'

'All we're at liberty to tell you is that five boys were named in the report—three are now dead,' Grady replied. 'The initial complaint from Tynan is the only connection we have between the three victims.'

Jason looked from one man to the other, searching for clues or answers. 'I'm guessing this Wilkins and Beckston you mentioned are the remaining two of the five?' Neither man gave any indication if he was right or not, so he shrugged his shoulders. 'Well, it doesn't really matter,' he said, 'I won't be in the States long enough for you to solve the case.'

'We know Reggie was around Vegas at the time Jamison Clark was killed.' Grady tossed out the tidbit.

'So was I.'

'You didn't have a motive to kill him.'

'I don't believe Reggie or Roger knew anything about Jamison Clark, about the party, or the complaint filed by his grandfather.'

'All right, Inspector Keane. We appreciate your talking with us,' Grady said.

'Are you following up on the accident?'

'We're looking into it.'

'And the Christmas party? You suspect a fight or attack of some kind, something that might have been grave enough to have provoked these murders?'

Hampton made a dismissive gesture with his hand. 'We didn't ask you here in your professional capacity, Keane. We have our own methods when it comes to a murder case.'

'A polite way of telling me to keep out of your investigation?'

'You could say that.'

'I might be more help if we were to share a little professional courtesy.'

'Thanks for the offer,' Grady said drily. 'We'll call you if we need you.'

'All right,' Jason replied. 'But if you start investigating my family members, I will be inclined to make this case my business.'

'You have no authority over here,' Hampton warned. 'We don't want some Brit hamming up our investigation.'

'Perish the thought,' Jason replied. 'Naturally, if I learn anything of importance, I will report it to you immediately.'

'As a professional courtesy?' Grady asked.

Jason quipped, 'Of course; an equitable exchange for the civility you've shown me.'

As neither detective had anything more to say, Jason stood up and left the room. He had hoped to learn something. Instead, he now had twice as many questions and the same amount of answers as before—zero!

'KARI?' THE TELEPHONE receptionist said, 'you have a call from New York. I put it on line three.'

Kari said thanks and pushed the button. She said 'hello' but was ill-prepared for the instant attack.

'What the hell do you think you're doing, Kari?' It was Roger. 'Is this your way of taking petty revenge against me? Are you out to ruin my family?'

'Roger!' she gasped. 'I don't know what you're talking about. And if anyone has a right to be upset, it's me!'

'I knew it!' he jeered. 'You're using your poison pen to get back at me for dumping you!'

'You conceited, egotistical jackass!' she snapped at him. 'My writing an article had nothing to do with the end of our relationship!'

'Yeah, right. You sic the police on my mother and it had nothing to do with us!'

'I wrote a story about three murders,' Kari clarified. 'I didn't know your mother was in any way involved.'

Vehemence was thick in his reply. 'I'll bet you didn't. She sounded close to tears when I talked to her. My mother hasn't seen any of those men since she graduated from high school. Being questioned by you and a couple of police bullies was pure torture for her!'

'I'm sorry for your mother, but I—'

He didn't let her finish. 'So how did you come by your information, Kari? I see you've gone from writing obituaries to having your article on the front page. It read that you were the reporter who connected a third murder victim in Vegas to the other two men in Salt Lake. How'd you manage that?'

'I—I did some research on the Web. The three men all had a common background: the graduating class from Jordan High. That's all there is to it.'

'That's all, huh?' He obviously didn't believe her.

'Yes, I got a copy of the list of juniors and seniors for the year Pacheco and Kenny graduated and searched for other names on the Web.'

'Several hundred names—I'll bet you did!' He swore in disgust. 'I knew something smelled like week-old fish when I spoke to Jason last night. The two of you are in this together!'

Rather than deny it, she gathered courage from the fact Jason was involved. 'Your cousin was only trying to be a decent guy. He wanted to help me get a story printed and apologize for your behavior!'

Roger uttered a cruel laugh. 'Now that's rich. You lead me down the matrimonial path, pretending to be as virtuous as a newborn baby. Then, when I find out you're a slut, Jason apologizes for it!'

Kari grit her teeth. 'I'm not a slut!'

His words were cutting and brutal: 'You're no virgin either!'

'Neither are you!' she fired right back. 'I thought we had something special, that you were something special. You had me believing—'

'What?' he challenged. 'Believing I would marry someone like you, someone who is soiled and used?'

'Good lord, Roger! What kind of narrow-minded monster are you?'

'A woman is nothing without her virtue,' he sneered. 'It's the most precious gift she has to give. She can love more than one man, have sex with more than one man, even have children with more than one man, but she can only surrender her virtue once. It should be a sacred treasure given only to the man she is going to marry.'

'This isn't the nineteenth century, Roger. There are very few twenty-something virgins around. You can't expect—'

'Expect what?' he interrupted again. 'Expect a woman to remain chaste until her wedding day? Are you defending a woman's right to act like a slut?'

'Leave me alone. I let you make a complete fool out of me. That should be enough…even for a slimy, underhanded snake like you!'

'Next time I talk to Jason, I'll fill him in on what a back-stabbing witch you are.'

'This is me, hanging up on a disgusting, degenerate, rat-maggot!' Her voice rose an octave, 'You can go to hell!'

She slammed down the receiver, just in time to see Marge Taylor standing a few feet away. One eyebrow was cocked in disapproval.

'Sorry,' Kari muttered ignominiously. 'I didn't mean to raise my voice.'

'Please tell me you weren't speaking to our editor?'

Kari felt the glow of embarrassment heating her cheeks. 'No, of course not. It was some hack trying to give me a hard time over an article in the paper.'

Taylor let the matter pass, but walked over and glanced down at Kari's monitor. There were three lines written on the blank page, but nothing of interest.

'I haven't seen a fresh follow-up story on the murders yet.'

'There are no new developments,' Kari said. 'I've spoken to several people from the same graduating class as the three victims, but none of them had anything to add to the story. The only other link I've uncovered is something the police won't discuss. There was a call made to complain about those three men once, but it was while they were still in high school and never became a formal charge. It's doubtful it has any relevance.'

'Scott is going to become anxious if you don't deliver something pretty soon.'

'Yes, ma'am.'

'Have you spoken to the relatives of the three dead men?'

'Yes, but they are clueless about the murders. So far, there simply doesn't seem to be any motive to tie the crimes together.'

Taylor paused and put a hand up to cup her ear. She feigned listening. 'What's that?' she taunted Kari. 'Do I hear the obituaries calling?'

'I'll find something,' Kari said quickly. 'I'm going to contact my source and pick his brain for more information.'

'Good idea. You need to come up with another article, before you end up sitting down at the city hall, awaiting word on the new water development projects.'

Kari groaned. 'Yes, ma'am. I hear you.'

As soon as Taylor walked away, she dug Jason's number out of her purse. Here she was, calling him again, and there was little chance he had anything more to tell her. She dialed his cell phone number but it went to voicemail. Instead of leaving a message, she dialed his motel, but it also went to the recorded message. She waited for the *beep* and cleared her throat.

'Jason, this is Kari.' She hated the meekness of her voice. 'I know we didn't part under the best of circumstances the other night.' She hesitated. 'But I would like to see you again.' She groaned at the weak delivery and finished with: 'Call me.'

Replacing the telephone receiver in its cradle, she stared at the nearly blank screen on her monitor. Roger's call had caused a raging storm within her chest. His acid words stung her wounded pride and raised her ire at the same time. Roger had never pretended to be overly moral or religious. For him to spout off about her not being a virgin was not only hurtful and cruel, it was hypocritical! No, she wasn't a virgin, but she was a decent girl. Concerning her sex life with men, she had made only two mistakes—he was both the second and the biggest!

Kari tapped her nails against the desk top. She was at a dead end. She needed another angle, something outside the norm. More than her next story, she hated the feelings of shame and inadequacy Roger had provoked. She needed to share time with someone special to counteract his treachery. She groaned inwardly, finishing the thought—she needed to be with someone like Jason.

TWELVE

JASON RETURNED KARI'S phone message and agreed to meet at her place. He arrived to find her waiting in her car. He parked next to her, then quickly joined her in the passenger seat of her car.

'So where are we going?' he asked, buckling the seatbelt.

'I called Tynan and he offered to talk to us.'

'Us?'

'Yes, I told him I would bring you along. I think that's the reason he agreed to talk to me.'

'The police warned me to stay away from this case this morning.'

Kari was surprised by the news. 'They talked to you?'

'A couple of charming fellows—Hampton and Grady.'

She snickered. 'Yes, I am familiar with them both. They're the ones who grilled me about you.'

'About me?'

'My source,' she explained. 'Of course, I didn't tell them it was you.' She glanced over at him. 'So how did they know to bring you in for questioning?'

'Aunt Sally must have told them I was visiting. They wanted my opinion about Roger and Reggie. They are two of the three new suspects.'

'Why would the boys be suspects?'

As Kari drove, Jason told her about the party and Tynan calling the police. Then he added the part about Warren Lloyd's death.

After a few minutes, Kari shot him a sheepish glance. 'I guess you know why I called?'

'Because you've run out of ideas?'

She laughed at his grasp of the situation. 'Well, I wanted to see you again too. But, yes, I've got to find another follow-up story and, unfortunately, it all revolves around your family.'

'The truth is what matters, Kari. Whether it's here in the States or back in Mother England, we need reporters to tell the truth, without adding personal bias.'

'I hope we can find the truth after so many years.'

'So do I, Kari,' Jason replied.

MARIA PACHECO NOW HAD the last name of Anderson. She had three kids, two grown and on their own, and the last, a seventeen-year-old, who had left for school by the time Grady and Hampton arrived. She wore sweats and was in the middle of cleaning the family room carpet. The two detectives had to knock twice and ring the doorbell before she finally heard them over the roar of her vacuum cleaner.

Grady smiled a greeting when she opened the door. He was quick to notice Maria did not seem surprised to see them.

'I thought you might come back,' she reinforced his assumption.

'May we come in?' Grady asked politely.

Maria glanced down at their shoes, as if to check for dirt, although she moved back and opened the door wider. She motioned them into the kitchen, where they sat down at a freshly cleaned table. She offered them coffee, but they both declined, so she took a chair opposite them.

Grady, who was more delicate when it came to inter-views, started the dialogue.

'Mrs Anderson, when we first met, our assumption was

that Paul was a singular murder victim. Since that time, we have come to discover two other men—both of whom graduated with your brother—have died in the very same fashion. It has forced us to look for any connections between your brother and the other two victims. The only link we've been able to uncover leads us back to the Christmas party during their senior year. I know this is difficult and it was a long time ago, but I wonder if you would go through what you can remember of that night?'

'Even the simplest fact could be important,' Hampton told her. 'Tell us exactly what you recall from the very beginning.'

Maria looked several years older than during their last visit. She had been wearing make-up and her hair had been brushed out. Today, she wore baggy clothes, house slippers, her hair was not combed, and the circles beneath her eyes were proof that she hadn't been sleeping well.

'After I read in the paper about Jamison Clark and Steve Kenny,' she began, 'I did a lot of thinking about that night.'

'Take your time.' Grady offered her encouragement. 'We don't want to rush you.'

'Jimmy and I—that is, Jamison Clark—had been dating for about three months. He was a senior and I was a sophomore. He asked me to come to the party, but he couldn't pick me up. He and some of the others—Steve Kenny for one—needed help to get the food and drink ready for the big party. Anyway, they asked Paul to come so I'd have a ride. There were going to be a lot of kids there; it was a major party. Paul was thrilled because it was the first time he'd ever done anything with the big-shot jocks.'

Maria stopped long enough to get up and pour herself a cup of coffee. She again offered Grady and Hampton some, they declined, and she sat back down.

'So Paul wanted to be a part of the jocks crowd?' Grady prompted her, returning to the story.

'Paul was not athletic or real popular,' she explained. 'I think it was an ego trip for him to be invited to one of the school bashes. Anyway, he borrowed Dad's car and we went together.' She took a moment to take a sip of coffee.

'Tell us how the party went,' Grady coaxed her to continue.

'Steve's older cousin was there. The kids all called him Special K, because he was old enough to supply the beer. It was also because hardly anyone called Steve by his first name. To most everyone in school, he was Kenny.'

'Makes sense,' Hampton contributed. 'To keep from confusing the two, one is Kenny and the other is Special K.'

'I thought there would be a couple kegs of beer, but there was also a lot of hard stuff and some pills being passed around. By the time we had been there an hour, several kids were drunk and a couple were sick or had passed out.

'The house was big, with five or six bedrooms. I saw several guys taking girls upstairs to have sex. The drinking was out of control and the music was so loud you could hardly hear to talk. Jimmy and I danced a few times, but he had been drinking and kept trying to feel me up. When he said we should go upstairs, we had a fight. I was a virgin…only sixteen by three weeks, and I didn't want my first time to be with a guy who was slobbering drunk. He got mad and called me a tease and a couple dirty names.' She scowled at the memory. 'I told him to drop dead and went to find Paul.'

She didn't readily continue, so Grady nudged her gently. 'And what did Paul do?'

'He was having a good time. He'd been drinking and was hitting on some blonde from his English class. I told him to take me home and he refused. I kind of made a scene about it and Amy Burlington, a senior I knew from choir, offered to give me a ride home.' She took another sip of coffee. 'She took me home and went back to the party.'

Hampton gave Grady a sharp look and he prompted Maria to continue. 'Please, tell us about what else happened that night, anything you might have heard around school afterwards?'

Maria did not meet their eyes—not from guilt, more like embarrassment. 'Paul never told me everything that happened. As for Jimmy, we broke up and didn't speak to each other after that night.'

'But you heard rumors,' Grady suggested.

'Paul did say he was glad I left and he admitted the party got a little out of hand. He was involved in something, but he never would tell me what it was. Some of the other kids, who stayed around later, said there was an attack or fight of some kind. Paul was still at the house when the police arrived and they warned him not to drive home, because of the amount he had been drinking. He called our folks and told them the car battery was dead and he was staying the night. He said one of his friends would give him a jump the next day so he could get the car back home.'

'Then your folks never knew about the police?'

Maria gave a negative shake of her head. 'That was pretty much the end of it, except for Paul acting all kinds of weird. At first, I thought it was because he was mad at me for making a scene, but he was moody and withdrawn for a long time.'

'What about the other boys, the jocks?'

'I didn't spend any time around them after that night. Paul went back to his own life too. He didn't have any interest in hanging around with the football players any more. And, because I was no longer dating Jimmy, I lost track of all of them.'

'Do you know anything about Warren Lloyd, the boy killed in an auto accident a few weeks after the party?' Grady asked her.

'Warren had been at a family reunion or something over the holidays. I remember hearing how mad he was that Sally had gone to the party and gotten drunk.'

'Did your brother seem satisfied that his death had been an accident?'

'I asked Paul about it after Warren's wreck. I remembered Sally Cline had been at the party and asked Paul if he thought that might have something to do with Warren's wreck.'

'And what did he say?' Hampton asked.

'He told me to *never* ask him about Sally or Warren again.' She now looked at Grady, a serious fix to her gaze. 'And I mean he told me in a way that I never forgot.'

'Can you explain that a little more?'

'Paul wasn't the kind of guy to raise his voice; he never had a temper. But when he told me to butt out, it was like threatening to hit me in the face if I didn't listen. It was the only time he ever scared me.'

'Did you hear any more about Tynan or Sally Cline?'

'Just that Warren had gotten Sally pregnant before he was killed. It wasn't a total surprise, 'cause the two of them had been dating for several months.'

'Do you personally have any thoughts about the party, the car accident, or the murder of your brother and those other two guys?'

'I can't see this being something from that far back. I mean, what's the point?'

'Anything you can tell us about Special K?' Hampton asked. 'With him providing the booze, he might know more about the car accident than the other boys.'

'I only saw him that one time.' She cocked her head to

one side. 'Gave me the creeps, you know? He had tattoos on both arms and one on his neck, plus he was wearing earrings in both ears. Not many guys were doing that kind of gross rapper stuff back then. Someone said he'd been in jail…which I can believe. Like I say, a weirdo.'

Grady caught Hampton's look; they mutually decided they had finished the interview. They bid good day to Maria and didn't compare notes until they were back at the car.

'Special K—Tom Kenny,' Grady said. 'He's the guy we have to look at.'

'Out of jail since last year. I'll bet you a cup of coffee he is making sure no one can point a finger at him for Warren's death.'

'We need to find him.'

'The party opens a new venue for us,' Hampton said. 'What if there was a rape at the party?'

'I was thinking about that too,' Grady admitted. 'And I'm thinking Sally Cline might have been the victim.'

'Be another reason for Warren to go after these guys.'

'Another reason for someone to kill him too.'

Hampton was thoughtful. 'It could also add to our list of suspects again.'

'Meaning the twin boys?'

'Mother raped, father killed, that could cause a man to want revenge.'

'Jason Keane was pretty comfortable during the interview. I like the guy as the source for the reporter. He admitted to being in Vegas when Clark was killed, plus he would have a head for names.' Grady rubbed his chin with the back of his hand. 'As for the two boys, Reggie was driving a rig through Vegas, both going and coming a day apart. He was in the right place to kill Clark. However, his brother, Roger, was in Portland at the time. We confirmed his flights and hotel.'

'Let's leave a message for Reggie to contact us. We can do it through his company's dispatcher.'

'Good thinking, Ham. I'll have Peggy get hold of them.'

Hampton changed the direction of their conversation again. 'Speaking of our dispatcher, she left word this morning…the uniforms in Ogden can't locate Larry Wilkins. They've had his place staked out, but he hasn't shown.'

'For crying out loud! We'd better put out an APB on him.'

'I called his house myself,' Hampton informed Grady. 'His wife claimed Larry would be home by tomorrow. He is supposedly off working somewhere.'

'We'd better go round him up in the morning…before the killer finds him first!'

THIRTEEN

TYNAN STOOD A LITTLE under six feet tall and was lean, but rugged looking. He opened the door and his aged face brightened with a smile. 'Jason Keane and the reporter, I presume?'

'I'm glad you agreed to see us, Tynan,' Jason said.

Tynan reached out to shake his hand, then held the door open wider. 'After listening to Sally talk about you and your father all these years, I feel I know you. She and Elwood were always close.'

'Yes, sir,' Jason replied. 'I've felt the same way about Aunt Sally too.' He cocked his head toward Kari. 'And you're right, this is Kari Underwood, a news reporter.'

Tynan led the way into the kitchen and bid them sit down. 'I was about to have a cup of freshly brewed coffee.' He grinned. 'Have to limit how many cups I have any more. The doctor tells me I need to cut back.' He removed two more coffee mugs from the cupboard and placed them on the table.

'Do you remember that old joke,' he asked, looking over his shoulder. 'I cut out drinking, cut out women, cut out smoking...now I'm *cutting out* paper dolls?' He grunted with humor. 'I've been sharpening the scissors.'

'Maybe you ought to switch to decaf,' Kari suggested.

'That's like candy without the sugar, young lady. I make a man's cup of coffee. My brew would make John Wayne proud if he were still alive. You know.'

'Reggie warned me about your coffee,' Jason remarked.

'His description was, if he couldn't drink the stuff, he could always use it in the crankcase of his truck.'

Tynan laughed and poured three cups of steaming liquid. He placed a cup and spoon for each of them, sat down and smiled at Jason. 'Always felt bad taking Sally and her mother away from your father. I loved her madly, but I'm sorry Elwood had to grow up without his mother and little sister.'

'Love sometimes chooses the direction of the heart,' Jason allowed. 'The way my father explained it to me, Grandmother was completely overwhelmed with her affection for you.'

'She was the world to me too,' Tynan avowed. 'I didn't know she was married when I met her.' He lifted his bony shoulders. 'Didn't really think about it. I just knew she was meant to be with me. I mean, it's like we had no choice in the matter. The two of us were swept up inside a tornado. There was nothing either one of us could do about it.'

Kari spoke up. 'Roger told me how you were there for him and Reggie growing up. He said you taught them to fish, hunt, and play ball. You were a substitute for the father they never had.'

'I like to think I was there when they needed a man in their lives.'

'The police came to see you.' Jason got down to business. 'They had me down at the station for questioning too.' Jason added a spoonful of sugar and began to stir the hot liquid. 'The detectives asked me about a police report you filed years ago, but I didn't know anything about it.' He looked up so he could study the man's reaction. 'They said it was about a party. Can you tell us what happened?'

Tynan added a single sugar to his coffee and stirred it in before answering. 'They come to see me too. Don't understand all the fuss. It was a long time ago, before the twins were born.'

'I wouldn't ask, but the authorities are looking hard at Aunt Sally's boys. They have questions and there aren't any answers. Was this about Sally having too much to drink?'

Tynan took a sip of his coffee. Jason couldn't imagine anyone being able to drink something so hot, but the old gent held the cup long enough to take a second taste, before he lowered it to the table. After some moments he looked Jason square in the eye.

'It was all pretty harmless, Jason. Some kids put together a Christmas party and it gets a little out of hand. I can't imagine how it could be related to the death of those three men. That's what I told them two detectives.'

'It's the only link they can find between them,' Jason said. 'I'm afraid they are going to think Reggie was somehow involved. He was near Las Vegas when the first victim was killed. He could end up a suspect.'

'Suspect? That's crazy!'

Jason tried again. 'The police are looking for a motive and can't find one.'

'What possible motive could Reggie have?'

'None that I know of; it's the reason why we came to see you.'

Tynan pondered on that for a short time. With a sigh of resignation, he told Jason about the party, the way Sally had come home drunk and disheveled, then about summoning the police.

'But they never filed any charges,' Jason said.

'No, they weren't able to find the man who provided the alcohol.' He shrugged. 'That was the end of it as far as I was concerned.'

'Why did they only list those particular five names on

the complaint?' Kari asked. 'There must have been dozens of people at the party.'

'By the time the police arrived, those were the only boys still at the house. The cop threatened to haul them off to jail, but none of them would tell who bought the liquor. That was the one person the police would have charged, only they never found out who he was.'

'What about Warren Lloyd?' Jason asked. 'One has to wonder at the coincidence, him dying within a few weeks of the party.'

'The police at the scene ruled it an accident.'

Jason fixed a stare on Tynan. 'What about you and Aunt Sally? What did you two think?'

'There were rumors that Warren had been trying to find out who was responsible for getting Sally drunk. Needless to say, the boy was not happy when he returned home after the holidays. I grounded her for a month. Sally and Warren talked on the phone quite a bit and I heard her crying a time or two, but...' Tynan flinched at the memory. 'It was a difficult time for all of us.'

'Us? Your second wife was living with you at that time?'

'Yes, she wanted us to plan a life of our own. She and Sally never did get along, so she didn't cut her any slack over getting drunk. Maybe we could have handled it differently. For Warren's sake, I wish we had.'

'So what are your thoughts concerning Warren's death?' Jason asked.

'I think Warren found out who provided the booze for the party. I don't know if he threatened to go to the police or what, but he ended up dead a short time later. Sally confronted one of the boys who had been at the party right after the wreck, but he claimed Warren had lost control and ran off the road during a grudge race.'

'Who with?'

'He wouldn't tell her, but she heard someone say it was a guy the kids called Special K...don't know why.' Tynan looked very old, his shoulders bowed under the weight of his next words. 'Anyway, Sally suffered a lengthy depression after Warren's death and never fully recovered from the loss.'

Jason pondered the information. 'If Lloyd was murdered, it would give the boys a motive to go after them.'

'That's pretty far fetched, Jason. There's no proof Warren's death was anything other than an accident.'

'I'm only saying the police are looking for a motive for the killings. Their line of investigation leads me to believe they think the twins have one.'

Tynan dismissed the idea. 'I'm sure neither of them would go out and kill three men over something which might have been an accident. And how could they know if they were even the ones involved?' He grunted. 'It makes no sense.'

'Three homicides and no clues make the police quite zealous.'

'You say you were in Las Vegas when the first man was killed?'

'Yes. He was killed in Henderson, a short drive from my motel. The guy's name was Jamison Clark, and Reggie was on the road around that area at the same time.'

'Even so, there's no way Reggie would be mixed up in these murders.'

'The party brought about the ruination of Sally's life,' Jason argued. 'Killing Warren left her an unwed mother with two children to raise.'

'Yes, she stayed at home with me. It was a hard time for all of us.'

'The end of her dreams and future,' Kari contributed.

'She was naturally bitter,' Tynan admitted. 'She wanted

to dance professionally, or to maybe become a dance teacher. The pregnancy was difficult for her. She put on a lot of weight. Then, when she attempted to get back into shape, she tore up her knee. An operation repaired most of the damage, but the career she wanted was lost to her.'

'And the twins were to blame.'

Tynan blinked at the mist which came to his eyes. 'She blamed the world for a long time. It wasn't only giving birth to the boys. She became a hermit. By the time the twins were old enough to take care of themselves, she had cut herself off from the outside world.'

'It cost you a life alone too,' Kari said. 'Your second wife didn't want any more children to raise.'

He did not contradict the claim but gave an affirmative tip of his head. 'Yes, she wouldn't accept a household filled with chores, crying babies and a young mother who was sour on the world. After several demands and fights, she packed her things and left.'

Kari shook his head. 'All of that misery caused by a little pre-marital sex with a man she intended to marry. It doesn't seem fair.'

'Everyone has their *what-ifs* in life,' Tynan postulated. 'We all have to live with our disappointments and mistakes.'

Jason queried. 'You said Warren was out of town. Did Sally go to the party alone or with friends?'

The question caused Tynan to frown in thought. 'Let's see, it was Sally's best friend who picked her up. She also brought her home.'

'Do you remember her friend's name?' Jason asked. 'Maybe she could fill in some blanks for us.'

'Um, her name was Amy…Amy Burlington—at least, it was back then. I know she got married but have no idea who the guy was.' He remained thoughtful. 'Growing up,

she and Sally used to stay over at each other's house sometimes. They stayed close friends all through high school.'
He wrinkled his brow in contemplation. 'I think Sally lost
touch with her when the boys were born. I doubt she has
seen or talked to Amy in years.'

'Thanks, Tynan,' Jason said. 'No need to tell Aunt Sally
we spoke about this. She would be upset for no reason.'

'I still can't imagine the Christmas party being the reason behind these murders. It happened so very long ago.'

'I agree, but we have to check it out.'

'Thank you for the coffee,' Kari said, having tried a single sip. 'It was a little strong for my taste, but it was very
nice meeting you.'

'Good luck to you two,' Tynan said, displaying a fatherly
smile. 'I imagine you're going to need it.'

Jason reached the driver's side of the car first and
opened the door for Kari. She slid into the seat and he
went around and got in on the passenger side.

'We need to talk to Amy Burlington,' Jason told Kari,
as he secured the seatbelt.

'I'll do a database search and find out where she is living now.' She hesitated. 'Do you think I ought to call Detective Grady? He said he wanted to be kept informed.'

'Amy might not add anything to the inquiry. Plus, the
police probably know about her already.'

'All of this...' Kari paused. 'You don't think Reggie
could be involved, do you?'

'He strikes me about as gentle as a lamb,' Jason replied.

'I could easily believe it of Roger.' She harrumphed.
'Thinking of him, I could believe anything evil or bad.'

'While you follow up on Amy, I'll do a little research
on the two remaining names on the list.'

'The police told you their names?'

'It was part of their questioning,' Jason said. 'John Beckston and Larry Wilkins.'

'If you want, I'll look them up at the office and give you a call,' Kari offered. 'I can get that information in a matter of minutes. It's going to be a lot harder to find Amy. I'll probably have to contact her parents or siblings to locate her.'

'All right.' He agreed to her offer. 'Once I know where to find them, I'll try and track them down. I'm sure the police are watching them, but I might have some joy.'

Kari raised an eyebrow. 'Joy?'

'Sorry, we sometimes use the word *joy* instead of *luck* back home.'

She smiled. 'Well, the two words are a lot alike. For me, when I have good luck, it fills me with joy.'

Jason chuckled. 'I often feel that way myself.'

NEMESIS SMILED. There he was, shuffling along the dark street, hands shoved deep in his pockets, a man without a care or conscience—Larry Wilkins! He missed a step and nearly went down. Casting a dirty look at the sidewalk, he muttered an oath and kept walking. He appeared headed toward a rundown hotel, now converted into a cheap boarding house. With two neon lights out, the sign read…OMS, instead of ROOMS.

Moving swiftly, Nemesis caught up with the man before he reached the entrance. Wilkins gave him a sidelong glance, distrust strong in his eyes, until Nemesis produced the bottle. Seeing the familiar label, he stopped in his tracks.

'Hey! I thought it was you—Larry!' Nemesis greeted him like an old friend. 'You remember me, don't you? We worked together on the pipeline job; I drove one of the trucks when you were flagging traffic.'

The man's head bobbed up and down, his gaze fixed on

the nearly full bottle of good whiskey. 'Sure, I 'member you, buddy.' Larry was immediately warm and sociable. He stuck out a paw, patting Nemesis on the shoulder like a long-lost brother. 'How ya been?'

'I'm hauling dirt and rock in North Salt Lake,' Nemesis said. 'I don't know anyone around this part of town.' He held up the whiskey. 'How about you and I having a few drinks?'

'Sure!' Larry's eyes lit up like neon bulbs. 'I've got a room right here.'

Nemesis put up a stop-sign hand signal. 'Hey, I don't want a bunch of guys seeing us come in together. They might think we're a couple of homos or something.'

Larry leaned over to speak low. His breath hit Nemesis and nearly staggered him with the foul odor. 'Not ta worry, buddy.' He slurred his confidence. 'Jake's the night clerk and he don't do nothing but watch television. He only peeks out if'n somebody rings the bell.'

Nemesis grinned. 'What are we waiting for? Let's get to work on this here bottle!'

FOURTEEN

I**T WAS AFTER NINE** in the morning and yet the woman answered the door in a faded flannel nightgown and fuzzy pink slippers. She was without make-up, with frizzy, uncombed hair. A half-smoked cigarette dangled from between her pale lips.

'Yeah?' she asked, regarding Hampton and Grady with unmasked suspicion. 'What do you want?' Before they had time to answer, she added: 'If you're selling something or we owe you money, you're out of luck. We're broke.'

Hampton was the one to answer. 'I'm Detective Hampton and this is my partner, Detective Grady. Are you Mrs Wilkins?'

She removed the cigarette and flicked the ashes out the door, but a breeze caused some of it to land on Hampton's jacket front. She eyed them with open distaste and answered. 'Until the divorce goes through and I get around to changing my name, yeah.'

Grady inquired, 'Then Larry Wilkins doesn't live here any more?'

'He comes by now and again, but he moved out some time back.'

Hampton was immediately irked by the news. 'I called and talked to you yesterday. When I asked if he was living at home, you said yes!'

She dismissed his concern with another drag on the cigarette. 'Larry told me to keep saying he lived here. He needed to be able to look at any job offers that came along. He's been out of work for a coupla months.'

'You told me he was working construction for the gas company.'

'Well, he was, until they laid him off. It ain't like I was lying or nothing.'

'Where is he now?'

She lifted her shoulders in a shrug. 'I ain't seen him for a while. He comes by long enough to see the kids and pick up his unemployment check. I make sure they send it here, so I can go to the bank with him to cash it.'

'So he stops by every week for his check?'

'Mostly, though he sometimes picks up work that pays in cash…you know, like last week he was doing yard work and hauling trash.'

'Where's he staying?' Hampton wanted to know. 'Do you have an address or phone number for him?'

'Dunno. Last time I seen him we had our usual fight about money and he left.' She took a final puff of her cigarette and flipped the butt on to the lawn. 'Like I told you, I make sure his checks come here. Soon as he runs out of unemployment, I'm fixing to divorce him. I've already talked to Social Services. They are going to help me pay the rent and support my kids.'

'Any special reason why you two are getting a divorce?' Grady asked. 'Has Mr Wilkins gone though some changes recently?'

'Larry has always had a temper. He got fired from his job at the airport a few years back—couldn't even handle moving luggage. Then he was caught stealing some supplies when he was doing janitor work for the county. Ever since, he ain't been able to hold a permanent job. Good thing he had that flagman job long enough to earn unemployment. Otherwise, we wouldn't have had nothing but food stamps to live on.'

Grady faced the woman, gravely serious. 'Mrs Wilkins, we really need to find your husband. If you are holding anything back, please tell us. He could be in serious danger.'

She scrutinized him as if she thought he might be lying. 'Danger? From what?'

'It's related to a case we're working on.'

'You don't mean those guys he used to hang with during his high school years?'

Hampton was instantly alert. 'He mentioned them to you?'

'Only said a coupla his pals from school had been murdered. He didn't talk like he was scared or nothing.' She uttered a snort of contempt. ''Course, that's the way he is, always playing the big man, though I never seen him back it up with action. Besides, I can't see what the death of a high-school buddy or two could mean after so many years. We never even exchanged Christmas cards with anyone from his schooldays.'

'Then you never met any of those men?'

'Didn't know nothing about them, 'cept for the stories Larry would tell. He liked to brag about the gang he ran with back in high school, like he was the hottest thing on campus.' She skewed her face into a mask of disgust. 'Guess it was to make up for his shortcomings in other areas.' She added a vulgar wink. 'If you know what I mean.'

Hampton gave a nod of understanding. 'Yes, well, we have reason to believe the man who killed those other three might also be after your husband.'

'You ain't making this up?' she wanted to know. 'You ain't trying to scare me into telling…?'

Grady lost his patience and practically shouted: 'Tell us where he is, Mrs Wilkins. His life might depend on it!'

'OK, OK,' she whined. 'It ain't like I took an oath in blood or anything. Besides which, I already told one of the guys he used to work with where he was staying.'

'You did what?' Hampton nearly screamed in frustration. 'When? Who was it? Did he give you a name?'

The woman took an involuntary step backward, surprised at the assault of questions and the harsh tone of voice.

'Take a valium, mister,' she told him sourly. 'It was just a phone call. I'm getting to it.'

Hampton's fingers flexed, battling the desire to wring the answers from the woman's throat. Grady stepped between his partner and the woman to prevent his acting on the impulse, and instilled a calm into his voice.

'Please tell us about this phone call and tell us where Mr Wilkins is staying.'

'The guy said he had worked with Larry on the pipeline job and thought he might get him on where he was working now...a sand and gravel outfit I think it was.'

'Did he give you a name?'

'Joe something.'

'You didn't recognize it as one of your husband's friends?'

She snorted. 'Jack Daniel's or some other brand of whiskey has been his only friends for the past coupla years.'

Grady got the address from the woman and the detectives returned to their car. Hampton was still steaming when he closed the door.

'All we ask is a little co-operation from people,' he growled. 'We are trying to save her husband's life and she gives us that snotty damned attitude!'

Grady was also miffed. 'Yeah, she lays all the blame at

his door for being a bum, but he's the one who has to live with her! I don't see her being much of a prize.'

'And you wonder why I'm not married any more. You hear the way she belittled him?'

Grady started the engine. 'Yeah, the man's good enough to stay married to for twelve years, good enough to sire her three kids, good enough to support the family all that time. Then, when he hits a bad streak, they have a break-up, and she spouts about his not being able to satisfy her needs!'

Hampton grunted his contempt. 'I keep telling you, your wife is one in a million. You're a helluva lucky man to have her.'

'I'd hate to think, if something ever happened to split us up, that she would run around telling perfect strangers I wasn't man enough for her!'

Hampton simmered and gave his head a negative shake. 'Never happen, Grady. I've been around you two. The light of love shines in her eyes every time she looks at you. I'll bet she hasn't got a single complaint.'

'And I haven't got a single complaint about her,' he replied. 'That's the way it should be between a man and his wife. Any real complaints should be kept private and worked out as a team.'

Hampton chuckled. 'I sure do like your thinking, Grady. If I was ever tempted to chase after a man, you'd be my pick.'

'Yeah, like you'd ever give up the luscious scent of a woman, the feel of her soft body in your arms, the subtle sway of her hips or sweet kiss of her lips—'

'Cut it out, Grady!' Hampton said sharply. 'You're turning me on!'

'But not for me,' Grady quipped.

'No, definitely not for you!'

Grady pulled out of the driveway. 'You familiar with where the guy is staying?'

'Yeah, it's over a few blocks. It used to be a decent motel…thirty years ago.'

Hampton picked up the radio mike and contacted dispatch. He gave the address where they were heading, but before he could ask for a patrol car for back-up, the dispatcher interrupted him.

'Uniforms are on site at that location already, Ham. A 911 call came in a little while ago. I believe they have someone there you were looking for.'

'Thanks, Peggy,' he replied. 'On our way.'

Grady glanced over at his partner. 'You know Peggy is available,' he said. 'She always talks extra nice to you. Maybe you ought to act on that.'

'She's smart as a whip,' Hampton came back. 'She knew better than to say Wilkins has been found dead. If she would have used his name, we'd have had a media circus blocking the door.'

'You can't be sure it's Wilkins, or that he's dead.'

'Trust me, Grady, I'm right…on both counts.'

'See? You read exactly what Peggy was saying. You better ask her out before one of the other horn-dogs finds out her divorce is final.'

'Just drive the car,' Hampton growled, more angry about the news than Grady's ribbing. 'You're too old to be playing cupid.'

It took five minutes to make the drive. They spotted several squad cars and numerous unmarked vehicles at the scene. 'There's the hotel,' Grady said. 'Looks like the crime scene boys got here ahead of us.'

'Probably were called in before anyone identified Wilkins.'

The coroner and lab team had already cleared the body

for removal, but waited until Grady and Hampton had time to look over the crime scene. It was the exactly the same as the others—duct tape, electrical wire, and a quarter stuck between the victim's teeth.

'We should have been notified about this right away,' Hampton complained.

'Rookie cop caught the call,' a CS technician spoke up. 'He didn't know about the on-going case. Just figured this was a dispute gone bad between winos.'

'Same lack of evidence as the other two, I suppose.'

'Looks that way,' the technician replied. 'We kept the victim here until you arrived. The place is such a mess, it will take a week to process all of the trash.'

A uniform policeman entered the room, waited until Grady gave him an expectant look and asked, 'What?'

'There's a man outside, sounds Australian,' the uniform replied. 'He said he had spoken to you at the station.'

'Average build, about six-foot, with an air of superiority?'

The cop raised his brows. 'Yes; name's Keane. Said he's an inspector.'

Grady looked at the lead man on the CS team. 'You said you're done here?'

'The meat wagon is waiting for the body, but we're finished.'

'Send the inspector up,' he told the uniform. 'I'm curious to see the Brit in action.'

Once Kari had given Jason what information she could find on the two men from the list, he spent the evening tracking them down. Beckston was at work, so he wasn't able to reach him. As for Wilkins, he had gotten the man's whereabouts from his wife, moments after the police had left his house. When he entered the squalid room Hampton greeted him.

'How the hell did you end up here?' was his less than cordial greeting.

'I was right behind you at the Wilkins's house. Mrs Wilkins told me her husband sometimes stayed in one of these run-down hotels. They offer cheap rates, perfect for a wino…which is how she described him.'

'And you guessed our location?'

'Hard to miss a dozen police vehicles parked on the street.'

Hampton gave Jason a hard, menacing look, trying to intimidate him with his size and years of experience. Jason had met his share of men like that before and held his ground.

'You don't back off easy,' Hampton allowed after a few long seconds, rewarding Jason's staunch resistance with something akin to a compliment.

'It takes a special insanity to frighten us Brits. You must remember that, unlike you Americans, we in the CID don't routinely carry a sidearm.'

Hampton grinned. 'You got me there.'

Jason gazed over at the body. The electrical wire was still around Wilkins's neck, having drawn blood when tightened to the point of strangulation. Duct tape secured his hands and ankles, plus a short piece had been placed over his mouth. There was a tiny slit between his lips, where a bit of blood and saliva had seeped out and slid down his chin.

'Same as the others?'

'Right down to a quarter between his teeth, face down.'

'Anything special about the coin?' he asked, without looking at Hampton.

'Just a regular two-bit piece. It is always with tails showing upward,' Grady was the one to speak. 'We don't know if that means anything or not.'

Jason took a few moments and scanned the room with a slow but alert concentration. Then he poked in the trash, looked in the bathroom and under the bed. Then he moved over to study the body again. Leaning down next to Wilkins's mouth, he closed his eyes and inhaled, just enough to sort out the scents. Lifting his head, he took a second survey of the room.

'Did you find a whiskey bottle?' he asked. 'I'd say average grade or better.'

Grady looked at the technician. He gave a negative shake of his head.

'There are a number of discarded bottles sitting about or stuffed in the rubbish. A few empty beer bottles, but most are inexpensive, aftershave bottles,' Jason said.

'Yeah, a down-and-out wino's drink,' Hampton profiled.

'If you take a whiff at Wilkins's mouth, there is the definite odor of whiskey. I'd guess the killer shared a bottle with him, then took it when he left the scene.'

Grady removed the tape from Wilkins's mouth carefully and sniffed. 'He's right, Ham. It smells like whiskey.'

Jason looked at the man's hands, noted the dirt and grime under his nails, and moved around to the back of the victim. He observed the twisted wire, and gently ran his hand along the back of Wilkins's head. On a second pass, he felt a very slight lump and examined the dirt-encrusted hair. Carefully pushing some aside, he stared at the spot for a moment. Then he began to inspect the shirt collar and along the back of the chair.

'You find something?' Grady asked, unable to be silent any longer.

'It could be nothing,' Jason said. 'But there is a slight

abrasion here below the top of his skull, a minute fissure in the skin, which could have been made by a person's teeth.'

Hampton and the technician both moved closer for a look.

Jason pointed at the spot. 'The location on the head is too high above the chair back to have been bumped. But if Wilkins threw his head back, while the killer was leaning too close...'

'He hit him in the mouth!' Grady exclaimed.

'There might be blood,' Jason said, again studying the chair railing and looking on the floor. Before he could find anything, Hampton reached in and curled back Wilkins's shirt collar.

'There!' he cried. 'It looks like a spot of blood!'

The technician used a strong light and magnifying glass to scrutinize the tiny blotch, then announced, 'It does appear to be a droplet of blood.'

'You label that and guard it with your life,' Hampton warned the man. 'I want that blood tested against Wilkins, just as soon as is humanly possible.'

Grady bent and inspected the dead man's face from several inches away. 'No visible nicks, cuts or scrapes on his neck, other than around front, from being strangled with the wire. The blood could be from our killer. Being out of sight like it was, even a careful man would have missed it.'

'Damn, let's hope it's his,' Hampton said. 'We are in dire need of a clue.'

The technician promised, 'I'll put a rush on it and give you a preliminary as soon as possible.'

'We appreciate it.' Grady spoke up. 'This is one perp we really want to catch.'

The body was removed, leaving only the three detectives in the room. After a final look around, Grady was the one to speak first.

'Good catch on the whiskey and bump on the head, Keane.'

'Yes,' Hampton agreed. 'We would have discovered whiskey from the man's stomach contents, and likely the bump too, but it would have taken time.'

'You both were at the previous crime scenes, so you expected the killer to be careful and meticulous. I would guess he had a special reason for priming Wilkins with whiskey. Any idea as to what he wanted?'

'Can't be the location of the other man on the list. He's in the phone book,' Hampton replied.

'It's a mystery to me too,' Grady said.

'Maybe he wanted to toy with Wilkins for some reason,' Hampton suggested. 'For all we know, they might have reminisced about old times.'

Jason could not add any light to the conversation. Rather than stand about, he needed to get back in touch with Kari.

'I appreciate your allowing me to look at the crime scene,' he told the two detectives. 'It is a courtesy you didn't have to extend.'

'Hey, we're all trying to solve the same case,' Grady responded. 'And you did pick up a couple clues that would have taken us another few hours to come up with.'

'That's very gracious of you,' Jason said. 'I'll be in touch should I learn anything more of value.'

'Just don't end up a victim or try solving the case on your own…OK?' Hampton warned.

'I'm on holiday,' Jason told them. 'The only reason I came to see Wilkins was for Miss Underwood. The young lady is desperate for a story.' He gave them an expectant look. 'Might I request you grant her a short interview concerning this murder?'

'We're going to look like fools, having this guy killed while we were trying to find him so we would protect him.'

'I suspect Miss Underwood will be sympathetic in her article...more so than the other media outlets.'

'Yeah, all right. Once I clear it with the captain, I'll give her the details,' Grady agreed.

Hampton said, 'All but the part about the vic having a quarter stuck between his teeth. That doesn't go into print. We've got to stay mum about that.'

'I understand completely, gentlemen. I shall keep that information to myself as well.'

'All right then, we're on the same page,' Hampton said. 'See you later...and stay out of trouble.'

Jason grinned. 'That, Detective, is always my first inclination.'

FIFTEEN

It had taken Kari all of the previous afternoon to track down Amy Burlington. Her mother returned her call late that night and gave her the information she needed. Married, divorced, and married again, Amy's last name was now Dawkins. Mother of two, she was owner-operator of Angel Love Day Care, located in South Jordan, a few miles south of Salt Lake. Kari called Amy first thing from work and arranged to meet with her after lunch.

After attending a short news brief, Kari spoke to Jason on the phone. He had just left the crime scene in Ogden and suggested she contact Detective Grady for what she could print. The urgency to stop the killer caused Kari to rush through an editors' meeting, so she could interview Amy.

She arrived to discover Sally's old girlfriend had two other women—one was a teenager actually—to help her tend a dozen or so children. As it happened, the kids were outside on the playground, so Amy led Kari to her office where they could speak privately. Kari wasted no time in explaining why she was there.

'I had heard about Steve Kenny,' Amy said. 'I never really knew Paul very well and Jamison liked to act a big shot…quarterback of the football team, you know.'

'I attended a news conference this morning. Larry Wilkins was killed last night.'

Amy groaned and pain showed on her face. 'Larry and I were on the same debate team. He was very bright until…' She studied Kari as if deciding how much she dared tell her. 'He started drinking after the Christmas party. A lot. By the end of our senior year he was an alcoholic, a completely different person.'

'What can you tell me about the night of the party?'

Amy grew pensive. 'Sally had been going out with Warren Lloyd for several months, but they had a number of squabbles and fights. I know Warren wanted to get engaged, but Sally wasn't ready to commit.' Amy paused as if sorting out the story so she would tell it right. 'I imagine you know Warren went to a family reunion over the holidays. It left Sally more alone than usual. As for the rest of the story, I've never told anyone about that night.'

'Four men are dead, Amy. I'm trying to make sense of it.'

'I really don't know how I can help.'

'Tell me what happened that night. It might be more important than you think.'

'Well, Sally had a thing for Steve Kenny,' Amy began. 'It started back in grade school, but he never gave her a second look. He was friendly toward her and all, but he never asked her out.'

'How did she end up at his Christmas party?'

'That's kind of sad,' Amy said solemnly. 'Sally had been brooding and sour because Warren would be gone over the Christmas holidays. When Steve invited her to his party she was ecstatic. She saw it as a chance to be with the guy for whom she had been carrying a torch for years.

'Sally didn't have a car, so she begged me to take her. The guys weren't able to pick up their dates because they were busy setting things up for the big bash.' Amy bit down hard and hissed the next words. 'It was the most dirty rotten trick you can imagine!'

'What do you mean?'

'When Sally and I arrived at the party, we found out

Steve hadn't ask her to come for himself, but for the sake of his cousin. It destroyed Sally—her girlish dreams, her longtime infatuation—it crushed her.'

Kari felt a tingle of apprehension. 'Did you know his cousin?'

'No. I'd never seen him before, but Maria Pacheco—she was going with Jamison Clark at the time. She said Steve's cousin had seen Sally when she was cheerleading and wanted to meet her.'

'Maria…as in Paul Pacheco's sister?'

'Yes; we were not close friends, but we knew each other. I ended up taking her home that night.'

'And this cousin, she knew him?'

'Just from what Jamison told her. Maria said Steve's cousin had been to some of the football games and saw Sally doing her cheerleading thing. The guy had the hots for her, so Steve invited her to the party.' She swore softly. 'When Sally found out the truth, she totally caved in. She began to drink and got all wired and silly. She danced with several guys and I saw her kiss a couple of them. I was embarrassed for her but she refused to leave.'

Amy grew silent until Kari prodded her. 'Please finish the story. It might save someone's life.'

'Well, Maria was much too young to be there. Jamison was eighteen and a senior, but Maria was only a sophomore and didn't have a driver's license yet. The two of them got into a noisy argument when he wanted to take her upstairs and have sex. She came crying to me some time around midnight and begged me to take her home.'

'Why not her brother, Paul?'

'Paul had never been to one of the school parties before. He was having too much fun being one of the boys. I told Sally we ought to leave. I said we would take Maria home and then she and I could go have pizza or something.'

Another sigh. 'She was about half-looped and refused to go. She said to come back after I'd taken Maria home.'

Kari waited as Amy again paused. This time it seemed due to a battle with her own conscience. When she started the story again, there was a grave tone to her voice, full of regret and self-incrimination.

'Maria lived about twenty miles away, because the party was being held in Herriman—less chance of anyone calling the police way out there. The place belonged to Kenny's uncle, a retired rich guy who owned several houses. Anyway he was in Florida for the winter. The place was nice and isolated, with several bedrooms, two or three baths and a pool table.'

'What happened when you got back?'

'I was surprised to see there were only a few cars left. Most of the kids had gone home. I found Sally, passed out in a bedroom...' Amy's voice cracked with emotion. 'There were six boys still there, including Steve's cousin. Sally was the only girl and she had...' Another swallow to clear her throat. 'Her clothes. They had obviously dressed her after having sex. Her panties were missing and her blouse was buttoned up wrong.

'I blew up!' Her voice grew strong with ire. 'I called the guys animals and rapists! But they all swore Sally had asked for it. I knew John Beckston better than the others. I dragged him into a corner and demanded he tell me the truth.' She could not hold back her tears. 'John said it was Sally's fault. He said she was staggering drunk and told Steven Kenny how she had always loved him and how much she wanted him. Kenny and the others took her into a bedroom and they all had sex with her! All but John himself. He backed out...' her fury returned, 'not because he was such a decent guy,' she rasped hotly, 'but because he didn't want to be the last one! The idea of having sex after five other guys turned him off!'

'Did Sally know what had happened?'

'At first, she seemed to think nothing had happened. The pills and liquor numbed her senses, and she was deathly sick from all the stuff she'd drunk. By the time I got her home I had stopped three or four times so she could puke. The last stop or two were for the dry heaves and she suffered terribly. She sobered up a little before I got her home, but she still looked like a hollow-eyed ghost.'

'That's what upset Mr Cline, when he saw Sally's condition,' Kari finished the story.

'Her stepmother was furious and Mr Cline swore—I'd never heard him use a coarse word before. We didn't tell them about the sex, only that she had drunk too much and got sick. Mr Cline called the police. He said he would see all of those kids in jail for getting Sally drunk.'

'Steve's cousin, did you get his name?'

'He had a nickname, like a cold cereal or something, but I believe his real name was Tom.'

'What about Warren?' Kari asked. 'When he returned, did Sally tell him about the sex?'

'Sally made me promise to never talk about that night, but Warren might have found out from one of the guys. He and John were in several classes together. They had known each other since junior high. I don't know if John said something, or if Warren wormed it out of Sally, but their relationship suffered.' She made a face. 'Of course, it didn't suffer very long, because Warren was killed in a car accident a few weeks after the party.'

'Thanks, Amy,' Kari said earnestly, 'you've been a big help.'

Amy lowered her head. 'Maybe if I'd have been a better friend, she wouldn't have ended up in that bedroom.'

'It doesn't sound like you could have stopped her.'

Amy scowled. 'Maybe not from making a fool of herself, but I wouldn't have stood by and let five guys gangrape her!'

Kari placed a consoling hand on her shoulder. 'It wasn't your fault.'

'I know,' Amy murmured, 'but it doesn't help ease the guilt. I should have been stronger, even if it meant calling Sally's father.'

Kari said good-bye and left. She had additional information…a possible story to write. She should have been eager, but she was hesitant as well. What if the killer was caught and the sexual assault had nothing to do with the murders? It was her duty to report her findings, but she hated the idea of hurting the Cline family.

HAMPTON AND GRADY spent thirty minutes with Reggie Cline in an interrogation room. They questioned him about his whereabouts on the dates of the murders and got a DNA sample from him. When finished, they thanked him and watched him leave the room.

'He admits to having a gun.' Hampton was first to speak up.

'Yeah,' Grady said, 'but most truckers carry protection. Same thing about the electrical wire and duct tape…standard equipment for anyone hauling freight.'

'He seemed pretty straightforward,' Hampton concluded. 'I don't like him for being our killer.'

'I guess our next move will depend on what the lab give us about the DNA sample. It's the first drop of evidence we've had since Pacheco's death—pardon the pun.'

'If it doesn't match Reggie's DNA, that would eliminate both Cline boys,' Hampton said. 'Brothers carry enough of the same DNA to rule them both out.'

'Roger Cline was in New York when Wilkins died, and in Portland when Clark was killed, so he's pretty much in the clear anyway.'

Ham said, 'Let's go talk to Beckston again. With him being the last of the five names on the list, and us knowing about what went on at the party, maybe he'll open up.'

'Good idea,' Grady agreed. 'We'll hit him with the news about Wilkins and see if it doesn't shake loose whatever he's been holding back.'

SIXTEEN

Kari was sprawled on the loveseat, lounging about in a pair of sweats and bare feet, when the doorbell rang. She sprang up from the chair and padded quickly over to peek out through the peep hole.

When she saw that Jason was the visitor, her heart took flight, until she did a quick self-inspection. Ratty hair, no make-up, slovenly clothes—a great way to make a good impression!

She opened the door and summoned forth a bright smile. 'Jason!' She allowed some of her delight to enter her voice. 'I was hoping you'd call. This is a nice surprise!'

'I don't mean to intrude, but—'

'Come in!' She stepped back and waited for him to enter. Once he was inside the room she closed the door. 'Can I get you something? Are you hungry?'

'No, I've already eaten.'

'How about something to drink? I've got Pepsi or Sprite?'

'I don't want to keep you up. I know it's getting late.'

'Sit down on the couch,' she invited him, 'while I get you a glass of Pepsi and some ice. I'm waiting for a call back from Detective Grady.' Flashing another smile his way, 'I located and visited Amy. She gave me some more information about the party.'

'Good for you.'

'I've got the story ready, but I want to stay on good terms with the detectives. I hope he gets back to me pretty soon, because the editor is holding a spot for my report. There is a deadline. Don't know what they'll do if I can't finish the story.'

Jason didn't seem to notice how she rambled on. He moved over to sit down, while she went to the kitchen. She sensed he was following her movements with his eyes.

'It's too bad they didn't find Wilkins in time,' she said over one shoulder, as she opened the refrigerator and took out a two-litre bottle of Pepsi. She put ice in two glasses and continued. 'The news briefing today didn't shed much light on the killer, I'm afraid. But this new information could at least give us a stronger motive.'

'They called in Reggie for a sit-down today,' Jason replied. 'I met him for dinner and told him it was standard procedure. With Roger being two thousand miles away he has a pretty good alibi for last night.'

Kari filled both glasses with soda and returned the Pepsi bottle to the fridge. She carried the drinks over to Jason. She handed him one and placed the second on the coffee table, next to the couch.

'Would you excuse me for a minute?' she asked. 'I'll be right back.'

'Sure,' he said. 'I should have phoned first, but—'

'No.' She forestalled his apology, 'I'm glad you stopped by. I wanted to see you again.' She tipped him the wink and pointed to the phone. 'If it rings, be a dear and answer it before Detective Grady hangs up.'

Her playfulness had a positive effect. A softness entered Jason's features and a half-smile tugged at the corners of his mouth. Rather than gawk inanely, she spun about and hurried off to the bedroom.

Kari was like a quick-change artist. She ran a brush through her hair, applied a touch of make-up and peeled off her sweats. Then she grabbed a peach-colored, chiffon

blouse and a black, snug-fitting, knit skirt from her closet
and dressed again, all in about two minutes flat.

Taking a deep breath to steady her nerves, she re-en-
tered the living room area. Before she could reach the
couch, Jason looked at her—and stood up!

'What?' she asked, puzzled by his odd reaction. 'You're
not leaving?'

'No,' he answered, displaying an awed expression. 'I
was...uh, it was an automatic response,' he explained
sheepishly. 'You surprised me. You look positively stunning.'

She laughed at his explanation. 'I've never had that effect on a man before.'

'Well, it's been some time since I was around a woman
as special as you.'

Oddly, it was the most satisfying approval she had ever
been given. Roger had been smooth, debonair and flatter-
ing, but the polish had seemed professional, as if he had
given the same praise or compliments a number of times
before. To hide her pleasure over the singular action and
remark, she commented: 'I assumed you were a debonair
lady's man. Is that the norm for all British men?'

Jason chuckled. 'We have our share of buffoons and
unsavory sorts. A man is either a gentleman or not. His
nationality has nothing to do with it.'

Kari displayed a modest smile. 'The same holds true
about being a lady.'

They moved round to the sofa and sat down together.
She took one quick sip of her drink and placed the glass
back on the coffee table. Then, making eye contact with
Jason, she took a deep breath. 'I'm not sure you're going
to like what I have to say. It's...' she lowered her lashes to
hide from his peruse. How could she tell him something
so appalling? Was it even necessary?

'It's about my Aunt Sally, isn't it?'

She wasn't surprised he had guessed. 'Jason, what I learned from Amy might not even be a factor in this case. The killer might be doing this for reasons of his own. I don't feel right about…'

'Sally did more than drink too much at the party didn't she?' He asked the question, but his cool tone of voice belied his suspicions. 'I spent some time looking over her high school yearbook again. There must have been a hundred kids who had signed messages and wished Sally well. The one thing missing was a note from any of those five boys. Not one of them had signed her yearbook. Very odd when you consider Paul had drawn her picture and Kenny and Clark were her football chums.'

Kari blurted out the details of her conversation with Amy. There was no way to lessen the impact of what she knew. She talked for a full two minutes, recalling every detail of their conversation. She finished with, 'I'm sorry it turned out this way.'

But Jason accepted the news without flinching. 'It makes sense,' was his grave response. 'Reggie said the police came at him like a suspect. They took a DNA sample and wanted to know if he had an alibi for any of the murders. They either know or suspect those five names were specifically singled out because they were the guys who had sex with Sally and may have been involved in Warren Lloyd's death.'

'Except for Beckston,' Kari pointed out. 'He claims he didn't take advantage of Sally.'

'The police have to look at Reggie. He uses electrical wire and duct tape on his job.'

'Yes, and I know the killer binds the victims with duct tape and uses electrical wire to strangle them,' Kari acknowledged. 'It was in one of the follow-up news conferences last week. They wanted to put it out in the open, in case there were other victims in nearby states. I guess they are having a hard time keeping the Feds out of the investigation.'

'The Feds?'

'Jamison Clark was killed in Nevada. If a serial killer murders in two different states—that makes for a possible FBI case.'

'I understand. We sometimes encounter the same quandary with the Met. It often concerns jurisdiction or secondary investigations, that sort of bother. Anyway,' Jason continued, 'Reggie allowed the police to search his vehicles or apartment if they were so inclined, but they weren't ready to do it just yet.'

'There!' Kari said with a degree of confidence, 'the fact they didn't go forward with a search proves they don't truly suspect Reggie!'

'I doubt he is very high on their suspect list.'

'The car accident has to be the motive,' Kari said. 'It's the only possibility that makes sense.'

'It seems likely the sexual attack is what set the car accident into motion.'

'Tom Kenny, Steve's cousin, has to be the killer,' Kari said. 'He provided the alcohol for the party, and he also had sex with Sally.'

'The detectives are looking for him.'

Kari said, 'Still, it's hard to believe he would kill his own cousin.'

'Detective Grady mentioned he had mental problems and has been in and out of prison for most of his adult life.'

Kari arched her brows. 'You seem to have gotten very cozy with the two detectives.'

'Yes. I told you, they allowed me to look around at the crime scene as a professional courtesy.'

'I checked the employment record of Tom Kenny. He was an electrician's apprentice for a time—might explain the use of duct tape and electrical wire. With his mental condition, he's the…'

The phone rang. It was Detective Grady, so Kari and he spoke back and forth for a time, comparing notes and information. She wanted to clarify exactly how much she could say in her news-breaking story. When she hung up the phone she regarded Jason with a curious frown.

'How strange is that?' she said. 'The autopsy showed Wilkins had been drinking a mixture of aftershave and good whiskey. But they found no liquor bottle in his apartment, only numerous empty bottles of aftershave.'

Jason said, 'I suggested the killer might have plied him with whiskey. Perhaps he wanted to talk to him.'

'What about?' Kari wondered. 'He was the fourth of the five men on the report. I can't imagine what he could learn from him.'

'It may be he used a bottle simply to gain access to Wilkins within the privacy of his room, but a swallow or two would have been sufficient inducement.'

Kari searched through the known facts in her head and said, 'So our killer must be trying to prevent the victims from telling the truth about the death of Warren Lloyd. The testimony from any one of them could put him in jail.'

'Tom Kenny owned the truck, so he was probably driving. Steve is his cousin and Jamison Clark was his best friend. That means at least two boys, Wilkins and Beckston, would have only been hearsay witnesses.'

'So?' Kari wondered.

'Yet the killer still murdered Wilkins,' Jason concluded. 'Perhaps it was to keep his identity hidden. He couldn't trust Wilkins not to talk. And if that's the case,

John Beckston is still on his list. And it sounds as if Tom Kenny is psychotic and delusional.'

'Yes, Detective Grady confirmed that he was being treated for a mental illness and went into hiding after being released from jail. It all fits. Tom hasn't checked in with his parole officer and the police can't find him. Being paranoid, he could be killing these men out of fear they would tell the police about Lloyd's death.'

'A sick mind might indeed think that way. Did the detective say anything else?'

'They might have a DNA sample of our killer, but I'm only to mention they have collected some new evidence.'

'It isn't going to look good, the police having a list of names and not protecting Wilkins.'

'I stated in the article how Wilkins had left his wife and was practically living on the streets.'

'So what are you going to say about the party?' Jason appeared wary. 'If you're going to mention Aunt Sally, I...'

'It isn't part of the story,' she said quickly. 'If our man is Tom Kenny, the sexual misconduct is past history. Yes, it might have been a motive for killing Warren Lloyd, but it isn't necessary to provide any personal information. It adds nothing to the current situation.' At his raised eyebrows, she continued. 'Don't you see? The real motive is to hide the fact Tom Kenny went looking to find Warren Lloyd. Whether Warren was chasing him or vice versa, it makes no difference. Warren died that night and Tom was responsible. That's the single motive we've discovered for these murders, the only motive we have to exploit.'

'OK, so how much *are* you going to put in your article?'

'I have to keep the details vague. They want to find Special K and don't want him to go deeper underground. As for Beckston, they are watching his house and he is co-operating.'

'So you won't mention the killer has one more victim to go?'

'I'll say the police have discovered a feasible motive—a twenty-seven-year-old homicide. Also, they are looking for a person of interest, but do not yet have him in custody. Other than that, the story will be about Wilkins being victim number four.'

The next half-hour was hectic for Kari. She edited her article with Jason watching over her shoulder. When finished, she made a call to her office and emailed the story to the editor's desk. She felt a rush of excitement when told the story would be on the front page.

'You are my savior, Jason!' she told him jubilantly. 'Until we started working together I was about one day away from landing back in the obits…probably to languish there for ever.'

He smiled at her enthusiasm.

'I'm sorry.' Kari instilled a compassionate tone to her voice. 'I had no idea when we wrote our first story that your aunt would be involved. Worse, that Warren's death might be the motive for this killing spree.'

Jason displayed a sadness. 'Is it any wonder Aunt Sally never gave another man a chance? Pregnant by her first love and he ends up dead before she had even told him. Next she goes to a party, has too much drink, and is taken advantage of by several boys. I can't imagine handing two complex wedding presents like that to your future husband.'

'I know something about how it feels to be used by a man,' Kari said quietly. 'I can understand a little about how she must have felt.'

Jason squirmed uneasily and placed his glass on the coffee table. 'This isn't going to work,' he said tightly. 'It's like trying to bridge the ocean.'

'What do you mean?'

'You know what I mean,' he said. 'I like you...more than anyone I've met since my wife died, but...' He started to get to his feet, but Kari grabbed hold of his arm and pulled him back down.

'What's the matter with you liking me?' she asked.

'This whole relationship is irrational—you and my cousin, Roger, the murders, my aunt, everything! Besides that, our residences are an ocean apart.'

'Jason Keane!' Kari snapped, immediately piqued. 'How dare you say something so negative! If we like each other, that ought to be enough!'

He smiled at her outburst. 'It doesn't strike you that there might be a spot of bother in attempting a relationship when the time difference is several hours? Besides which, you will surely have a number of options. You're beautiful, charming and clever—everything a man could ever want in a woman.'

'And you're handsome, intelligent, compassionate, a gentleman in every sense of the word! What woman wouldn't want to be with you?'

'I chase criminals for a living.'

'And I'm an underhanded, sneaky, do-anything-for-a-story reporter. Who is going to cast the first stone?'

'Perhaps you're reacting to the situation we're in. It's not every day you end up on the rebound from a brutal split with someone like my cousin, then become embroiled in a bizarre string of killings. We should probably go our separate ways and not see each other again. That would be the rational thing to do.'

Kari slid closer to Jason. 'I don't want to be rational,' she murmured, gazing directly into his eyes.

'What do you want?' he asked softly. 'Do you even know?'

'I—I...' she had to swallow her uncertainty, 'I want you

to stay here a little while longer. I want to get to know you better. I want us to be…to be…'

Jason didn't force her to finish the last sentence. His arms went around Kari and he pulled her to him. When their lips touched she responded eagerly. She blotted out everything else—the awkwardness of being a world apart, any concerns about Roger, her newspaper story—everything ceased to exist except the sweet sensation of Jason's kiss.

After enjoying several delightful moments, Jason pulled back and Kari relaxed, snuggled securely within his embrace.

'I must be bonkers,' Jason lamented.

'What's so bonkers about a young couple making out on the couch?'

'You know what I mean.'

Kari rotated around enough so that she could peer up at Jason. She fabricated a pout. 'Are you going to hurt my feelings and tell me you didn't enjoy kissing me?'

Jason lowered his head and placed his mouth on her own. After a delicious few seconds, he raised back up. 'No,' he whispered, 'I would never say that.'

'So what's the problem?' she asked. 'You wanted to kiss me and I wanted you to kiss me. That should be all that counts.'

'When did you decide you liked me?' Jason asked.

'Actually, I liked you from the very first, when I was at Sally's house. I thought you were very sweet, especially the way you were willing to help with the dishes, so I would be free from the chore.'

'Yes, I recall the saying: *every woman loves a man with dishpan hands!*'

She giggled. 'What about you, Jason?' she wanted to know. 'Did you take special notice of me when I arrived?'

'From the moment you got out of Roger's car.' The confession instilled ardor in his voice. 'You stepped out in that stunning black dress and the sun was like your own private spotlight.'

'You didn't know me.'

'I saw you smile. It was honest and natural. Your whole face lights up when you smile. There's nothing fake or forced about it. That's when I—'

The musical sound of his cell phone interrupted them. Kari uttered a pronounced sigh, but Jason was already shifting his body so he could pull it from his belt.

'I hate those miserable things,' Kari told him. 'They are about as irritating to have around as a spoiled child throwing a tantrum!'

'There aren't many people with this number,' Jason explained, before he flipped the cover open and lifted the cell to his ear. 'This is Jason,' he said. After a second, he said: 'Oh, yes, how are things in the...what do they call New York, the Big Apple?'

Kari cursed Roger under her breath and decided it was a good time to visit the bathroom again. Even having the man's voice in the room was more than she could stand.

'No, the only thing new is that another man is dead... Wilkins,' Jason replied to a question, as she left the room.

Kari checked her make-up in the mirror. Her hair had become a little mussed from laying her head on Jason's chest. It didn't need brushing out, but she used her fingers to fluff the sides back into place. She returned to the main room to hear the end of his conversation.

'I...yes, tomorrow night?' Another pause. 'Yes, I'll talk to you then.'

Kari waited until he said his goodbye and put away the cell before she returned to the couch and sat down.

'Roger again.' She made the statement. 'How does that swine know to call you every time we're together?'

'He thinks I'm pining for my homeland, sitting all alone at some dimly lit restaurant,' Jason replied.

'I was afraid he was calling because you had started seeing me.'

'How would he know that?'

'He knows,' she told him. 'He called me at the office, concerned about the story in the paper. I didn't tell him anything, but he guessed you and I had gotten together and he was not happy about it.'

'I imagine I'll hear about it tomorrow, after he gets back from New York.'

'Another of his insurance business trips?'

'Yes, a fire destroyed one of the buildings his company insures. He has been over there trying to work out a settlement. I'm sure it takes a lot of calculating when computers, software, office furniture and the like go up in flames.'

'I remember him saying he handled a lot of major insurance policies, some for high-end CEOs who treated him like royalty.'

'He's flying back tomorrow afternoon.'

'What are you going to tell him about us, Jason?'

'There's nothing to tell.'

Kari raised her eyebrows. 'Nothing?'

Jason gave her an off-hand shrug. 'It's none of his business.'

'But he knows and…' She groped for the right words. 'Don't you feel…uncomfortable about seeing me? I mean, it's like you are following behind him and picking up his discards.'

Jason reached out and placed his hands on her shoulders. His eyes bore into her own, his face drawn into a tight frown. 'Don't ever say that, Kari. You're not damaged goods, something no one else would want!'

She sighed. 'I didn't mean to sound so negative, but I'm concerned about you. How do I know you aren't just feeling sorry for me?'

'And how do I know you're not using me to get back at Roger?'

'I wouldn't!' Kari replied heatedly. 'Don't you dare suggest such a thing!'

'Well, I wouldn't either!' Jason retorted firmly. 'I know why I'm infatuated with you. You're everything a man could ever want in a woman. But it's hard for me to believe a girl like you would settle for someone like me.'

'Settle!' Kari exclaimed. 'I let you kiss me and I kissed you back, didn't I?'

'Yes,' he admitted.

'Do you think I kiss every guy I meet?'

'I would hope not.'

'Well, I don't!' She was adamant. 'I've told you the truth about Roger and me, every sordid detail. He coaxed me along like a starry-eyed, love-sick teenager. I thought he was sincere and fell for every one of his lines. Then he did me dirt; he used me and discarded me like a pair of disposable gloves! I hate him for the contemptible cad he is, but it has nothing to do with how I feel about you.'

'How can it not?' Jason fired back. 'I'm his cousin. We met at his mother's house!'

'You aren't like him, not in any way, shape or form!' Kari contended. 'I saw that from the very first time I met you. I know you're a decent, caring person.'

She didn't allow Jason to debate the issue further. She slipped her arms around his neck and cajoled him down to her. Then she sealed her lips over his in a hot, searing kiss, and clung tightly to him. When she finally pulled back, she gasped for air.

'There!' she said, in a tone that brooked no denial. 'Doesn't that prove anything?'

Jason was breathing hard too, and his complexion was darkened by the flush of arousal. 'Whoa!' was his single declaration.

'Whoa? What's that mean?' she asked.

He carefully removed himself from the passionate embrace. 'It means I should be going.' She frowned, as he stood up, but he was quick to smile. 'Unless you're prepared for our relationship to go to the next level.'

Kari felt a warmth of anticipation. The idea was wildly tempting, but she battled to maintain her prudence. 'No,' she murmured, also coming to her feet, 'I don't think we're ready for that just yet.'

They stood together for a few awkward moments, neither of them daring to speak. Eventually Jason leaned forward and placed a tender kiss on her lips. It was a simple show of affection, not a prelude to a sexual union. Yet, the contact stirred as yet unbidden feelings deep within Kari. The yearning to make love was compelling.

'I'll say goodnight,' Jason said, moving a step away from her. 'If I don't see you before, would you care to dine with me tomorrow night?'

Kari cooed the reply sweetly: 'I'd like that.'

For a moment, Jason simply stared at her. 'I'd better go,' he said quickly, 'before I do something we'll both regret.'

Kari did not attempt to talk him out of leaving. She knew it was a good idea to end the visit. They were still at an early stage in their courtship. There were contributing factors for each of them to consider concerning their relationship. For the time being, it was appropriate and wise for their romance to be limited to a kiss or two. They still had a lot to learn about one another.

She followed Jason to the door. He opened it and then pivoted around to face her. Another warm sensation surged through her veins as she met his gaze. There was something very special within the depths of his eyes, a sensitive longing which had been missing when Roger looked at her. Roger had been about lust, Jason was about desire.

'I'll see you tomorrow,' was all he said.

'Yes,' she replied, 'tomorrow.' She rose up on to her toes and touched her lips to his. The simple action felt like the most natural thing she had ever done in her life.

He left her with an unassuming 'Goodnight' and disappeared down the hall.

Kari waited until he was out of sight before she closed the door. As she pushed the lock into place, she felt both wonderful and anxious. Jason was so much more than she had first imagined. He was kind, considerate, masculine, everything a man should be. He had lost a woman he loved, but he was still young. He had a lot more life to live.

Even with such positive thoughts, she still suffered some very real concerns about Roger. Nothing could change their history together. Roger might try and persuade Jason not to date her; they might argue or fight about her. She prayed it wouldn't happen, but it was a definite possibility, something she had to consider.

'God,' she murmured softly, 'why couldn't I have met Jason first?'

SEVENTEEN

THE CAPTAIN STOPPED at Grady's desk, obviously unhappy. 'I just came back from meeting with the news media. When the chief explained about how the killer managed to find the latest victim, while his own inept department could not…those reporters were practically screaming for our blood!'

'It's not our fault, Capt'n. We've been doing everything we can.'

'How can that be?' he demanded. 'We had this man's name on our list of potential victims! It was our job to protect him! The chief wants to know why someone wasn't watching him.'

'We couldn't find him,' Grady replied. 'We staked out his house, but the wife lied about his whereabouts. Even when Ham and I confronted her, she didn't want to tell us where he was staying. By the time we tracked him down…'

'Dead in some god-awful wino apartment.' The captain finished the tale.

'Same MO as the other two—three if you count the one in Vegas,' Hampton put in, sitting at his own desk. 'There was another coin…showing tails.'

'What about the fifth man?' the captain wanted to know. 'We've got a patrol car at his house and he has been warned not to move about without telling us. He works at the Point of the Mountain. Being a guard at the state prison there, he knows how to handle himself.'

'Did we get anything more from the murder scene?

What about the drop of blood found on the inside of the victim's shirt collar?'

'We owe the Brit for that catch,' Hampton allowed. 'He noticed a bump on the back of Wilkins's head.' With a grunt to cover for a full explanation, 'We'd have found it during the check of the body, but it did help save some time.'

'I don't know about allowing an inspector from a law enforcement branch in England to visit our crime scene.'

'It was just a courtesy,' Hampton said. 'The guy's family is mixed up in this because of an old complaint. He isn't pushy or looking for personal credit, and he is observant.'

Grady changed the subject. 'The blood doesn't belong to the vic, so we're thinking he managed to put up a bit of a struggle. We should have an initial finding back pretty soon.'

'Our killer probably didn't expect a drunk to give him any trouble,' Hampton added. 'Having him bound in the chair, we're guessing he might have tossed his head back and maybe caught the perp in the mouth or nose.'

'Do we have any suspects with whom to try and match DNA?'

'We got a DNA from Reggie Cline,' Grady told him. 'If need be, we can also run up and get a sample from Tynan Cline. He's the grandfather, but not a blood relation.'

'You said Reggie, the truck driver, doesn't have an alibi?'

'No, but he doesn't seem right for any murders. Even so, we can compare his DNA. We've only spoken to his brother, Roger, on the telephone, but we don't need him for testing. Being brothers, one of them is all we need.'

'Are we still convinced the party is the answer as to the motive?'

Hampton answered, 'We think so. The party looks to

be the reason for the car chase that left a boy dead. It's the only circumstance we've found that places our four victims together. Pacheco didn't usually hang with the jocks.'

'How about the man who provided the booze?'

'Special K—aka Tom Kenny,' Grady replied. 'Haven't been able to locate him yet, but we have to like him for the murders.'

'What about this fifth man, the one we're protecting? Might he be involved in the murders?'

'Beckston was on graveyard shifts for two of the three murders here, and he hasn't been to Vegas in a few years. We're pretty certain he's clean.'

The captain pointed out, 'With his life on the line, he ought to be telling everything he knows about the party and the car accident.'

'He offered up the name of Special K, but he claims to not know of any reason for these murders.' Grady gave him an uncertain look. 'And he admitted the other boys pulled a train on Sally Cline, but swears he didn't take a turn. As for the night Warren Lloyd died in the auto crash, he was on a date—with the girl he's now married to.'

'He's the last man standing who was listed on the police report! You'd think he could give us something more.'

'He's scared, Capt'n,' Hampton jumped in. 'He was evasive about the party, until we pinned him down with what we knew. Then he told us it was the two Kenny boys and Jamison Clark who went out to find Warren Lloyd. They were supposed to talk to him and try and smooth things over.'

'And Lloyd ends up dead.'

'He swears it was an accident. The boys said they were shouting out the window, trying to get Warren to stop when the truck and car bumped. Warren lost control and went off the road. Don't know if Beckston actually believed it happened like that, but we think he was being truthful about what he was told concerning the wreck.'

The captain said, 'So it's either the truck driver or Tom Kenny?'

'That's our entire list at the moment. The DNA ought to confirm one or the other.'

'What about the reporter? Did she have anything more to offer?'

'She managed to track down Sally's old girlfriend and confirmed the same information we got from Maria. I told her what she could print.' Grady winced. 'She's the only one who didn't crucify the department for Wilkins getting killed.'

'We really need a tip or break on this one,' Hampton commented. 'We've got to locate Tom Kenny.'

The captain didn't look pleased. 'You told me the guy was on meds and has been getting treatment for manic depression.' His jaw worked, the muscles twitching from grinding his teeth. 'That hardly sounds like a cunning killer who didn't leave a shred of evidence at the first three crime scenes. And why stick a quarter in the victims' mouths? What's that prove?'

'There was something else queer about Wilkins's death,' Grady said, retrieving a form from his desk. 'We had them do a rush on the autopsy and Wilkins had quite a mixture in his water basket.'

'What kind of mixture?'

'About half was a good-label whiskey—possibly Jim Beam—and the other half was cheap aftershave...a poor man's booze. We found some empty aftershave bottles in his room, but there wasn't any sign of a whiskey bottle.'

'The Brit thinks our killer may have plied him with liquor to get information or something.'

'You told him the findings of the autopsy?'

'Uh, no,' Grady replied. 'He detected the whiskey from smelling the mouth of the corpse.'

'Got a good nose on him,' Hampton admitted. 'All I could smell was vomit and the old sot's body odor.'

'The killer might have only used the whiskey to get an invite into Wilkins's room,' the captain suggested.

'Why give him so much?' Hampton asked. 'He managed to bind and strangle the other vics without any trouble. We're thinking he used a gun or knife to threaten the three before Wilkins.'

'Plus, if our killer is Tom Kenny, Wilkins probably would have recognized him. He must not have been afraid of him, or he wouldn't have let him up to his room. It's still quite a puzzle.'

The captain scowled at them both. 'You men are in the profession of solving puzzles. I want you to go over every piece of information again until you find something. And I want Kenny in custody by the end of the week!'

'Right, Capt'n,' Hampton replied.

'Yeah, we hear you loud and clear,' Grady also responded.

As soon as the captain continued to his office, Hampton leaned over to Grady. 'Got any bright ideas about how we can find Kenny?'

'I'm ready to consult a psychic or palm reader…anything! This case is kicking our butts!'

DEE SAT ACROSS FROM Kari. The two of them were alone in the break room, so Dee was her usual candid self.

'You look quite rosy today, kiddo,' she said. 'Did you do something naughty between the sheets to lift your spirits last night?'

'Dee, you've got the dirtiest mind of any woman I know.'

'Sure, blame me for the way you've been acting all morning.'

'Me?' Kari was incredulous. 'What are you talking about?'

'Humming a tune, cheerful, smiling...you are the girl-friend I love again.'

'In case you hadn't noticed, my article on the serial kill-ings was on the front page.'

'Nope,' Dee was not buying it, 'seeing your byline isn't the same as having your battery charged.'

'Did I mention you have a dirty mind?'

'I'm saying it isn't the way a girl acts after she breaks up with a man she adores, regardless of what she has written.'

'I thought we weren't going to bring up that slimy snake!'

'I'm just saying, for a guy you cared so much about, you sure got over Rat-maggot in a hurry.'

'I had help.'

Dee giggled. 'OK, now you're talking. Tell me.'

'Tell you what?'

'Everything!' she replied eagerly. 'The who, the when, the where, the how good it was, everything!'

'Slow down, Dee. It wasn't even a date.'

'OK, then it was either his place or your own. I'm bet-ting his!'

'You'd be wrong.'

Dee giggled again. 'Then it was your place! I knew it! I knew it!'

'I thought you said I was the one acting like someone on happy pills.'

'Is it someone I know? Have we talked about him before?'

Kari knew there would be no putting Dee off. She would hound Kari until she 'fessed up the truth.

'Jason came over for a short visit last night. That's all.'

The news caused Dee to pause. 'Kari, Kari, Kari,' she lamented woefully. 'Hello! His cousin is the slime-sucking pig who dumped you like last week's garbage. There is nothing for you but misery with that family.'

'Jason is not anything like his cousin.'

'I know he's a nice guy and he is nothing like Rat-maggot,' Dee volunteered. 'But it doesn't matter. This guy doesn't even live on our continent! Do you know how much a plane ticket costs to London?'

'All right,' Kari said, 'I'll admit there's a problem with our potential dating in the future.'

Dee put a hand to either temple as if struck by a migraine. 'I try and I try, I talk and I plead, but you never listen.'

'I know you're trying to be a friend, Dee. And I realize falling for Jason is going to have some drawbacks.'

'I'm sorry, kid,' Dee said, 'but I've done a lot of thinking about this. While he sounds sincere, I can't see you and him having any kind of a happy ending together.'

'Then I'll take an unhappy one,' she replied. 'I've grown very fond of him and I know he cares for me. I'm not going to throw that away.'

'Kari, your dates will have to be over the Internet, via emails or a chat room. I can't imagine getting much of a thrill out of kissing a monitor goodnight.'

'I'm not giving up on Jason,' Kari said brusquely. 'He's the kind of man I've always wanted in my life. If I have to write letters and use phone calls in the place of actual dates, I'll take it!'

Dee arched her eyebrows at the force behind Kari's avowal. 'I begin to think you are serious about this guy.'

'Yes, I am.'

'Then I wish you the best of luck and every kind of

happiness known to mankind...or womankind...or any other kind!'

Kari laughed. 'I think that covers about everything!'

Dee was smiling again. 'You know me—I like to be thorough.'

'And we both need to get back to our desks. I've got some more research to do.'

'Ah, yes, and I have more ads to critique. What glorious lives some of us mortals lead.'

REGGIE HAD CALLED JASON. He wanted to spend the day together. Jason said that sounded good and drove over to Reggie's apartment. Reggie had just finished his shower and shave. He was shirtless when he answered the door.

'Cousin!' he greeted Jason. 'I'm glad you were free today. I don't know how much longer you'll be around, and I've got a long haul scheduled for tomorrow or the day after. Dispatch is going to let me know sometime today.'

'Is your mother meeting us for lunch?'

'Yes, she took a vacation day from work.' He narrowed his gaze. 'I thought we could do a little something with her so she doesn't sit at home and drink. This business about boys dying from her high school class must be driving her crazy.'

'I understand.'

Reggie walked to the closet and began to push the hangers to one side. After a short inspection he growled an oath. The phone rang, preventing him from telling Jason what he was upset about. Rather than picking up the phone, Reggie looked at the name on the caller ID and hit the speaker button.

'Roger, did you take my gray-and-silver dress shirt?'

'Geez, little brother, some people take time to say *hello* before they accuse a guy of something.'

'That would be for people who don't have a brother who steals shirts out of his closet!'

Laughter from the other end. 'I didn't think you'd miss it!' he said. 'You never go anywhere or do anything. I met a girl and needed a quick change, and the poor orphan shirt seemed lonely and out of place in your closet.'

'When did you take it?'

'I don't know, a few days back. I've already sent it, along with two of your other shirts, to the laundry. I didn't want you calling me cheap or inconsiderate for bringing them back dirty.'

'I was going to wear that shirt today.'

'Sorry about that,' Roger replied, his voice lacking any real sympathy. 'I called to tell you, I don't think I'll be able to get together for a day or two. I'm going to be beat from the flight home and I've got a lot of work at the office to catch up on.'

'Well, it wasn't my intention to get dressed up for you, Roger. I'm going to lunch with Mom and Jason.'

'Tell Cuz I'll call him when I get home, would you?'

'Yeah, I'll tell him.'

'Maybe the three of us can get together, once I get caught up,' Roger said. 'And don't worry about your shirts. I'll pick them up at the laundry, first chance I get, and drop them off at your place.'

'You're all heart, Roger,' Reggie said drily. 'Talk to you later.'

Reggie reached over and shut off the phone, then grinned at Jason. 'Good thing Mom doesn't like to eat out at anyplace too fancy. The only thing left in my closet is a green polo shirt Roger doesn't like.'

'Casual dining suits me.' Jason was agreeable.

'You know, Jason, I've been thinking. Why don't you check out of the motel and stay here with me? I've got a second bedroom that I never use and I'd get to see a little more of you before you have to head back to England.'

'I wouldn't want to impose on you.'

'Are you kidding? When I'm on the road, this place sits empty for days on end. You could save what—a hundred bucks a night? Plus, I keep quite a few groceries on hand. You can fix your meals here, and I'd be happy to have you around. No telling when, or if, I'll ever get over to London. I'm not much for flying.'

'If you think I won't get in your way?'

Reggie laughed. 'You're talking to a guy who has never brought a girl to this apartment. I haven't even been on a date for the past three months. No, it would be great for the remainder of the time you're here. I'd like the company, and if you've got things going, that's fine too. I'll give you a spare key so, if I'm on a trip when you leave, you can just drop it in the mail box.'

'That's an invitation I can hardly turn down. I have something planned for this evening, but I can check out of the motel and bring my things over, after we have lunch with your mum.'

Reggie said, 'That'll work, and you can do me a favor too. When you go to get your things, you can drop me off at the garage. My rig is being serviced and it will save me a bus ride.'

'Certainly. It's the least I can do, Reggie.'

LOUIS GRADY ENJOYED his three kids, but he was always glad when they were all in bed for the night. It was the only time he had a little peace and quiet with Leta. After his normal ritual of kissing each of the children and saying goodnight, he went into the living room and sat down on the couch.

Leta entered a few moments later and sat next to him. 'How goes the latest caper?' she asked, casting a sidelong glance at him. 'Anything new on your serial killer?'

Grady extended his arm across the back of the couch and encircled his wife's shoulders. She immediately slid in close. He loved that about her. She was like a wonderfully affectionate cat. It took only the slightest encouragement and she was ready to cuddle up to or kiss him.

Leta had been a foster child, in and out of homes from the time she was six years old. She'd finally been adopted at eleven; the couple had been in their early sixties. She liked to joke she had grown up with a two-generation gap, instead of the single one most teens had between them and their parents. He discovered early on in their relationship that she needed a great deal of affection, and she always returned it with interest.

'Every lead has been a dead end to this point, Kitten.' He used his pet name for her. 'Ham and I are trying to paint with clear water.'

'No evidence yet? I thought you found DNA?'

'The crime lab is getting the single drop of blood we found tested, but we won't know for a few more hours if it belongs to our killer.'

'Do you have someone to check it against?'

'We have narrowed down our list of suspects to two men,' he replied. 'We have the DNA of one of them and the other was related to one of the victims. We'll be able to tell if either of them is the guy we want.'

Leta turned her body enough to kiss Grady on the cheek. He decided that wasn't good enough and pulled her round until she was sitting on his lap. Being a diminutive five-foot and a hundred pounds, he often lifted Leta off of her feet and carried her about like a child.

'You're not feeling frisky?' she murmured softly. 'Not after a full day at work?'

'I'm no more tired than you,' he answered. 'You have the tough job, tending three kids for sixteen hours a day.'

'I do get to feeling very old sometimes. I wonder if you won't go looking for someone younger and prettier.'

Grady kissed her and gave her a warm smile. 'They don't make them prettier than you, Kitten. And I sure wouldn't have the energy to try and keep up with a younger girl.'

Leta uttered a girlish giggle. 'Answers like that will get you in trouble,' and she leaned around and nipped him on the ear. Her arms were around his neck, so he only had to slip a hand under Leta's legs to lift her up and carry her to the bedroom. He hadn't swept her away like that in a long time...too long.

Before he could stand up with her the phone rang!

'You're off duty,' Leta murmured breathlessly. 'Don't answer it!'

Grady hoped it was a telemarketer or some charity, but paused to listen for the speaker.

A second ring and the announcement to leave a message played. There was a momentary gap, then Hampton's voice barked loud and clear.

'We've got a possible on Kenny's location, Grady. The night shift is tied up with a job up east. Chief says for us to log some OT and check it out.' There was a short silence. 'If you're busy or something, I can go this alone. I've got plenty of back-up.'

Grady groaned his disappointment and gave Leta a quick peck on the lips. She hurried to remove herself from his lap so he could get up and answer the phone.

'I know your missis must hate me, but it ain't my fault,'

Hampton continued to talk. 'I had myself a nice frozen dinner in the oven and was looking forward to watching an episode of NCIS on my DVD player. I'm not happy about—'

Grady grabbed up the receiver. 'I'm here, Ham.' He cut him off. 'What've you got?'

'The lab boys called right after I got home. The drop of blood was a DNA match to Steve Kenny...you know, the Y chromosome or whatever a guy and his brothers pass to their sons. Anyway, it's proof our perp is related to Kenny. We've got our man. It has to be Special K—his cousin.'

'So what now? Did you say we've got a location on him?'

'The chief gave the go-ahead to stick his picture on the early edition of the news. Don't you watch television?'

'I sometimes catch the weather and sports,' Grady admitted. 'That's about it.'

'Well, we got a tip that Kenny is staying at a rundown, vacant house in Herriman. The place burned down while the owner was gone some time ago.'

'Let me guess—the same house where the Christmas party was at?'

'You got it.'

'Who called in the tip, Ham?'

'Some guy who said he often walked his dog back in the hills. He didn't want to give his name, but said he's seen our perp hanging around at the old house and at the local store too.'

'I'll pick you up on the way.'

'See you in about ten minutes,' Hampton replied as he hung up.

'Sonuva b,' Grady lamented, quelling his sexual desire. 'Gotta go, Kitten.'

'I won't wait up.' Showing a coy smile, 'And you owe me.'
Grady chuckled. 'That's one IOU I'm going to pay up on.'

EIGHTEEN

NEMESIS SAT IN the stolen pick-up and watched the cars surround the old Kenny house. Luckily, he had been able to get out before they had the place completely surrounded. His current location was a quarter-mile away, concealed by abandoned cars and several antiquated, rusted pieces of farm machinery. The one-time farm had sold off most of its acreage for another housing development, a common practice all over the Salt Lake Valley. The old farmhouse near by was decayed and had no doors or windows.

When he left the burned-out house he had driven to this remote secondary spot. It allowed escape via several different back roads and two highways.

However, there was little danger of being discovered. He watched the police as they flashed their lights back and forth; the headlights on their cars were all pointed at the house. He counted two suits and four uniformed cops, also a police dog. They were busy rummaging around inside the charred remains, doing a thorough search of the house and yard.

After a few minutes two of the policemen and the dog began to search the surrounding hills and brush, all of them unaware that the killer of four men was watching their every move.

With the house no longer being a safe place to hide, the places to move to or find shelter were limited. Also, photos having been shown on the four major news networks, it would make moving around or finding another place very difficult. Nemesis had little time to finish what he had started. He had managed the first three victims with ease and had outsmarted the police with Wilkins, the fourth man on his list. But Beckston was still out there, being watched around the clock. It would be suicide to try and get to him.

Nemesis smiled to himself. There was still a chance. If things worked out, if the police didn't find something in the rubble to put them on his scent...he might still succeed.

KARI COULD HARDLY contain herself until the first coffee break. Dee regarded her with a wary gaze, more suspicion than curiosity, about her date.

'So let's hear it,' she said wearily. 'I can see you're about to bust a button trying to keep it to yourself.'

'It was great!' she said, trying not to sound too much like a schoolgirl. 'We went to Red Lobster and then to a movie. Jason wouldn't hear of me paying for anything. He is a bit of a chauvinist, but also the most polite gentleman I ever met.'

'Most men who treat a woman like a lady are a little on the chauvinistic side,' Dee admitted. 'My Harry always pays when we go out for a meal or movie. Different story when we shop,' she added. 'That's my domain.'

'Anyway, we had a great time, but the movie got out pretty late. He knew I had to work, so he kissed me at the door and said goodnight.'

'What?' She arched her eyebrows. 'No dessert?'

'I keep telling you, Jason isn't looking for a one-night stand.'

'Not being anything like his cousin might have some drawbacks,' Dee said pointedly.

'Actually, Jason's concern is our living an ocean apart. I'm not sure how we can bridge that problem.'

Dee said emphatically, 'Well, it sounds as if you're only going to miss a goodnight kiss anyway.'

Taylor chose that moment to stick her head into the break room. She looked anxious. 'Telephone call for you, Underwood.' She was direct and to the point. 'The guy says he has some information on those murder victims.'

Kari said an 'OK, thanks!' and hurried over to the break room phone. The red light was blinking on line three, so she punched it and put the receiver to her ear.

'This is Kari Underwood,' she answered. 'How can I help you?'

'Miss Underwood.' A strange, masculine voice came back over the line, 'I need to speak to you.'

'Who is this?' she asked impatiently. 'If this is a crank call, I'll call the police and have them—'

'No, no, you'll want to hear me out!' came the immediate reply. 'You don't know me personally, but I'm sure you know my name. This is Tom Kenny.'

Kari gasped in surprise. 'Special K?'

The name caused him to hesitate. 'I haven't been called that name in years…from back when I used to run with my cousin and a younger crowd.'

'What do you want?' Kari grabbed a sheet of paper and scribbled his name for Dee. Her friend's eyes widened, she threw up her hands and mouthed 'What should I do?'

Kari shook her head, uncertain as to what she should do.

'I seen the paper today and my picture was on television.' His voice sounded nervous and uncertain. 'I-I've been hiding out, ever since you broke the story about three murders. One was my cousin.'

'The police are looking for you, Mr Kenny.'

'I know!' He sounded desperate. 'That's why I'm calling you.'

'Me?' she asked. 'Why me?'

'You're a reporter,' he replied. 'You've got connections. You can write my side of the story. I know they're after me. I've been hiding in an old burned-out house, but it ain't safe no more.'

'Why do you say *they* are after you? Who are *they*, Mr Kenny?'

'The cops! The killer! Everyone is after me! You're the only one I can trust.'

'The police think you killed those men, Mr. Kenny,' She was blunt. 'How do I know you didn't?'

'I swear! It wasn't me!' He practically sobbed into the phone. 'I got scared when I seen your story. I was afraid the killer would come after me next. I've been hiding and running...' It sounded as if he took a deep breath to regain his composure. 'I been in prison and I can't go back—I won't go back! I'll do one of them cop suicides first! I'll force the cops to kill me!'

'Do you have any proof of your innocence?' she asked. 'Do you know who the killer is?'

'No! I don't know nothing! But the killer is after me and so are the cops. I know someone's been watching me... following me. I know I'm gonna die. I know it!' His voice broke, but he sniffed to regain control. 'That's why I called you. You are the smart one, the one who figured out that someone was after us.'

'Us? Meaning you and your cousin?'

'And Jimmy and Larry. I never knew the other guy— Paul something. He only showed the night of the party. His being there had something to do with Jimmy wanting to make time with his sister.'

'Yes, I know who was at the party. I also know the police think you killed Warren Lloyd.'

'No!' he wailed. 'It was an accident! We only wanted to talk to him. I was going to offer him some money to keep quiet. But he spooked and tried to run. I only bumped his car to make him stop. That's all. We only wanted to talk!'

'I'm sure the police will take that into consideration.'

'You got to help me, Miss Underwood.'

'What can I do?' she wanted to know. 'The police are the people you need to talk to. They can protect you.'

'They think I'm the killer! I ain't got no alibi for any of them murders. I been on the run since I got out. Ain't no one going to stick up for me.'

'If you're innocent, the police aren't going to frame you.'

'I'm the only one left, ain't I?' he asked. 'I read where Johnny works as a guard at the state prison. He has protection at work, and I'll bet the cops are keeping him safe at home. Working graveyard shifts like he does, I know he's got an alibi for the murders; the cops know he ain't the killer. I'm not only the last suspect, Miss Underwood, I'm the last victim too!'

'The police have the killer's DNA,' she informed him. 'If you are not a match, you're off the hook for the murders.'

'Yeah?' He didn't sound as if he believed her. 'I never heard about them finding any DNA.'

'It was recovered at the last murder scene. It hasn't been released to the news media yet. I was going to call one of the detectives this afternoon to verify if they have a match.'

'I never gave no DNA,' Kenny said. 'How they gonna know it ain't me?'

'We need to get a sample. If you're innocent, they will protect you—the way they are doing for John Beckston. You'll be safe until they find the real killer.'

'You ain't lying to me?'

'I've no reason to lie to you, Mr Kenny. Why don't you contact the police and get this all taken care of?'

'It could be some rogue cop who's doing the killing.' He

didn't sound rational. 'If I give myself up, they can sure enough kill me too.'

Kari realized she was talking to a very frightened, mentally unstable man. Reason and logic was not going to convince him of anything.

'What do you want from me?'

He pleaded with her. 'I need to meet with you, to prove to you I ain't no killer.'

'How will you do that?'

'I'll give you a sample of my DNA. You can take it to the police and get it tested. Once it proves I'm not the killer, they'll have to leave me alone.'

'What about the real killer?' she asked.

'I ain't gonna stop hiding until he's caught. He ain't found me yet, and he ain't gonna find me after we meet.'

'You're asking me to trust you. Why should I do that?'

'How long have you been a reporter?'

Kari was caught off guard by the question. 'Uh, only a short while...since the murders of your friends began. It was my first story.'

'So this was your big break,' he said thickly. 'I'm glad running for my life is good for something. What were you before?'

'I began by writing obituaries.'

He uttered a sarcastic chortle. 'That's just fine. You can write my obituary when the cops or that serial murderer gets me!'

'Let's not let that happen,' Kari said quickly. 'Let me help you.'

'You can help, by writing my *story*.' He sneered the word. 'That's all you newspaper people care about, ain't it, the story?'

'I admit, interviewing you would be a big boost to my career.'

'Sure,' he was growing more confident, 'and you'd have the scoop all to yourself. It'd make you the number one reporter in the whole country.'

'Why don't you let me accompany you to the police station? I would be your insurance that no one railroaded you for these murders.'

'No dice, lady. I told you, I don't trust cops. It's you and me or nothing!'

It was obvious she was not going to alter his thinking with any rational argument. He was not going to give himself up. He was paranoid, believing that the police would try and pin the murders on him. He wanted to be cleared of the crimes, without offering up himself as proof.

'All right, Mr Kenny,' she agreed. 'Where can I meet you?'

'I rented a room at the Motel 6, downtown, number 211. Be there at 4.30 sharp.'

Kari glanced down at her watch. It was 10.20. 'OK, I'll be there.'

'If I see a cop or anything suspicious, I won't show. You understand me?'

'Yes, Mr Kenny, I understand.'

As the line went dead, Kari immediately dialed in the number for Jason. The cell went to voicemail without even ringing. She hurried to dial Reggie's apartment and was relieved when it was Jason who answered. She told him of the call and the meeting she had arranged.

'You've done your part, Kari,' Jason said with a calm that helped to slow Kari's heart rate. 'Let me take it from here.'

'But I could...'

'Please, trust me on this, Kari.' Jason's voice was soothing but firm, as if there was no room for argument. 'I'll make it clear to the police that you are responsible for this information, but you must let the professionals handle it.'

'All right, Jason,' Kari said. 'I do trust you and I'll wait to hear back.'

GRADY WAS BUSY typing a report when the phone rang at his desk. 'Get that, would you, Ham?' he asked. 'I'm about finished.'

'Slowest damn typist I ever seen in my life,' Hampton complained. 'Ought to have the department set you up with one of them computer programs that allow you to orally dictate your report.'

'Two minutes, Ham. I'll be done in two minutes.'

With a grunt, Hampton lifted up the receiver and put it to his ear. 'Yeah? Detective Hampton here.'

'This is Jason Keane, Detective. Do you remember me?'

'Let's see—smart-ass Brit, works for the CID, with a penchant for sticking his nose into our murder investigation. That the Jason Keane I'm talking to?'

Jason laughed. 'Yes, but you left out the smart-arse Brit you're going to owe a big favor to.'

'OK, so what's the big favor?'

'I've some information for you about Tom Kenny. I'll give it to you, but I'd like a bit of consideration down the road.'

'What kind of consideration?'

'Nothing illegal or unethical, just the first call to Kari Underwood if this works out. As she is the one responsible for this tip, I believe she deserves an edge on writing the story.'

'I'd have to clear something like that with the chief. I can't withhold information from the general press.'

'You and I know how this works, Detective. I'm only

asking for a little consideration on the first call,' he said. 'That isn't much for what I have to tell you.'

'If you've got something worthwhile, I'll talk to the chief and see what we can do for your reporter friend,' Hampton replied. 'That's as much as I can offer. Now, what do you have?'

'First of all, is there anything new you can tell me about Tom Kenny? I know he's the most likely suspect you have.'

'About as we had figured. The guy's a total nut job, skipped out on his parole officer and probably stopped taking his meds the day he was released from prison. He had pretty decent grades in school but totally flunked out of life. His shrink told us a man suffering from his kind of paranoia might become desperate enough to do anything to keep from being sent back to jail. We figure it's what triggered this string of murders.'

'Do you have any hard evidence?'

'We found his prints in a burned-out house last night, plus there was wire and duct tape that matched all of our victims. Also found a glass cutter kit. It's him all right.'

'The spot of blood, from the last crime scene, have you matched the DNA to Tom Kenny?'

'You know how this works, Inspector. That information hasn't been released to the public yet.'

'For what I'm offering, you will owe me more than one favor. Miss Underwood said that Grady told her you'd have a preliminary DNA result today.'

Hampton swore. 'Yeah, that's my partner, the one with the big mouth. He wasn't supposed to tell her anything that hasn't been cleared by the chief.'

'Miss Underwood promised not to print any details without his say-so.'

'She's getting kind of cozy with him, isn't she?' Hampton growled. 'Wonder if I ought to mention her to his wife!'

Jason took up her defence. 'She did tell you about a gang rape the night of the Christmas party.'

'We pretty much figured that out from talking to Maria Pacheco. It gives additional motive for those boys wanting to keep Warren Lloyd quiet.' Hampton again put an edge to his voice. 'So your news is something we already knew.'

'Yes, but what about the DNA?' he persisted.

'All right, it's Kenny,' Hampton told him gruffly, 'but it isn't official yet...you understand?'

'Yes. Did you find a sample of Tom Kenny's DNA to run it against?'

'Don't need it,' he replied. 'Father and son share the same Y chromosome, as do brothers, uncles and so on. The DNA matches Steve Kenny to our killer. It means they are definitely related.'

Jason thanked Kari's good sense in calling him. Tom claimed to be innocent, but he was delusional and paranoid. If he was off his medication he might not even be aware of having killed those four men.

'I'm waiting,' Hampton prompted. 'What do you have that is so newsworthy?'

'I know where Tom Kenny is going to be at 4.30 this afternoon!'

NINETEEN

THE POLICEWOMAN HAD volunteered. She was about Kari's age, attractive and arrived dressed in a business suit. Her protective vest was hidden under her suit jacket and she wore a wire, so the police could hear everything being said. Grady and Hampton were given rooms to either side of 211 and checked in like businessmen. For back-up, there were four men doing maintenance, wearing coveralls and carrying concealed weapons. SWAT was on alert, parked a block down the street, ready to move at a moment's notice.

At precisely 4.30, the policewoman climbed to the second floor of the motel, approached the door and knocked.

'You alone?' came a voice from inside.

'Yes, it's me, Kari Underwood.'

The curtain moved a few inches but Kenny stayed out of sight. 'You don't look like a reporter.'

'If you wanted a known television anchor, you should have called a TV station,' she responded with some calm. 'You called me...remember?'

'What did you say was your first job at the newspaper?'

The policewoman hesitated. 'I started as a proof reader.'

She stood and waited, but there was no response. 'Mr Kenny?' she asked. 'Are you still there?'

The door flew open. Kenny grabbed the woman, spun her about and put a gun to her head. His eyes swept the balcony walkways and he stared at the men in coveralls, all of whom were watching him anxiously.

'The lying slut!' Kenny wailed, forcing the hostage to start walking to the stairs. 'I trusted her!'

'Don't do anything foolish!' Grady warned, easing himself out through the door behind Kenny. He had his gun aimed at the man, ready to fire if necessary. 'We only want to talk to you.'

Hampton also had his door open, but was too late to box Kenny in. He had already passed that room and was moving toward the stairs. 'We know the killer is after you,' Hampton spoke in a soothing voice, while also pointing his gun at the suspect. 'We are here to help you. We can protect you.'

'You're a liar too!' Kenny snarled. 'You think I'm the killer. You raided my hiding-place and want to send me back to prison!'

'It's true, you violated your parole,' Grady tried to reason with him, 'but we can work that out. We know you've been running for you life. Let us help keep you safe until we catch the killer.'

'No!' Kenny shrieked, yanking the policewoman along until they reached the top of the stairway. 'You're going to put me behind bars. You want me stuck back in a stinkin' cell. I know you! You're all out to get me. You think I don't know how you've been watching me?'

'Take it easy, Kenny,' Grady tried again. 'Put the gun down and let's talk about this. We haven't been following you. We didn't know where you were.'

But Kenny's face was red. Blood rushed through his veins, a raging inferno of flames and heat. He could no longer think or reason. He cocked the pistol and held the muzzle against the policewoman's head.

'I'm taking her with me!' he cried. 'I'll never go back to prison! You'll never—'

The policewoman panicked. Ducking quickly, she batted the gun aside, then dove headlong down the stairs!

Kenny's expression of surprise changed to shock as bullets from two guns tore a path through his chest. Three… four bullets struck him. He had no chance to fire his weapon and it spilled from his fingers. He staggered backward against the railing and slumped to the floor, landing on his side. A groan escaped his lips, as he drew his knees up, curled into a fetal position.

The policewoman had slid down several steps. She wasn't injured, except for a couple scrapes on her forearms. By the time she had righted herself, Grady and Hampton were standing over Kenny. They both held their guns ready as Grady reached down and picked up the man's gun.

'You stupid damned idiot!' Hampton growled at Kenny. 'We didn't want to shoot you. We only wanted to talk.'

Kenny rolled his head enough to look up at him. His eyes were glassy, but a sneer came to his lips. 'I…always hated…cops!' he whispered harshly. Then he went limp.

Grady put away his gun, knelt down at the man's side and checked him for a pulse with his free hand.

'Looks like paperwork and office duty for us, Ham. I'm pretty sure it was me who killed him, what with me being the better shot.'

Hampton snorted. 'Lucky he was so close. The way you were shaking, another step away and you would have missed him altogether.'

'Hated to have it end this way,' Grady said seriously. 'Would have liked to have taken him alive.'

'Guy was crazy as a loon,' Hampton replied. 'He would have undoubtedly gotten counseling and prison for the rest of his life…at the taxpayer's expense.'

Grady glanced at the policewoman. 'You OK?' he asked. 'That was a dangerous stunt, diving down those stairs.'

She was on her feet, busy assessing her scrapes, but managed a weak smile. 'I'll have a couple of bruises, but I thought he was going to pull the trigger.'

'You did good,' Grady told her. 'Come your next review, Ham and I will vouch for your actions here today.'

She smiled her appreciation and gingerly went down the steps.

'Case closed,' Hampton said, patting Grady on the shoulder. 'I'll make the call to the captain.'

JASON WAS ALONE AT Reggie's apartment when the phone rang. He didn't know if it was for him or his cousin, but he answered it anyway.

'Jason! It's Kari!'

'Good thing you keep calling me on Reggie's phone. My mobile has stopped working.'

'Yes, I've tried it twice and it goes directly to voicemail.'

'I think the battery has stopped holding a charge. I'm going to take a trip to the store to replace it.'

'Well, anyway, I wanted to let you know what happened. The police got Tom Kenny, but he forced them to kill him. Detective Grady just spoke to me. He wanted to thank you for not letting me try and handle the interview with Kenny on my own.'

'I'm glad it worked out.'

She laughed. 'Anyway, I'm still at work, busy finishing up the story.'

'Suppose I won't be seeing you this evening, then?'

'I'm sorry, but it looks like this may take some time. They want to include a chronological history of Tom Kenny and that is going to take some research. It will be a major front-page story, with no limit to the number of words. So I have to get it all down in print before the presses run. I might be here till midnight.'

'Do you need me to pick up some take-away and bring it over?'

She laughed. 'We call it take-out, and no, the editor has sent out for pizza.'

'Then I'll check with you tomorrow.' He looked absently at his watch, for it showed the calendar date. His vacation was passing very quickly. 'Goodnight.'

THE CAPTAIN STOPPED AT Grady's desk. He had a rare smile on his face.

'The review board convened for less than an hour and ruled the death of Tom Kenny to be a good shoot. You two can consider yourselves ready for another case.'

'Something still don't feel right about this,' Grady said. 'What about the quarter? What did it mean? And why did Kenny ply Wilkins with whiskey?'

Hampton cleared his throat. 'Yeah, wish the guy had lived long enough to explain about that. Also, was he killing his old gang in a certain order, or did he kill them as he found them?'

'Good questions,' the captain said, 'but you found the evidence at the burned-out house. We verified his prints on some of the trash he had left around. He was our man.'

'And the DNA strain makes it clear we got the right guy,' Grady admitted. 'The "Y" test proved it was a blood relative, a man—had to be Tom Kenny. I'm mostly curious about what the quarter meant.'

Hampton said, 'Our answers died with the perp. I don't suppose we'll ever know all of the whys or wherefores.'

'Did you see the reporter's scoop?' Grady asked the captain. 'You notice how she had nothing but praise for the department?'

Another rare smile. 'Yes, I called and spoke to her. As she did us a favor, I gave her the information about the quarter for a follow-up article. It's a detail I left out for everyone else. Considering her tip is what allowed us to catch Kenny, I don't think the other media outlets can complain about bias.'

'I'm just glad she didn't try and meet Kenny on her own,' Hampton said.

Grady bobbed his head in agreement. 'Thank God, she didn't try to be the hero. She set up the meet and called the Brit. He knew the only move was to contact us.'

'A smart reporter, and a British cop who wanted nothing from this case but to help,' Hampton remarked drily, 'who'da thunk?'

The three men laughed and the captain left the desk.

'You think it was something as simple as flipping a coin?' Grady asked his partner. 'Could it have been at the party, to see who got to have sex with the girl next? Or was it about who would be the ones to go talk to Warren Lloyd?'

'Might be that simple,' Hampton replied. 'Beckston claimed he never knew anything about a quarter. Don't know if he was telling the truth or not, though.'

Grady tapped his pen on the desk top. 'If he knew and didn't speak up, it was because it was something he was still ashamed of. He might have been there when they flipped to see who killed Lloyd. No way he would want to own up to that.'

'Yeah, conspiracy to commit murder would land him on the other side of those walls where he works as a guard. Whatever he knows, he has no need to tell us now. There's no one left alive who can rebut his story.'

'Case closed, Ham.'

Hampton gave him a resigned look. 'Yep, case closed.'

TWENTY

'I TOLD YOU, Wilma, I'm meeting a couple of the guys for a beer,' John Beckston told his wife sharply. 'Can't you stop your whining for one damn minute and let me have a little fun with my friends?'

'You spend half of the grocery budget when you go out with your *friends!*' she shouted. 'Buddy and Deb need new shoes. I hate that we sent them back to school with stuff from the thrift store. We didn't buy them one new thing to wear this year.'

'Gripe and moan, that's all I ever get,' he yelled back. 'I work my butt off, I pull double shifts, I work holidays— all so I can bring in a little extra money. No matter what I do, it's never enough.'

'Coming home drunk isn't the answer, John!'

'If you hadn't waited until you were middle-aged to have kids, we wouldn't have this problem.'

'We agreed to wait,' Wilma fought back. 'I wish I hadn't waited until I was thirty-eight to have our kids, but it's too late to worry about it.'

'Well, as soon as Deb is out of first grade and going to school all day, you can get a full-time job and buy whatever you want. 'Til then, I'm going to bust loose once in a while. I only get two nights off a week. I'm taking one of them to unwind and have some fun.'

'Yes, and then you come home drunk and smelling like some cheap whore!' Wilma fired back. 'You think I don't know when you've been around another woman?'

'For hell's sake, let it go!' he snapped. 'I'll be back when I get back.'

Wilma might have said or yelled, even screamed something at him, but John was not listening. He slipped behind the wheel of his late model Toyota, glad to be free of the police stake-out and the intolerable surveillance. It was nice to have his life back—such as it was.

The going-home traffic had cleared from the highway, but there were still a great number of cars on the road. John cussed at several, calling them names for the stupid way they drove, and ended up at Riley's Roundup. The bar was off the main drag, a bit on the sleazy side, where he usually met up with another guard or two from work. Riley often had a friendly waitress or barfly to keep men company. For the price of a drink or two, a guy could manage a cheap feel. When lucky—and he had the money—it was occasionally more.

The worst thing about the place was its lack of parking. There were maybe a dozen stalls behind the bar, but with four to six people working there, it took only a few customers to fill the small lot. It meant parking across the street and risking life and limb to get to the front door. He didn't give it a second thought tonight. He was celebrating his freedom from cop shadows and a fear someone was out to kill him.

John spent four hours at the bar, along with every cent he had on him, before finally calling it a night. There were three girls working the tables, but some army reservists had come in early and had been spending money like they had their own printing press. Manny Valdez showed up from the prison, but he had his two brothers with him. John spent a little time with the trio, but the night was pretty much a bust.

The fresh air hit John in the face as he left the bar. He looked back and forth, trying to remember where he had parked. The street-lights were not great along that stretch, but the bar's neon sign helped to light up the road. John spied his ride and started across the street. It wasn't until he was several steps into the road that he heard the roar of an engine. He froze, seeing a pick-up bearing down on him. Being half drunk, he was slow to react—too slow!

The grille hit him with such force it knocked him fifty feet. Even as he hit the hard pavement the truck continued forward and he was caught beneath the wheels. Both the front and rear wheels rolled over John, crushing his chest, ribs and torso.

John's whiskey-fogged brain worked feverishly to sort out what had happened. His eyes caught the gleam of taillights, as the pick-up sped on down the road, but he had no other sensation.

Damn! That was close, he thought. *Must have somehow bounced right over me. I don't feel a thing.* He smiled at his luck. *Wait'll I tell Wilma. She ain't gonna believe it. She just won't...*

Blackness suddenly blocked his vision. The smell of blood was in his nostrils and a salty, somewhat familiar taste filled his mouth. Before he realized his eyes had closed, he was sucked into an ocean of darkness. Caught within a whirlpool of eddies and swirling currents were several brilliant memories and vivid images. The pictures which flashed through his mind were mixed...the fun and good times of youth, the first time he held his children in his arms, the numbing guilt from watching a girl he admired being sexually attacked, even the endless nagging of his wife of twenty-five years. Beyond the complex reverie, he realized a grim certainty...he would never see the light of day again.

KARI LEARNED OF the hit-and-run the next morning. Although tired from a short night and very little sleep, she wanted to cover the story. However, there was no evidence to support the notion that Beckston's death was murder. It was likely John had been a victim of another drunk driver. There were several bars and night spots along that poorly lit part of town. Two careless and impaired men—one driving, one crossing the street—it was an open-and-shut case. The police would look for witnesses and try to determine the identity of the person driving the vehicle, but it was unlikely they would consider Beckston's death premeditated murder. Thinking about it rationally, it did seem a stretch.

Her phone rang and she answered to discover a surprise caller—Amy Dawkins!

'I read in the newspaper about how you helped the police catch Tom Kenny,' she began. 'Then, this morning, I heard John Beckston was killed in a hit-and-run last night.'

'Yes, I was about to call and talk to the police about it, but I'm pretty sure they don't believe John's death was in any way related to the other murders.'

'Maybe not, but there is...' she seemed to take a deep breath, 'well, there's something I didn't tell you before.'

Kari sat up straight, fully alert, feeling she was about to learn something important. 'What is it, Amy?'

'You remember I told you that John and I were friends?' She didn't wait for an answer. 'We sat together in successive classes from the time we were in junior high. It wasn't a romance or anything, just a couple of kids who got on well together. I never dated him, but we often confided in each other.'

'All right, you were good friends. What didn't you tell me?'

'After the Christmas party John was withdrawn and apologetic to me. He avoided Sally because he was ashamed of what had happened. He blamed the whole thing on everyone drinking too much. He claimed it was the first time he'd ever gotten drunk.'

Kari gnashed her teeth, waiting for Amy to get to the point. When Amy paused, she used the moment to prompt her back to her reason for calling.

'You said there was something you needed to tell me?'

'Yes,' a heavy sigh came through the line, 'it could be important, and with John dead now, I don't see how it can hurt anyone.'

'Just say it straight out, Amy,' Kari coaxed. 'I'm not going to criticize you for holding back information.'

'I'm pretty sure Warren Lloyd isn't the father of Sally's boys.'

Kari had to replay the words in her head twice before they registered. 'What?'

'Sally liked Warren, but she didn't know if she wanted to marry him—not back when they were dating. I told you how she carried a torch for Steve Kenny all those years. Maybe it was wishful thinking, but she didn't want to give her heart to Warren. She told me they had fooled around some, but she had never gone all the way with him. It was after she discovered she was pregnant and Warren had been killed—that's when she claimed the babies were his. No one would hold it against a poor girl for getting pregnant by her boyfriend, the guy she was going to marry. It was her way to cope and I think she said it so often she began to believe it herself.'

'But…but if she didn't…?' Kari swallowed the notion,

considering the ramifications. 'If Warren isn't the father—who is?'

'I didn't want to say anything for her sake, Kari. I was trying to protect Sally...and also John. It wouldn't have done his marriage any good if it came out he had been a party to gang sex—whether he actually took part in the act or not.'

'Sally got pregnant from the Christmas party!'

'Yes, and it was not a pretty thing. You remember how I said we didn't find her panties? Well, it was because there was blood on them. She didn't bleed a lot, but she was still a virgin and there was a little. I guess the first pig who had his way—I'm thinking Steve or Tom Kenny—didn't bother to remove her underwear.'

'And you kept quiet all these years?'

'John was afraid the truth would ruin him and the others, some who were going to college. For himself, he was afraid there might be some kind of debt involved—possibly helping to pay for eighteen years of child support—for a rape he never committed. Don't you see, Kari? It was better for everyone. Sally claimed her two boys were love children from the man she had been ready to marry, while John and the other boys were able to continue on with their lives.'

'It turns out you didn't have to protect John's career,' Kari said in a cool tone of voice. 'Not much college needed to become a prison guard.'

'He didn't have a lot of ambition in school. I think it pretty much stayed that way when he got into the work force. Anyway, it seemed better for everyone if the rape was forgotten.'

Kari returned to the case. 'So Warren found out his virtuous girlfriend had gotten drunk and had sex with several guys,' she surmised. 'That would have definitely set him off.'

'John swore to me the Kenny boys and Jamison Clark were only trying to stop Warren when the accident happened. They wanted to talk him out of going to the police or Mr Cline, but he thought they intended to beat him up and ran from them.'

'Yes, a detective told me John's story, and the fact he was on a date the night of the car crash.'

'I believed Warren's death was an accident.'

'So you kept quiet about the attack.'

'It would have been the word of two high-school heroes, who had just won the state title in football. Plus, Wilkins's dad was a church bishop and Paul Pacheco's father was on the city council. I told you how they claimed Sally got tanked and asked Steve to make love to her. The case would have never gone to court.'

'Did you read my article about the murders, about how the killer stuck a quarter between the teeth of the first four victims?'

Amy grunted. 'Sounded rather melodramatic.'

'Do you know if leaving a quarter with each body meant anything to John?'

'I never heard about it. Maybe it was a statement about how much Tom thought their lives were worth, something like that.'

'OK, I just wondered. The police never discovered what it meant either. Perhaps the killer taunted them—you know, *heads you live, tails you die*—that sort of thing.'

'I suppose,' Amy replied back. 'Or it could have been a private joke between the group. Tom might have thought they would release the information and put terror into the hearts of his victims, something like that.'

'Well, whatever it meant, it's over. Once again, I really

appreciate your calling me, Amy. The information clears up a number of things.'

'If you decide to print anything about Sally, please don't say it came from me.'

'I don't want to cause her any more misery. It's information I'm glad you shared, but it's more for my personal use than publication.'

'I couldn't imagine it making a difference,' Amy said, 'but I thought someone ought to know about the twins.'

Kari thanked her again and hung up the phone. She picked up her cell and located the number she wanted from the menu. There was one call she had to make. It probably meant nothing, but it was a piece of evidence that had to be cleared up.

TWENTY-ONE

HAMPTON GLANCED AT Grady when he took the phone call. He grinned when his partner made a face and gave a shake of his head, while listening to one end of the conversation.

'Miss Underwood,' Grady said pleasantly, 'I thought we might hear from you today.' A pause. 'No…we don't believe it's related. Just a hit-and-run like we have a dozen times a year.'

Another pause.

'Yes, we are looking into it, but there's no reason to think…' He listened for a few seconds. 'We'll certainly be checking all the angles. You know we do a thorough job here.'

He let her speak again.

'Yes, the quarters still are a mystery to us to, but there was no quarter stuck between Beckston's teeth. He was drunk and probably didn't see the vehicle coming.'

Another short wait.

'What's that?' he frowned. 'You want me to do what for you?' After listening again, 'Well, yes, it's a hassle and a lot of unnecessary expense, but I suppose we can check it out. Can you tell me what this is about?'

'I see,' he replied to something else. Then he began to bob his head up and down. 'Yes, yes, I know we owe you a favor or two. I'll get the information for you.'

Hampton was chuckling by the time Grady hung up the receiver. 'That didn't take long,' he said. 'Let me guess, she thinks we got the wrong man for the serial murders?'

'The reporter shares the same concern we do about the quarters. She doesn't buy the toss of the coin to see who had sex next or who went after Lloyd.'

Hampton snorted. 'Do we?'

'What if we've made a mistake, Ham,' Grady asked. 'We've been working on the idea that Kenny worked alone to do these murders. What if he had an accomplice or was innocent altogether?'

'You know, I really hate it when you start that *what if* stuff.'

'The six men who are now dead were all involved in the gang rape at the party and are responsible for the death of Warren Lloyd. Suppose it was the intent of the killer to get every one of the six guys who were involved all along?'

'And when we nailed Kenny, there was no need to continue security on Beckston—is that what you're saying?'

'I'm only throwing the idea out there, Ham.'

'Yes, but we cleared everyone else with the DNA from the Wilkins murder. And you saw Kenny with your own eyes...holding a gun to a policewoman's head! He was as guilty as homemade sin.'

'The reporter made a strange request,' he told Hampton. 'She wants me to check the DNA of the victims against Reggie Cline.'

That raised the senior detective's eyebrows. 'Did she say why?'

'She believes Sally Cline was impregnated the night of the Christmas party and not by Warren Lloyd.'

'That tidbit came out of thin air. Didn't we check the time frame on the boys right at the start?'

'Could have been either way,' Grady said. 'Sally said they crossed the line the last time she saw Warren, before he and his family left for the holidays.'

Hampton suggested, 'I can see her naming Warren as

the father. I mean, who wants to tell their kids they were born out of a gang rape?'

'That makes sense,' Grady admitted. 'But I don't know what good it will do now. I don't see any sense in telling the Cline boys that Warren wasn't their biological father.'

'Is that why she wants the information?'

'She didn't say.'

'Can't match all the pieces to a puzzle if you don't know what the picture is supposed to look like.'

Grady laughed. 'My partner, Socrates Hampton.'

He showed his teeth in a silly grin. 'Think of it this way, pard...we've got the gal reporter and her British cop friend still checking things out. Maybe they'll solve the rest of the mystery for us.'

'I don't think I'll put off lunch waiting for one of them to call back with an explanation,' Grady replied. 'I'll ask for a complete DNA of everyone involved...alive or dead. That should suit our nosy reporter, and then we can get back to work.'

Jason had spoken to Kari on the phone and discussed the death of John Beckston. He fixed himself a cup of tea and read the newspaper. Reggie had left the previous evening. The trip was to California and he preferred to go through Vegas at night, so as to miss the worst of the traffic congestion.

After a couple of hours Jason drove to the Fashion Place Mall. He waited until the stores opened and began to search for the battery he needed. When he found the right store the phone tech offered to replace it for him. However, the tech discovered there was nothing wrong with the battery. The phone itself was broken. He thanked the young man for his effort, explained to him politely that he was British, not *Australian*, and stuck the mobile into his pocket.

As Jason was leaving for England soon he decided he

would do without a mobile phone until he got home. In any case, he would be at Reggie's apartment. Considering Kari or one of the Clines were the only people he talked to, he hardly needed a mobile at the present time.

He could not shake the uneasy feeling over the untimely death of John Beckston. There was a fine line between the coincidence of an accidental death and the cunning execution of a planned murder. What if the serial killer had waited until he was vulnerable, then ran him down? If so, the murderer was still out there!

Kari had told him the police detective suspected no connection to the other murders. There had been no quarter stuck between his teeth to send an ominous message. And the preliminary DNA test proved Tom Kenny was the likely killer.

However, Kari also said she had something of importance to talk to him about, but she wanted to do it in person. He gave her a rough estimate of when he would be at Reggie's apartment and promised to call her if he was delayed.

Jason went over everything he could remember from the murders. He had been told about the quarters, and it raised the question—what did it mean? There was the account of Tom Kenny and how he had, in fact, forced the police to shoot him. It was one of many unanswered questions. Kari described the man as being excitable and sounding paranoid. She claimed he had practically babbled and wept on the telephone, declaring his innocence of the deaths of his one-time friends and his cousin.

Yet they found his prints and the killer's items in the old Kenny house, including rubber gloves. He must have had lucid moments, such as when he killed his victims. It was possible Tom had used Steve Kenny, to keep track of the other men. If so, why kill his cousin?

Beckston dying the day after his personal surveillance was taken off; the meaning of the quarters; the idea that a madman could kill three people before leaving a single clue—it all added up to one big unanswered question: Was Tom Kenny the one and only killer?

Grady took the call at his desk. Hampton had started to leave the room, on his way to get them both a cup of coffee from the break room, but stopped when Grady raised a hand.

'Yeah, I remember,' Grady was saying. 'You did us a favor by checking on it.' He listened a moment and frowned. 'That can't be right. Maybe there wasn't enough for a good test.' Then after a curt response on the opposite end, 'No, I'm not saying you made a mistake. I'm only asking you to run it again. We got our man; it has to be a false reading of some kind.'

Hampton moved over next to the desk as the inflection of Grady's tone became more irate. By the time Grady had hung up the phone, he had parked his haunch on the corner of his desk and was staring at him, awaiting an explanation.

'I'll be a sonuva...' Grady shoved back from the desk. 'It doesn't make a bit of sense, Ham! Somebody must have screwed up!'

'Hello!' Hampton growled the word. 'I could only hear your end of the conversation. If you want my support for being peeved, you should have put the call on the speaker!'

Grady put his hands to either side of his head as if to ward off a migraine headache. 'You remember when the reporter gal asked me a favor?'

'Don't you go there!' Hampton wailed. 'Anything with her name on it has to be trouble.'

'She wanted me to have them run a DNA comparison test between Reggie Cline and the victims. Turns out Jamison Clark is the father of the twins and not Warren Lloyd.'

Hampton was relieved. 'That's not so bad. We kind of figured there was a little extra curricular activity that took place during the party. It could have gone either way for the two boys.'

'That's not the wrinkle here,' Grady told him. 'They ran the complete DNA test for Tom Kenny against the blood found on the shirt of Wilkins and it didn't match!'

Hampton was stunned. 'Hold on! They told us he was the man we wanted!'

'He shares the same "Y" chromosome as the killer, but the full DNA shows he was only a relative, and not our actual killer.'

'But he's the *relative* we liked for the murders!' Hampton exclaimed. 'Now you're telling me there's another Kenny out there?'

'I told the lab to run the test again.' Grady continued to rub his temples. 'It has to be a mistake. We only had three suspects. Reggie and Roger Cline turn out to be the sons of Jamison Clark and we cleared both of them of the murders. Tom Kenny was our only viable suspect, the one with the motive, and he practically admitted his guilt when we caught him.'

'If not him, then who?' Hampton wanted to know. 'Who do we have left?'

Grady dragged out his notes and scanned the pages for the information. 'Steve Kenny's dad died several years ago. Tom Kenny is an only child and his father lives in Maui and has a construction outfit. He hasn't been back on the mainland in nearly ten years. There was another uncle, the one who owned the house in Herriman, but he never married and also passed away a few years back.'

'So what?' Hampton cried. 'You mean we're looking for a child out of wedlock?'

'Who the hell knows!'

'It was only a single drop of blood,' Hampton said. 'Maybe there wasn't enough for a good test.'

'The lab says the results are conclusive.'

Hampton began to rub his forehead as well. 'The chief isn't going to be happy about this.'

'Yeah, we went from heroes to goats in about two seconds flat.'

'Killing an innocent man will do that,' Hampton said.

'Innocent of one of the murders, Ham, but he could have been working with someone. Besides, we can't forget about the Lloyd boy's death or the way Kenny held a gun to our policewoman's head.'

'I'm not forgetting anything, but it still leaves a foul taste in my mouth. We thought we had the right man. He had the tools right in his house, the place where he was hiding. Everything fit.'

Grady folded his arms and leaned back in his chair. 'The question is, what now? Do we start looking at Beckston's death as premeditated murder?'

'We go back to square one and check the evidence. We reinterview, we look at everyone who attended the Christmas party again. One of the two Kenny boys must have had sex with another girl.'

'But why kill the same five men? And how was Tom Kenny involved?'

'Six men are dead and we've lost our motive and our killer. We're in one hell of a mess.'

Grady groaned. 'I think it's time to take a vacation.'

'After we tell the captain we might both end up on vacation—permanently!'

Kari couldn't believe the news. She had listened to a very irate and unhappy Detective Grady before he practically slammed the phone down on her.

Gracious! You'd think it was my fault! she thought sourly.

Dee met her for the afternoon break and listened to the story. She was more than a friend, she was an intelligent, insightful person.

But she had nothing to offer, no ideas, no theories, no hypothesis at all. Indeed, where did a person look for answers to such a complex puzzle?

'Can you write a story about it?' she queried. 'Did they give you first shot at breaking the news?'

'No, Grady said to keep it quiet for now. The lab is going to retest the DNA of both men.'

'I thought they had tested positive?'

'On the "Y" chromosome test, not the complete DNA test. It seems the first chromosome test is much quicker. They used it to rule out the other suspects and match it to Tom Kenny. Now they've gone back through and ran the more conclusive test.'

'Who does that leave?'

'Absolutely no one,' Kari said. 'They have a clean sheet of paper with not a suspect or clue to work with. The DNA of the killer matches the Kenny strain, but it isn't Tom. And neither he nor Steve has any known male blood relatives who are unaccounted for.'

'What a *wracken-frack* mess! Can you say dead end?'

Kari looked at her watch. 'I'm going to see Jason. He should be home by now. Maybe I'll leave early and see what he thinks.'

'He isn't a detective on the case,' Dee reminded her.

'No, but he has insight and has seen a good many murders. He might be able to offer some kind of answer.' She shrugged. 'OK, it's pretty lame, but I have nothing else.'

Dee smiled. 'You don't have to con me, kiddo. You're eager to see him again.'

Kari didn't argue the fact. 'Yes,' she kept her voice hushed, 'but Ms Taylor would have a cow if she thought I was sneaking off early to see my boyfriend.'

'She won't get the information out of me,' Dee assured her, then grinned. 'Unless she threatens to pull off my fingernails with pliers. You know how I love my nails.'

Kari stood up. 'I'll see you later.'

Dee waved a hand, getting up herself so she could return to her desk downstairs. 'Don't do anything I wouldn't do,' she teased. 'Of course, that opens the door pretty wide.'

Kari laughed and started up the hall. She would pick up her purse and leave Taylor a message that she was following a lead. Once Grady got a second confirmation on the test results, she was going to have another front page story!

TWENTY-TWO

As it happened, Jason arrived about the time Kari was getting out of her car. She smiled at the timing and walked over from Visitor Parking to where he had parked his rental.

Jason gave her a head-to-foot appraisal without ever moving his gaze from her face. She felt an ardent glow inside her at the tenderness which came into his face. It caused a tingle of anticipation; she was enjoying the way he did not hide how much he liked what he saw.

'You're early. I wanted to catch a shower and change clothes before seeing you,' was his greeting.

Kari's light mood took an immediate downward turn. 'I didn't dare wait to speak to you, Jason. There's been… well, I wanted to speak to you before I wrote my next story.'

'Come on up to the apartment,' he offered. 'I wasn't expecting company, but Reggie keeps a tidy house.'

She hooked her arm through his and they walked together to the second floor of the nearest building. He led the way and stopped at the door to Reggie's apartment.

Jason unlocked the door and pushed it open, allowing Kari to enter first. She was impressed. Tidy was the right word. A desk with a computer sat in one corner, with a comfortable-looking recliner and a matching settee placed opposite a television and entertainment center. A small table and four chairs were next to the kitchen, which was also clean and organized.

'Make yourself at home while I shower and change,' Jason said. 'Would you like a cup of tea?'

'No, I'm fine.'

He responded with, 'I shouldn't be more than a few minutes.'

'I'll try not to get bored,' she replied.

Jason went through the kitchen and down a short hall-way toward the bedroom and bath. Kari tested the chair and decided on the sofa. About the same time as she heard the running of a shower the apartment door opened.

Roger Cline was silhouetted in the hallway for a moment before he stepped inside and closed the door. In his hand was a plastic garment protector which had several shirts on hangers. He came to a sudden stop and stared at Kari agape, stunned to find her sitting in the living room.

Kari rose to her feet, immediately consumed with a mixture of hateful rage and bitter shame. The last time she had seen this man's face he had sneered vile oaths and degraded her with his utter contempt. He had left her feeling lower than the most worthless human being on earth.

'Kari,' he spoke her name uncomfortably. 'I didn't expect you to be here.'

'I'm here with Jason. Had I known you were coming I would be someplace else,' she said testily. 'I don't relish the idea of being in the same room with you.'

Roger raised his free hand, palm outward, as if to stop her from continuing. 'Before you attack me physically—which would be completely justified—give me a chance to speak.'

Kari crossed her arms, still burning from the heat of fury and abasement. 'There's nothing you can say that I care to listen to.'

Roger stepped over to a closet door and hung the freshly laundered shirts on the doorknob. When he gazed at her, there was an odd expression on his face…it looked like regret!

'I don't blame you for hating me, Kari,' he said quietly. 'I deserve nothing but contempt for the way I treated you, and I don't expect you to forgive me.' He moved a bit closer and met her hot glare directly. 'But I would like for you to understand my…personal obsession.'

He waited a moment, as if giving her a chance to shout obscenities or start swinging at him. When she did neither, he took a deep breath and let it out slowly.

'My mother ruined her life by not saving her virtue until her wedding night. She had everything going for her—a dance career, a marriage to a wonderful man, a life full of love and happiness. It was all lost because she had a weak moment. She told me how, when Warren was leaving for two weeks over the Christmas holidays, they went too far. Reggie and I were the result of that single slip. Her life was forever changed. Even if Warren had not been killed in the car accident, she would never have the chance to fulfill her dream to dance professionally.

'All of my life, she has beaten three words into my head—*marry a virgin!* Anyone else wouldn't do. She has hammered it into me since my first childhood crush. She made me promise that I would never be second best when it came to my choice of a wife. Her mistake cost her everything, her future, her happiness, her whole life.' He shook his head. 'You know all too well how I reacted when I discovered you were not a virgin. And I admit it was a vulgar, disgusting display. But much of my reaction was because I had truly hoped you were the right girl. Everything about you seemed to point to flawless virtue. I was crushed because you turned out *not* to be the one. I took out my disappointment on you…wrongly, but it was something I could not help.'

'You have a screwed-up mother fixation, Roger,' she said bitterly.

He laughed at the remark. 'Yeah, tell me about it. Mom has pounded her notions into my head all of my life, and I am trapped by wanting to please her. She didn't have a life of her own, so I have to try and give her what happiness I can, by fulfilling her wishes. I know it's ridiculous, but I am bound by my pledge to her.'

'You're still a deceitful snake,' Kari told him. 'All you had to do was ask me. I would have told you the truth. You didn't have to work for a month to seduce me, then treat me like the worst kind of street prostitute.'

'For that, I apologize,' he replied. 'I know you didn't deserve that kind of treatment. It's my compulsive obsession, not your own. I shouldn't have blamed you.'

'You need help, Roger, professional help.'

'So did Freud, but instead he wrote the book on neurosis. Find any person working in the field of psychiatry and I'll show you someone who needs a psychiatrist.'

Kari didn't smile at his homespun philosophy.

'How are you and Jason getting along?' he asked, changing the subject. 'Finding the two of you here is a surprise. I didn't know he had moved in with Reggie.'

'We *were* getting along fine, until you showed up,' she told him meaningfully. 'And Reggie is being hospitable and saving Jason the price of a room. Besides which, he's not using the place for the next few days.'

'Well, I was just returning some shirts I borrowed.' He grinned. 'I kind of take advantage of my brother from time to time.'

'Nice guys are often taken advantage of.'

Roger started back toward the door. 'I don't want to ruin your plans for the day. I'll be going.'

'Wait a minute!' she said a bit too quickly. Recovering

her aplomb, she added, 'I-I was going to tell Jason something, but it concerns you and Reggie. You might as well stay and hear it first hand.'

'All right, if you aren't going to be uncomfortable with me here.'

'Just don't ask me to pretend I don't still hate your guts.'

'No, I wouldn't do that,' he replied. 'What's so important?'

'I learned something today and I think you should hear it from me, in case it winds up in the newspaper or on television.'

His face skewed at the remark. 'What are you talking about?'

'Let's wait until...'

Jason chose that moment to enter the room. He spied Roger and stopped, looking from one to the other. Masking his concern at once, he produced an uncertain smile.

'I thought I heard voices,' he offered. 'Roger, what brings you here?'

Roger pointed at the plastic-encased laundry hanging on the closet door. 'I told Reggie I'd get his stuff back to him. I swung by to drop off the shirts. I didn't expect anyone to be home.'

'Your brother offered me the spare room—' Jason began.

Roger lifted a hand to stop him. 'Yes, Kari told me.'

Kari smiled warmly at Jason. He had shaved and combed his hair, yet wore only his slacks. A glint of moisture glistened on his rather nicely proportioned chest and he had better muscle tone than she had imagined. He appeared anxious about having Roger present, but walked over to stand next to her. Perhaps to make a statement, he slipped his arm around her waist. She enjoyed the closeness and also the scent of his freshly showered body next to her own.

'Your reporter girlfriend said she had something to tell me.' Roger spoke up. 'Otherwise, I would have done the gentlemanly thing and left.' He grinned. 'Don't laugh, Jason. I know it would have been out of character.'

'So what news have you?' Jason asked Kari.

'I spoke to Detective Grady today and he gave me some disturbing information.' Jason removed his arm from her waist, pivoting around so he could face her. Roger took a step closer, so she was now facing the two men squarely.

'The police lab ran a full DNA on the victims and Tom Kenny—also on Reggie. It was to confirm their suspicions about the relationships of people involved with murders. What they found…' She had to inhale deeply as her voice became weak. 'Roger, you and Reggie…Warren Lloyd was not your father.'

'What!' Roger exclaimed at the statement. 'What are you saying?'

She kept her poise and clarified. 'The full DNA comparison showed Jamison Clark is your biological father. According to Sally's best girlfriend in high school, Warren and Sally never had sex together.'

Roger's face darkened. 'That's crazy! Mom loved Warren. They had an intimate date the night before he left for the two week holiday. She told me it was the only time they had ever gone all the way!' He stared at Kari. 'It's just as I told you a minute ago. It was their one mistake.'

'Her girlfriend has a different chain of events,' she countered. 'Perhaps she was mistaken about Warren, but…' Kari explained the relationship, as Amy had told it to her. She added why Amy thought Sally had been a virgin the night of the Christmas party. Next she described her conversation with Grady and their thoughts about Warren's death. After learning the truth about the party, they suspected Warren was going to make trouble for the Kenny cousins and the other four boys involved in the sexual attack. That was why he ended up dead in an auto accident.

Roger turned and walked away a few steps, his fists clenched at his sides. 'I knew about Mom being sexually assaulted, but...' He swore.

'You knew?' Jason challenged him. 'How long have you known?'

'I never told Reggie. I didn't want him thinking bad of her,' he replied. 'Mom had too much to drink and those guys took advantage of her. Granddad never found out about the attack, and Mom made me promise never to tell anyone.'

'And the DNA?' Jason spoke to Kari, 'Reggie has the same as Jamison Clark?'

'Yes, Clark is Reggie's and Roger's biological father.'

'Of all the vile, rotten news!' Roger cried. 'We are the offspring of a dirty, filthy, rapist! Is there no damned justice in this world?'

'They're positive about this?' Jason asked.

'No doubt whatsoever,' Kari confirmed. 'Sally Cline was impregnated the night of the Christmas party, by Jamison Clark.'

Roger was still fuming. 'I can't believe it. Jamison Clark!' He swore again. 'Mom once told me she tried to talk to Jamison at school, after the party rape. She thought she might be pregnant and was looking for support or a way out of the predicament. Jamison said it was her own fault. He said she got what she asked for!' Another bout of swearing and oaths. 'He got her pregnant and the sleazy bugger sat in judgment of her! If that worthless snake wasn't already dead, I'd take a club to him and beat him till he couldn't stand up!'

Jason sympathized with his rage, but said, 'You should

have told us about the sexual attack when I told you about the murders, Roger.'

'I didn't know the whole truth until after the murders started. The last time I visited Mom she confessed what had happened. She made me promise I wouldn't tell anyone, Jason...not even Reggie.'

'Yes, but some sod was killing those men.'

'Knowing about the attack would have made Granddad or Reggie and me suspects with a motive, Jason. Besides, I didn't think there was any way the murders could be connected to a party from way back then.'

'I suppose it's a little late to worry about it now.'

Roger put his attention on Kari. 'What about this newspaper story you mentioned? Is this going to be in it, a statement that Jamison Clark sired two sons from a rape at a party?'

'There's no reason to print anything concerning you or Reggie,' she replied. 'The attackers are all dead and you've been cleared of suspicion.'

Roger took a step toward her, acted as if he might reach out to take hold of her arms, but quickly recovered and let his hands fall to his sides. By the earnest expression on his face, she saw he was ready to plead with her.

'What about our mother?' he asked gently. 'Are the cops going to speak to her about this? Does she have to know we learned the truth about our father?'

Kari should have wanted to hurt Roger, but this was Reggie's mother too. Besides which, she had no animosity toward Sally Cline.

'I honestly don't know. They might speak to her again, as a matter of normal procedure, but I don't see any reason to publicize the attack at the party. And who is or isn't your father has nothing to do with the murder investigation, not any more.'

Roger sighed his relief, then regarded Kari with a somber look. 'Thanks, Kari,' he said, adding a degree of humility to his next words. 'And let me again apologize for the way I treated you. I wish you and Jason every happiness—should you end up together. I mean that.'

Kari had no reply. She stood rigid, while Roger gave a nod to Jason and headed for the door. He was quickly gone, leaving the two of them alone.

When the door closed, Kari took two steps toward the door, as if to call him back.

'Kari?' Jason wondered aloud.

She stopped and looked back. What she saw about broke her heart. He must have thought she wanted to give Roger another chance, as an uncertain kind of fear shone in his face, a dread that he had lost her.

'I...I won't stop you, if you want to go after him,' he said quietly. She rushed back and threw her arms around him. 'No, Jason,' she murmured, rising up on her toes to kiss him gently. 'You're the man I want in my life.'

He was still perplexed. 'You looked as if you wanted to stop him.'

'Yes,' she admitted, 'but not to renew our relationship. I didn't get a chance to tell him the rest of the news.' She shrugged. 'I guess it doesn't really matter. It will be in my news story.'

'What news?'

'They discovered one other thing when they ran the complete DNA tests.' Kari could not keep the dejected feeling from her words. 'The DNA trace found on Wilkins's shirt collar is *not* a match for Tom Kenny.'

It took a moment for that to sink in. Jason blinked and frowned in disbelief. 'How's that?' He was incredulous. 'But they had already established that Kenny was the right man!'

'The first test confirmed the Y chromosome was a match between the killer and Steve Kenny. They assumed it was Tom, because he would also have the same chromosome—all male relatives share it and pass it on to their sons.'

'Well, that doesn't make any sense,' Jason said. 'How could the test show it to be a relative and not be Tom Kenny? Where are the police going to find another Kenny?'

'That's the puzzle,' Kari answered. 'There isn't one—not that we know of.'

Jason remembered he was wearing only his trousers. 'I'd better finish getting dressed. I don't know if you're still hungry or not,' he said awkwardly, 'but I am famished.'

Kari smiled, glad to have the story set aside. 'I was hoping you weren't intending to go out dressed like you are. Unless we go to a drive-up window at a fast-food place, all of the higher-class establishments require a shirt and shoes.'

'I'll be ready in a tick.' He nodded at the freshly laundered shirts. 'Perhaps you could remove the hangers and get rid of the garment bag for Reggie. Just pop them into the cupboard there.'

Jason headed back to the bedroom while Kari removed the plastic covering and pulled the three shirts free. After hanging them in the half-empty closet she began to wad up the plastic, so she could put it in the trash. However, a copy of the bill was stuck to the side and she paused to look at it.

Twelve dollars for three shirts!

She thought of the tremendous waste of money. Who could afford such sky-high prices for doing…?

Something clicked in her mind. She stared at the bill for a moment and then tore it free from the plastic. Before Jason could return, she folded it and stuck the receipt in her purse.

Jason joined her moments later, wearing a freshly

laundered, turquoise-colored, dress shirt and his always-polished oxford shoes. He paused to glance at his watch. 'We still have time to beat the evening rush.'

'I'm ready when you are.' She flashed another smile. 'Besides, I need to get home early and write my story. Detective Grady is going to verify what I can say before I get it to the editor's desk.'

'You seem to be getting very chummy with that pair of detectives.'

She laughed. 'I'll probably send them Christmas cards this year.' Jason chuckled at the notion. 'I don't think I would count on getting one back from either of those characters. This case must be driving them mad.'

TWENTY-THREE

GRADY ROTATED THE swivel chair and watched Hampton hang up the phone. 'Anything?'

'Reggie Cline was four hundred miles away when Beckston died. I confirmed he went through the port of entry at the Utah-Arizona border within an hour of the hit-and-run.'

'Well, I checked with the hotel in New York and they say his brother was there during the time Wilkins was killed. Kept erratic hours, but the clerk remembered seeing him 'most every day. We got the same story concerning the first murder in Vegas. Roger Cline was in Portland at the time.'

'Their grandfather was at the Elks Club and Sally had the late shift at Smith's grocery. That pretty much clears all of them for the hit-and-run. As for the Lloyd family, they moved the year after their son died. The father passed away last year, the mother works at a hospital in Tampa, Florida, and Warren was their only child. And, of course, there's no reason any of them would have the Kenny DNA.'

'Don't know why we have to even check backgrounds on any new suspects,' Grady said. 'Unless someone planted the drop of blood, we're looking for a Kenny.'

'Looking for a ghost, you mean. We don't have another Kenny to check out. I personally spoke to the only other male relative we know of, the one working on Maui for the past decade. He hasn't been to the mainland in years.'

'We're missing something, Ham. I don't know what it is, but I feel like we're standing up to our noses in mud and asking for more rain. Who could have left a drop of blood on Wilkins other than the killer? And if the killer isn't a Kenny, where did he get a blood sample to plant for us?'

'This is crazy. We've got more questions than when we first started this investigation!' Hampton pounded his fist on the desktop. 'Maybe we ought to bring in the Feds and drop it in their laps. The first guy was killed in Vegas, so we've got murders in two states. We could justify turning it over to them.'

'Yeah, that wouldn't look like a bail-out, would it?' Grady moaned, the kind of noise a man makes when the world is about to end...and it can't come soon enough! 'You and I would be pounding a beat for handing off a five-murder case to the Feds, especially when we thought we had the thing all wrapped up.'

Hampton leaned back in his chair and suddenly looked years older. 'What's the reporter going to put in the paper?'

'The truth.'

'Ouch! Where's a good earthquake or meteor strike when you need one? Anything to take away the public focus from our murder case!'

'Even being gentle with us, Ham, I can see a lot of issues coming up. Not the least of which is the slight problem we have with our dead murder suspect: he's got the wrong DNA. She is going to write that we were still looking at other suspects, but have no reason to think anyone else is on the killer's hit list.'

Hampton folded his arms and scowled off into space. 'If Jamison Clark sired the two Cline boys, maybe one of the Kenny boys knocked up another girl about the same time. Maybe we've been dogging the wrong scent all along.'

'If that were the case, why take out the very same six vics? It's unlikely as hell the girl would have been gang-raped by the same bunch as the Cline girl.'

'Crap!' Hampton snapped. 'All we have is crap to show for all of our work. We haven't got one blessed clue as to who killed these men. I'm not even sure we have a motive any more.'

Grady lowered his head in defeat. 'I wonder if I can still get into my police uniform. I've put on a few pounds since I became a detective.'

'You're shooting pretty high,' Hampton sneered. 'How are you going to like riding a bicycle and writing tickets for parked cars?'

KARI STILL EXPERIENCED a tingle to see her reporting in print. The article announced the shocking news of how the suspected serial killer, who was shot during a standoff with police, might not be guilty of the four murders. It also pointed out the possibility that a fifth man, John Beckston, might have been the last to die at the real killer's hands. It explained how the incriminating evidence that led the police to Tom Kenny had been rebutted by DNA testing.

'How's the star reporter today?' Dee asked, having entered Kari's cubicle carrying two cups of coffee. 'I see you're still reveling in your glory.'

Kari laughed and thanked her for the cup of coffee.

'I can't tell you how much I need this after working to get the story out last night. Then I couldn't sleep because of all the weird thoughts which filtered through my brain.'

Dee sat opposite Kari and sipped her drink. 'I really thought this was a done deal,' she said. 'What about the hard evidence they had on this Kenny character?'

'Tape, wire, gloves—the works! And he had motive,' Kari added. 'He was terrified of going back to prison. He totally panicked when the police showed up…forced them to kill him, rather than go back to jail.'

'So how did the evidence get there?'

'I'm sure the detectives are wondering about that too. The only things that make sense are either Tom Kenny was set up to take the fall for the murders, or he had an accomplice, a cousin or something that no one knows about yet.'

'Why a cousin?'

Kari explained about the blood droplet.

'OK; for the sake of argument, Tom gets out of jail and is determined not to go back. He finds this love child—whom no one knows about—and gets him to help murder four men. When Tom gets caught, whoever the accomplice is kills the last man on the list.'

'Sounds preposterous when you come right out and say it.'

'You talked to the man, kiddo,' Dee said. 'Did he sound rational enough to commit four murders alone?'

'Not really, but it could have been an act to get me to meet him.'

'So you have no more to go on than the police?'

'Afraid not.'

'What did Rat-maggot say when you told him his father was almost as big a skunk as he is?'

Kari had explained about Roger arriving at Reggie's apartment and the subsequent conversation. She finished with, 'Roger was really steamed. I'm not sure if it was the fact that Jamison was his father, or that his mother had not told him the whole truth. He really takes her feelings to heart, and I believe it came across as a betrayal that she had lied about Warren being the father of her twins.'

'What about you and Mr Right?'

'Jason and I spent some time together, but I had to write the story. We had an early dinner together and that was it.'

'Doesn't sound like love to me.'

'It's complicated. Neither of us wants to get too carried away—Jason, because he still loves his wife, and me, because I'm on the rebound. Add to that, it's going to be very hard for us to date when we're so far apart.'

'I seem to have pointed that out at least once before.'

'I know, Dee,' Kari admitted. 'With his time here about to end, it's looming much larger than before.'

'Maybe you ought to make the best of what time you have left. Having been used by his cousin, you can't play the virtuous card. I'm surprised he doesn't push the issue.'

'Dee,' she didn't hide her exasperation, 'everything isn't about sex.'

'It is when you're getting serious,' Dee argued. 'You want to know you're compatible, especially if you're going to pine for him for several months between each date.'

'Where there is true love I believe the matter of sex will take care of itself.'

Dee displayed her sisterly smile. 'When do you see him again?'

'I'll see him after work.'

Dee laughed. 'I wish you luck, and you know I'll be here for you…whatever happens.' Then she stood up. 'I've got to get downstairs to my own desk. We can catch up at break, unless you're leaving the office.'

'Ms Taylor said she needed me to check on a public interest story for her. I'm sure it won't be as interesting as a murder case. If I'm not in the break room by ten, you'll know I'm off running around somewhere.'

Dee waved and left Kari alone at her desk. With the dull beginning of a headache, Kari reached for her purse. As she dug for the pain reliever she came across the folded laundry receipt. Glancing at it, she decided to do a check of her own, once she'd run the errand for Ms Taylor.

THE CAPTAIN STOOD with his hands on his hips. He was not a happy man and it showed in his curt demeanor.

'The chief is catching hell over this screw-up! In turn, he's giving me hell.' He narrowed his gaze at Grady and then Hampton. 'You two see where this is going, don't you?'

'We've been over everything a dozen times, Capt'n,' Grady told him. 'The duct tape and wire matched those found at the murder scenes. We had the disposable gloves, the glass cutter, along with Tom Kenny's fingerprints at the house. He was paranoid and off his meds. The guy would have done anything to stay out of prison. Everything fit.'

'So we should discount the drop of blood? Is that what you're saying, Grady?'

'If we dismiss that one detail, everything still points to Kenny,' Hampton pointed out.

'How do you explain the blood?'

'It can't be explained,' Grady replied. 'All of our records and background checks come up empty. We can't locate another Kenny.'

'You two ever read Sherlock Holmes?' the captain asked.

'I saw the movie,' Grady answered.

'I never was much for reading,' Hampton replied. 'What's your point, Capt'n?'

'Holmes used to have a saying concerning solving a puzzle. I don't remember the quote verbatim, but it went something like: *When you have eliminated the impossible what remains, however apparently improbable, must be the truth.* From this point forward, I want to start looking at every thing and every one with that thought in mind.'

'You mean like looking at a woman for the murders?'

'The DNA had the "Y" chromosome, so women are out unless they've had a gender change. Other than that, the field of men is wide open.'

'OK, boss,' Grady acquiesced. 'We'll start from the beginning and see what improbable answers we can come up with.'

'You might want to put this on the front burner, gentlemen,' the captain said, displaying a scowl. 'If I get busted down to a traffic cop, you'll be lucky to work as crossing guards at the nearby elementary schools!'

As soon as he had walked away, Hampton slid his chair over next to Grady. 'It's time for you to start tossing out your *what ifs*, pard. We need to find something, and we need to find it p.d.q.!'

KARI ENTERED THE LAUNDRY and waited until an elderly lady approached. 'How can I help you?' the woman asked.

Kari held out the laundry slip. 'Would it be possible for me to speak to whoever it was who wrote out this receipt?'

The woman glanced down at the handwriting. 'That would be Lucinda. What's the trouble—problem with one of the shirts?'

'No, it's nothing like that. I only need to ask her a question.' The woman grunted and walked into the back room A few moments later a young, moderately attractive girl of about twenty years of age came to the counter. She gave Kari an apprehensive look.

'Can I help you?'

'Hi!' Kari offered her a smile. 'I'm sorry to bother you, but I wanted to ask if you remember…is the date correct for when these shirts were dropped off?'

The girl glanced down. 'Yes…Mr Cline.' Her face brightened at once. 'He's a very nice man. He always pays a little extra for our work. Today, with the economy so bad, almost no one tips us.'

'Are you sure about the date? Do you remember which day of the week he was here?'

The girl paused to look at the calendar. 'It is correct,' she said. 'You see how we put an X through the day?' Kari observed how every day had been marked off until the present date. 'We do that before we open the doors—every day without fail. It is to make sure we don't have someone coming back to claim our service was slow or their order wasn't ready on the day we promised. You know how it is, even a judge will sue if he thinks he can make a few dollars. We have to be very careful.'

Almost breathless with anticipation, Kari asked: 'Did Mr Cline drop these off personally or did someone else leave them here?'

'It was Mr Cline.' The girl gave a little smile. 'I remember he was in a hurry at the time. But when he picked them up yesterday he talked a little about the weather, and gave me five dollars extra! That's the most he has ever tipped one of us.'

'Thank you very much,' Kari told her. 'You've been a great help.'

The girl was immediately concerned. 'There wasn't a problem with the laundry?'

Kari's heart was pounding, but she smiled, as she turned to leave, 'No, no problem at all. Thank you again.'

Once back in her car, Kari's mind raced at light speed. It was nearing quitting time, so she didn't go back to her office at the newspaper. She had access to the information on her laptop at home, but she needed to double-check the details. A dark cloud swooped down and lay heavily upon her shoulders. There was a very real fear she would discover something dreadful, something beyond belief. She needed to bring up her calendar of events, then call the airport and confirm some information. This could be something as simple as her misremembering the dates on her own calendar. But if she wasn't mistaken...

'Don't even think about it yet,' she warned herself. 'You make a blunder on something like this and you'll never be qualified to work at a newspaper again!'

TWENTY-FOUR

JASON WAS BORED so he spent several hours at the library, read some magazines and got on the Internet for a time. Using his personal log-in, he was able to check on some of the activities taking place in and around Sutton. He also went over his email, which was mostly a waste of time. Lastly, he looked at the weather back home. It had rained for four straight days. Not too uncomfortable, but it didn't equal the warm temperature and sunny skies he had been enjoying locally.

Returning to his car, to head for home, he knew the clock was running out. Kari occupied his thoughts and had infiltrated his heart. She was a wonderful girl, one he would gladly love. But he belonged back at the Sutton CID, solving crimes in his own district. Standing back and watching other detectives work only made things harder. He was a hunting dog, not a lap dog. He enjoyed the action, the solving of a mystery.

He had to pause thinking of that. Where had he encountered a better mystery than the one facing Grady and Hampton? All logic and evidence pointed to Tom Kenny as their killer. He had threatened to kill a policewoman when trapped. He had the motive, to keep from being sent to prison. He even had the history—paranoid, delusional and violent. Every piece of the puzzle fit…except for one drop of blood.

A short time later, he parked his car and entered Reggie's apartment. He glanced at the phone for messages. The light was not blinking, so he began to unbutton his shirt. He decided to check and see if Kari was still at work. When he picked up the phone, he saw there was a message—it had been played, but not erased. Reggie wasn't due back for another day, so who...?

He pushed the button to listen. It was Kari.

'Jason, I have to see you right away.' She sounded breathless and overly excited. 'I found out something. It's about Roger and it's important. I mean, really, really important! Call me, or come over as soon as you hear this message. Hurry, Jason. This won't wait!'

He started to punch in her number but stopped. The message was new, but the light hadn't been blinking. That could only mean someone had listened to the message!

Pausing to take a quick survey around the room, the only thing out of place was the dust bin. It had been moved from its usual spot—not far, but enough that he could tell it had been disturbed. He walked over and glanced into the receptacle. The only thing in it was the plastic bag Reggie's shirts had been in, the one from the laundry.

'Roger!' he exclaimed. 'What the hell?'

He quickly punched in Kari's number, but the line was busy. He tried her mobile, but it went to voicemail. Fearing something was very wrong, Jason made a quick call, then whirled for the door. He rushed down the hallway and took the stairs two at a time. He was in his rental car and on the road in seconds.

Running through two Stop signs, he risked speeding along whenever he could to make better time. It was only four miles and he made the trip in less than ten minutes. Nothing looked amiss as he pulled into the visitor's lot, but he was still apprehensive. Kari had been very excited about something.

With the car parked, he ran a hand over his hair—he

hadn't even looked in a mirror—and continued to hurry. He reached Kari's door and knocked lightly.

'Come in,' Kari called from inside.

Jason pushed open the door and stopped dead.

Kari sat bound in a chair with duct tape, and a .38 caliber Smith & Wesson was pointed directly at her chest. Holding the weapon was Roger Cline!

'Don't stand in the hallway, Cuz,' Roger said curtly. 'Get your butt in here and close the door.'

Kari displayed an apologetic expression as best she could while having tape over her mouth. Jason frowned in confusion, but Roger held up his phone. He pushed a button and Kari's voice again said: 'Come in.'

'OK, Roger,' Jason said, as he closed the door. 'You want to tell me what's going on?'

'First of all, don't get all protective or policeman on me. I don't intend to harm Kari in any way unless you try something stupid.'

'I'm listening.'

'There is a pair of handcuffs on the table,' he said, tipping his head in that direction. 'I know you're familiar with those. Slip one on your wrist and then back up to me with both of your hands behind your back.'

'Roger! What's got into you?' Jason cried. 'What's this all about?'

'Do as I say first, dear cousin. I'll tell you everything you want to know, once I'm sure you can't try anything.'

Jason followed his directions. Once his hands were cuffed securely behind his back, Roger had him sit in a chair. He used duct tape to wrap around his upper body and the chair back. Then he taped each ankle to a chair leg. When he had finished, Jason was as securely bound as Kari.

'It was those dumb shirts, Jason,' Roger began. 'That's

what brought us to this point. Reggie was bummed that I had taken his dress shirt and I wanted to get it back to him. All of the months of preparation, the precautions, a dozen covert flights back and forth on company jets with special friends—it was for nothing.' He shook his head. 'I paid cash for everything, never left a trail, never a print. I wore clothes and shoes from a different thrift store every time I went out, and then dropped them in Dumpsters or donated-clothing pick-up spots ten miles from the crime scenes.'

'You killed all of those men?' Jason was dumbfounded. 'But that's impossible!'

'They had it coming!' Roger sounded off harshly. 'The six of them raped my mother and killed the man who would have been Reggie's and my father! They were never going to pay for their crimes—ever!'

'I don't believe it.'

'Mom got a little drunker than usual one night and told me about the party. She showed me the photo of the five boys, taken from that night. Only Tom Kenny was missing. She said she had been lonely and wanted to dance and kiss a special boy, a guy she'd had a crush on for years. Next thing she knew she was dragged into a room and raped by five or six boys. I honestly didn't know she and Warren had never been intimate,' Roger admitted. 'She had claimed he was our father all along. But the party was what sent Warren looking for those guys. Mom tried to hide the attack from him, but he suspected what had happened. When he tried to find out the truth, it got him killed.'

'Kenny and Beckston told the police it was an accident.'

Roger uttered a cynical laugh. 'You think they would admit they ran him off the road intentionally? The same honorable men who took advantage of my mother and treated her like the worst kind of whore?'

'OK, Roger, the law should have—'

'Yes!' Roger cut him off sharply. 'The *law* should have done something, but they didn't. A bishop's kid, one the son of a councilman…two were high school heroes! The law turned their back on Mom's attack and Warren's death. The law allowed those guys to get away with rape and murder.'

'So you got even,' Jason said.

'It was brilliant,' Roger replied. 'I knew I could never get them all, not without the police finding the report Grandpa had made.' He bobbed his head. 'Yeah, Mom told me about that too. She talked a lot when she was drunk and melancholy.'

'I believed her drinking was because of Warren and the life she never had.'

'Yes, it was,' Roger said. 'And that's the reason I set this plan into motion. I had to wait until Tom was out of prison to act. He was the principal patsy, but let me keep this in chronological order. You need to know the whole truth to understand.'

'Understand what? That you're a cold-blooded killer?'

Roger patiently continued. 'I took care of Jamison Clark first because he lived out of state. Besides which, he deserved to die more than the others.'

'Why?'

'I told you how Mom confronted him when she learned she was pregnant, but I didn't tell you everything. When he laughed at her predicament, she called him a rapist and threatened to expose him and the others.' Roger snorted his contempt. 'Jamison took a quarter out of his pocket and tossed it at her. He said it was payment in full, because she had acted like a two-bit whore. He warned her that if she said one word about the attack then he and the others would smear her reputation to protect themselves.

By the end of the school year, everyone would think she was a complete tramp.'

'That's what the quarter between the teeth meant?' Jason said. 'Because Jamison had called her a two-bit whore?'

Roger lifted his shoulders in a shrug. 'It was payback for Jamison, but it meant nothing to the others.' He chuckled. 'Oh, I did decide to use it as part of my avenging character act. *Heads I win, tails you die* is what I figured for each one of those filthy vermin. Also, I left all the coins the same side up. Figured the cops might think it meant something, but it was only to keep them guessing.' He displayed a sinister smile. 'It was kind of like all of those ridiculous television shows. You know, the master criminal teasing the police with his cunning.'

'Smoke and mirrors, like a magic trick,' Jason said. 'You had the police chasing their tail.'

'I did my homework and knew where each man lived.' Roger continued with his story. 'Clark, Pacheco, Kenny and Wilkins...but I couldn't get to John Beckston. Mom said that Beckston told her girlfriend that he had only watched the rape. I decided to check the story with Wilkins before I killed him. I really hadn't made up my mind about his fate. Well, Wilkins confirmed that Beckston didn't have sex with Mom, but he also didn't do a damn thing to stop the attack. And afterwards he wouldn't stand up on her behalf either. He treated her like trash, the same as the others.'

'Six men, Roger,' Jason murmured. 'You're responsible for the deaths of six men.'

'I finished by setting up Tom Kenny for the murders. I pretended to be a pal and offered him a sanctuary, within the burned out remains of the old Kenny house. Then, when the time was right, I planted evidence and called the cops.' He paused. 'On a side note, I burned that house down the day after I learned the truth from Mom. It was vacant, but it was the first step to retribution.'

'And when Tom Kenny died at the hands of the police, you were able to run down Beckston,' Jason surmised.

'It was done…finished…forgotten,' Roger said. 'Justice was served, except they found a drop of my blood at the Wilkins crime scene.' He smiled at Jason's alarmed look. 'Yeah, I didn't know about the DNA until it showed up in the paper. Stupid drunk bonked me in the nose with his head while I was wrapping tape around his shoulders. I put up my sleeve at once, certain I hadn't bled on that smelly old sot. Apparently, I was mistaken.'

'But they tested Reggie!' Jason said. 'You should both have the same DNA as Jamison Clark! You're brothers! How come they didn't link him to the murder?'

Roger cocked his head at Kari. 'Your girlfriend—my ex-girlfriend—could field that question, if she could talk through the tape.' He grinned as she gave him a piercing stare.

'Fraternal twins can have separate fathers when the mother has multiple partners at the time of conception. It is extremely rare but does occasionally happen. After reading Kari's news article about the evidence not matching because of the DNA, I looked it up on a medical web site to figure it out. I'm sure Kari did the same thing. Once she had the laundry receipt, she put two and two together and got me!'

Jason conjectured, 'The slip from the laundry showed you were in town and not in New York during the time of Wilkins's death. You went to Reggie's apartment to try and recover the receipt and overheard the message on my telephone.'

'You and the lady were going out for a night on the town, so I knew you would show up here! Otherwise, I could have left her bound and been out of the country before she got loose.'

'What is your plan now?'

Roger said, 'I took this risk going forward. I knew I might have to disappear. One stupid drop of blood.' He gave his head another sorrowful shake. 'That was my only mistake.'

'You had me fooled. You did a fine job of acting,' Jason said. Roger didn't reply to that, but pushed and shoved Jason's chair around until he was back to back against Kari's chair. Taking his roll of duct tape, he bound the two of them together. Once finished with that, he tore a strip and pasted it over Jason's mouth. Lastly, he removed the keys from Jason's pocket, then shoved the couch over so that his cousin and Kari were pinned against the wall. Standing a few feet away, he paused to admire his handiwork.

'I'm sure that will hold the two of you for a few hours. It won't matter after that. I hope you don't mind, Jason, but I'm going to borrow your rental car. I left my ride a few blocks away, in case I was seen coming or going. I'm sure the police will locate the car in a day or two.'

He moved over to the couch, put a knee on the seat cushion, leaned over to Kari and kissed her on the cheek. He smiled at the confused look on her face.

'I won't be able to do that on your wedding day,' he said. 'I do wish you and Jason all the happiness in the world.'

Jason tried to speak, but the words were muffled from the tape. 'What's that?' Roger asked. 'You have something more to say to me?'

Jason nodded.

Roger paused, debating as to whether or not he should listen. After a moment's hesitation he peeled the tape away from Jason's mouth.

'I'm sure I'll regret this, but what is so important?' he asked.

Jason managed a tight smile. 'I made a call before I left Reggie's apartment...and the door isn't locked.'

Roger whirled about in time to see Grady and Hampton standing in the doorway! Both had their guns trained on him. As he had already put away his gun, he had no chance.

Grady and Hampton moved in quickly and put cuffs on Roger. Two uniformed policemen followed and began to move the couch.

Jason and Kari were quickly freed. Kari retrieved some lotion and applied some to her tender wrists, where the tape had removed the hair and abraded the skin. The uniforms took Roger to the lockup and the two detectives asked some questions and put the finishing touches on their reports.

'So your cousin was behind this from the beginning,' Grady remarked to Jason. 'He had us running in circles, like a couple of white mice in an endless maze.'

'That DNA is what threw us,' Hampton added. 'I've never heard of a case where twins did not share the same DNA.'

Grady interjected, 'And we had no reason to suspect her sons could have different DNA, not with Sally Cline claiming all the while that Warren Lloyd was their father.'

'Good thing you called us, Keane,' Hampton said. 'Another couple minutes and Roger would have disappeared off of the face of the earth.'

'Yes, and with his contacts all over the world, there's no telling where he would have gone.'

'So he used private jets to fly back and forth from Portland and New York,' Grady surmised. 'He really played us. If it hadn't been for you, Kari,' he spoke to her, 'the guy would have got away with all six murders.'

Kari agreed. 'Yes, returning the shirts he borrowed from his brother was the only mistake he made, other than for that one drop of blood.'

'And you, Jason, are you ready to go back and do some police work in your own back yard?'

Jason looked at Kari; he felt as though a knot were secured tightly around his heart. 'I suppose so,' he replied carefully. 'My vacation time is up.'

'You two make a good team,' Grady said, winking at Jason.

'I'll second that,' Hampton agreed. 'We owe you both big time for helping us solve this case.'

The two detectives had finished. They said their goodbyes and walked out together. Grady turned to his partner at the doorway. 'Well, I'm glad of one thing, Ham,' he said. 'At least we know what the hell the quarter meant!'

Alone at last, Kari walked over and put her arms around Jason. For a moment, they were like two weary dancers, too drained and jaded to keep time with the music, but unwilling to stop their embrace.

'Have you decided what we can do about us?' she asked.

'I don't want to lose you,' Jason whispered. 'Grady is right, we're a good team.'

Kari rose up on her toes and kissed him. It was tender, it was warm, it was what she wanted to feel at that moment. If only...

The phone ringing interrupted the romantic interlude. Kari stepped over and punched the speaker. 'Yes, this is Kari.'

'Drop everything, Ms Underwood!' Marge Taylor, her supervisor at work, cried. 'My sister just called me! They found her husband in the trash compactor at his work site. He was alone in the warehouse, but it has to be murder!

It would take someone outside the compactor to push the button and crush him. I want you on this...right now!'

Kari stared at Jason as the phone connection went dead. She offered a timorous smile and murmured sweetly, 'Jason?'

* * * * *

REQUEST YOUR FREE BOOKS!

2 FREE NOVELS
PLUS 2 FREE GIFTS!

MYSTERY **W(❂)RLDWIDE LIBRARY**®
™
Your Partner in Crime

YES! Please send me 2 FREE novels from the Worldwide Library® series and my 2 FREE gifts (gifts are worth about $10). After receiving them, if I don't wish to receive any more books, I can return the shipping statement marked "cancel." If I don't cancel, I will receive 4 brand-new novels every month and be billed just $5.24 per book in the U.S. or $6.24 per book in Canada. That's a savings of at least 34% off the cover price. It's quite a bargain! Shipping and handling is just 50¢ per book in the U.S. and 75¢ per book in Canada.* I understand that accepting the 2 free books and gifts places me under no obligation to buy anything. I can always return a shipment and cancel at any time. Even if I never buy another book, the two free books and gifts are mine to keep forever.

414/424 WDN FVUV

Name	(PLEASE PRINT)

Address	Apt. #

City	State/Prov.	Zip/Postal Code

Signature (if under 18, a parent or guardian must sign)

Mail to the Harlequin® Reader Service:
IN U.S.A.: P.O. Box 1867, Buffalo, NY 14240-1867
IN CANADA: P.O. Box 609, Fort Erie, Ontario L2A 5X3

Want to try two free books from another line?
Call 1-800-873-8635 or visit www.ReaderService.com.

* Terms and prices subject to change without notice. Prices do not include applicable taxes. Sales tax applicable in N.Y. Canadian residents will be charged applicable taxes. Offer not valid in Quebec. This offer is limited to one order per household. Not valid for current subscribers to the Worldwide Library series. All orders subject to credit approval. Credit or debit balances in a customer's account(s) may be offset by any other outstanding balance owed by or to the customer. Please allow 4 to 6 weeks for delivery. Offer available while quantities last.

Your Privacy—The Harlequin® Reader Service is committed to protecting your privacy. Our Privacy Policy is available online at www.ReaderService.com or upon request from the Harlequin Reader Service.

We make a portion of our mailing list available to reputable third parties that offer products we believe may interest you. If you prefer that we not exchange your name with third parties, or if you wish to clarify or modify your communication preferences, please visit us at www.ReaderService.com/consumerschoice or write to us at Harlequin Reader Service Preference Service, P.O. Box 9062, Buffalo, NY 14269. Include your complete name and address.

WWLI3

Reader Service.com

Manage your account online!

- Review your order history
- Manage your payments
- Update your address

> ### *We've designed the Harlequin® Reader Service website just for you.*

Enjoy all the features!

- Reader excerpts from any series
- Respond to mailings and special monthly offers
- Discover new series available to you
- Browse the Bonus Bucks catalog
- Share your feedback

Visit us at:
ReaderService.com

RS13

REQUEST YOUR FREE BOOKS!

2 FREE NOVELS
FROM THE SUSPENSE COLLECTION
PLUS 2 FREE GIFTS!

YES! Please send me 2 FREE novels from the Suspense Collection and my 2 FREE gifts (gifts are worth about $10). After receiving them, if I don't wish to receive any more books, I can return the shipping statement marked "cancel." If I don't cancel, I will receive 4 brand-new novels every month and be billed just $5.99 per book in the U.S. or $6.49 per book in Canada. That's a savings of at least 25% off the cover price. It's quite a bargain! Shipping and handling is just 50¢ per book in the U.S. and 75¢ per book in Canada.* I understand that accepting the 2 free books and gifts places me under no obligation to buy anything. I can always return a shipment and cancel at any time. Even if I never buy another book, the two free books and gifts are mine to keep forever.

191/391 MDN FVVK

Name _____ (PLEASE PRINT) _____

Address _____ Apt. # _____

City _____ State/Prov. _____ Zip/Postal Code _____

Signature (if under 18, a parent or guardian must sign) _____

Mail to the Harlequin® Reader Service:
IN U.S.A.: P.O. Box 1867, Buffalo, NY 14240-1867
IN CANADA: P.O. Box 609, Fort Erie, Ontario L2A 5X3

Want to try two free books from another line?
Call 1-800-873-8635 or visit www.ReaderService.com.

* Terms and prices subject to change without notice. Prices do not include applicable taxes. Sales tax applicable in N.Y. Canadian residents will be charged applicable taxes. Offer not valid in Quebec. This offer is limited to one order per household. Not valid for current subscribers to the Suspense Collection or the Romance/Suspense Collection. All orders subject to credit approval. Credit or debit balances in a customer's account(s) may be offset by any other outstanding balance owed by or to the customer. Please allow 4 to 6 weeks for delivery. Offer available while quantities last.

Your Privacy—The Harlequin® Reader Service is committed to protecting your privacy. Our Privacy Policy is available online at www.ReaderService.com or upon request from the Harlequin Reader Service.

We make a portion of our mailing list available to reputable third parties that offer products we believe may interest you. If you prefer that we not exchange your name with third parties, or if you wish to clarify or modify your communication preferences, please visit us at www.ReaderService.com/consumerschoice or write to us at Harlequin Reader Service Preference Service, P.O. Box 9062, Buffalo, NY 14269. Include your complete name and address.

SUS13